Jasper's Wife

Frances Parker-Smith

First published 2025
by Rowanvale Books Ltd
The Gate
Keppoch Street
Roath
Cardiff
CF24 3JW
www.rowanvalebooks.com

A CIP catalogue record for this book is available from the British Library.

Paperback ISBN: 978-1-83584-095-5

For Glenda, a lifelong friend.

Contents

Prologue

Kate's heart raced; beads of sweat trickled off her forehead into her hair.

He had his face pressed into hers. "You do as I say!" he shouted.

She could feel his evil, contorted face and his black eyes penetrating her soul.

He dragged her up the flower-shop stairs to the attic. Her arm was outstretched, pulling against him.

"No. NO!" she yelled.

He kicked the attic door open and flung her inside. Her bare legs scraped across the wooden floor, and blood dripped down them. She was shaking as she gasped for breath; tears gushed down her face and onto the floor.

He towered over her. "Seems you might be worth a bob or two." His evil laugh echoed in the empty attic. "The old woman wants her bastard granddaughter."

He kicked her bleeding legs, and she cried out in pain.

Sweat covered her naked body, mixing with the tears running down her face and dripping onto the bed sheets.

Jasper lifted her into his arms. "Kate, wake up. It's a nightmare. He's dead. He can't hurt you anymore. You're safe. Nothing will happen to you, my love." Jasper's words were soft and loving, as they always were following her nightmares. He kissed her eyes and lips as he stroked her hair. "Kate, I love you."

She opened her eyes. "Love me, Jasper."

Chapter One

Kate watched in horror as the sea raced up the gully towards her beach house. The rain was falling in torrents from the black sky, and the house creaked with each gust of wind.

With some haste, she threw on her wet weather gear and started to fill the Evoque with her important belongings. Fear gripped her; she was alone, no phone or electricity.

By the time she started the Evoque, seawater had already pooled under the beach house. She eased the car off the wet grass, its wheels spinning in the mud, and onto the firmer ground of the lane that led to her home.

She had stopped to look back at her sanctuary when the veranda dipped under the waves. Her eyes filled as she realised fate had dealt her the card that she dreaded; the sea had claimed her solitary life. She rested her head on the steering wheel and allowed the tears to flow. She had lost her haven, the place she had thought she would spend the rest of her days.

Suddenly, the Evoque door was yanked open, and Jasper pulled her into his arms.

* * *

Jasper's soft fingers meandered up and down her spine. She was dry, warm and safe. Jasper had always made her feel safe. They were in bed at the Carmichael House penthouse.

"The beach house is done for," Jasper said. "You can stay here as long as you want."

His uncaring tone hit her like a kick in the stomach, but she didn't deserve his sympathy after their last argument. He had wanted her to leave the beach house and live with him in his newly acquired property, River's End House, but she had refused. She could still hear the slamming of the beach house door and the Range Rover's tyres squealing as he drove away.

He'd wanted to look after her, and she had shunned him. She had been her stubborn self, and as far as the beach house was concerned, she had been selfish. All she thought of was warm days walking along the beach and painting. She had dismissed the unreliable electricity, the cold days spent struggling to keep warm and the storms.

A sob escaped her mouth.

"Kate, I'm sorry. I don't want to upset you even more," he said in the same uncaring tone.

Tears pushed out from under her closed eyelids as images of the violent, angry sea tearing at her home flashed into her mind. She could still feel the rain and wind that had lashed at the Evoque as it struggled to the safety of the underground garage at Carmichael House.

It was sometime later that a dripping wet Jasper had joined her. He had battled the storm to rescue her books and paintings because they were important to her. She didn't deserve him.

Her cheeks had been damp, her eyes red when he walked into the penthouse living room.

"Come here," he had said. He pulled her close, and his fingers stroked her lips.

Their eyes met, and he had murmured her name. His tongue moved along her lips, teasing her mouth open. Their tongues tentatively touched, tempting him to claim her mouth.

Desire had begun to build inside her; she wanted him, needed him. Her hands had cupped his cheeks as she eagerly kissed him.

They had staggered into the bedroom, removing each other's clothes between kisses. He had cupped her breasts and sucked her nipples, igniting the smouldering embers of desire. She wanted more; she didn't want him to stop. Her hands were in his hair and stroking his back. When he touched her sex, her orgasm had flashed through her.

"Number one," he whispered in her ear.

The fire of desire had taken hold, and she trembled as his fingers teasingly explored her sensitive sex. A second orgasm had whipped through her.

"Number two."

She had cried his name and dug her nails into his shoulders as he thrust deep inside her.

"Number three," he whispered again as their entwined bodies slowly calmed.

Several minutes passed as they lay there together, listening to each other's breathing.

"Kate, you're so quiet. It's not like you. Did I hurt you? It's been a while since we made love."

She stretched to his face, planting a kiss upon his lips. He moved her onto her back, deepening the kiss. Her legs wrapped around his waist.

"This isn't a good idea. You must be sore."

"I need you, my love. Make me whole."

He slipped inside her. She gasped.

"Kate."

"Don't stop."

One thrust and she fell over the edge. He had held her as her orgasm ripped through her body.

"Kate," Jasper said as he tilted her head, pulling her out of the memory of last night. He planted two soft kisses upon her eyes.

Her body tensed.

"I want you in my bed. I want what we had last night all the time."

She tried to free herself, but his strong hands held her in place.

* * *

Kate was sleeping when he left their bed. He slipped on a pair of boxers and padded into the kitchen.

As he made a coffee, Kate's words, "make me whole," repeated in his mind; he had never heard her say that before. The beach house had meant more to her than he realised. He had no idea how he was going to tell her that the storm had washed the beach away. There was no gully leading to her beach house. The sea had not only ravaged the beach but also her life.

His gaze moved to the bedroom doorway. Kate was standing staring at him, wearing one of his shirts. It was open, showing her full breasts. Their eyes locked, green on blue, as he stepped towards her, holding his coffee. She lifted the cup from his hand and began to sip the warm liquid. He wondered if she knew how beautiful and sexy she was. Age had been good to Kate; her aristocratic features had become more pronounced, making her very desirable.

"I'll send out for breakfast," he said, taking the coffee from her hand. "It might be too late though."

"Jasper… about last night."

"We are not going to analyse last night. It was beautiful. We loved one another." She went to speak, but he put his index finger over her mouth. "I love you, Kate, and that will never change. No matter how many times we argue. The question is: do you love me?" He paused, staring into her tear-filled eyes. "You loved me last night, but what about in the cold light of day?"

A long, awkward silence moved between them. A lone tear trickled down her cheek.

"I need words, Kate."

Her hands cupped his face. "I've always loved you, Jasper, from the very first time you made love to me. Remember the flower shop?"

"How could I forget," he said, his lips brushing hers.

Jasper's mind flashed to the lies her ex had spread that she was frigid, entertaining his drinking pals with untrue stories about how he had tried to fuck her. But Jasper had known that Kate wasn't frigid, just the opposite. The memory of the flower-shop sex was just as vivid as if it had only happened yesterday.

His musing suddenly stopped when she put her arms around his neck.

"I'll love you until I die."

He whisked her off her feet and carried her to the bed.

Chapter Two

After weeks of wind and rain, the weather had settled down. Jasper had reluctantly agreed to take Kate to the beach house. She clung onto his arm as she cast her eyes over what remained of her beloved sanctuary.

"The engineer's advice is to leave the beach house as it is, leaning towards the sea. The logistics of getting a crane to lift it are too risky. The whole area is unsafe. If we have another storm like that one, the fear is the sea will claim the whole coast."

"Where's the beach?" Kate meekly asked, gazing at the waves as they rolled over loose pebbles.

"Washed away."

"There's no gully, shrubs or trees."

The strings of Jasper's heart tightened at the sadness of her voice. He coughed to clear his throat. "The beach was in the direct line of the storm. Strongest wind, highest waves. The beach house didn't stand a chance."

"So much of my life is here. I mourned Oliver here."

Her eyes glazed over as she recalled the ending of her relationship with Bruce. She had loved him. He had been her rock when Jasper left. But Bruce had changed and had deceived her. She smiled as the heated arguments with Jasper sprang into her mind followed by their passionate lovemaking. No man thrilled her like Jasper, not even Bruce, who had satisfied her with his tender love. But she needed more.

"I will never again feel the peace and tranquillity of an early morning walk along the water's edge, the healing of the rhythmic lapping of the waves."

Jasper pulled her into his side and kissed her hair.

Tears slowly meandered down her cheeks as she put her arm around his waist. "Take me to River's End House."

Jasper thought he had misheard her emotion-ridden voice. "Did you just say take me to River's End House?" he said hopefully.

"I'm not promising anything, but I'm a realist, Jasper. My beach life is over and I can't live in the penthouse."

When they reached the Range Rover, Jasper opened the rear passenger door. "In you go."

"Jasper."

"I'm not waiting till we're in bed. There's no going back. I want the deal sealed."

"We are not young."

"What's age got to with it? I want you. Now."

* * *

The Range Rover coasted to a stop outside the River's End House kitchen door.

"Jasper, please stop grinning."

The grin turned into a beaming smile. "I can't. There's something about car sex, particularly when you take charge." Images of a naked Kate astride him danced before his eyes.

"Okay, I shouldn't have done it. But I just lost control."

"Kate, my love, you can do that any time. I enjoyed every minute."

He lifted her from the passenger seat and kissed her. Kate felt alive.

"How do I look?"

"Wonderful."

"Do I have that after-sex glow?"

Jasper grinned and wound his arm around her waist.

"It's a giveaway," Kate said. "They will know that we've just had sex."

"I don't give a flying fuck. I wouldn't have missed it for the world. Kate at her best."

"You didn't say 'I wouldn't have missed it for a bag of diamonds.'"

Jasper's hand rested on the kitchen door handle. He looked into her eyes. "You mean more to me than a bag of diamonds." Their lips touched. "And don't you forget it."

* * *

Jasper's head rested between Kate's breasts; he was sleeping. Her hands meandered through his soft hair as her eyes moved around the large bedroom. The king-size bed sat in the middle, facing two windows that were being pounded by the never-ending rain. Two walk-in wardrobes covered one wall, a his and hers. Jasper had filled her wardrobe with designer clothes: jeans, trousers, white blouses and t-shirts, long cardigans, jumpers, hoodies, lingerie, coats, jackets. The wet room had a large shower, and there were steps leading into the two-person bath. His-and-hers sinks faced a large mirror. A couch faced the open fire that had been blazing last night when they came to bed.

"Kate. Kate."

The urgency in his voice alarmed her. "Jasper." She held him into her breasts.

His breathing suddenly quickened, and beads of sweat trickled into her cleavage.

"You're lying," he gasped.

Kate suddenly realised that he was talking in his sleep. She kissed his head.

His hand moved to her breast. "Margot," he mumbled.

* * *

It was midday when Kate ventured downstairs; Jasper had kept her awake most of the night with his mumbling.

He introduced her to his staff: Robert the butler, Elsie the housekeeper, Ruby the cook and Ben the gardener. He insisted on introducing her as "Lady Carmichael". She didn't like to be referred to as "Lady Carmichael", so when she shook their hands and made eye contact, she whispered "Kate".

Opening one of the wooden front doors and walking over the gravel driveway onto the circular lawn, Kate was surprised to feel a peacefulness surrounding the old house. She had never been allowed to visit the house that the rich Landons owned, and had always wondered what it would be like to live in a grand house like River's End. Now she was lady of the house.

Kate gazed to the roof. River's End had once been a beautiful stone mansion that blended in with the greenery that surrounded it. Over the years, it had been extended to accommodate visiting friends and family. There were now three floors and at least ten bedrooms. Views of either

Wellsbury, the sea or river could be seen from all the rooms, but its most striking features were the stone chimneys that rose majestically into the sky.

A smiling Jasper marched across the grass towards her. His arms snaked around her, pulling her into a kiss.

"Do you like what you see, Lady Carmichael?"

"I do, but can you afford such a mansion?"

"Can *we* afford it, my love."

"We?"

"Grandfather built Carmichael Castle and the surrounding estate. This is our castle and estate." He paused, letting her think about what he had just said. "You are a lady, my love. In every sense of the word. You deserve to live in a mansion and not a beach house."

"I liked my beach house."

Jasper ignored her comment. "Wes Clayton is coming over. He's a project manager of sorts. Tell him what you want: furniture, carpets, books. Don't think about money." He took her hand. "Come. Ruby's made lunch."

After lunch, Kate spent the afternoon wandering around the house, trying to imagine herself entertaining the great and good just as the Landons had done. The only room she couldn't access was Jasper's diamond office.

He had divided the foyer into two halves, a his and hers. She knew why he had done that; they had a history of not being able to live together. That was one of the reasons she had moved to the beach house. To her left was her half, with Landon's original library and a room that Jasper had suggested she could use for the meetings she would need to have when she took charge of the declining shopping centre.

Kate eased the library door open. A square room with stone floor and wood-panelled walls that still had the original bookshelves. Large floor-to-ceiling windows filled one wall; she imagined that was where her desk would go. Her eyes settled on a large inglenook fireplace, which she would need, as she could feel the cold seeping towards her. The room wasn't damp, just cold, and it needed a good airing. For the briefest of moments, she felt she belonged in this room. However, it needed a lot of work. She made a mental list: thorough clean, chimney checked, furniture, thick-pile carpet.

She turned to face Jasper's half of the foyer: one room with a door secured by a security pad. A room devoted to his diamond business.

The shared rooms were the living room, dining room and kitchen, and stretching along the outer walls of the living room and dining room was an old Victorian orangery. When Jasper had shown her this, he had slipped his arms around her waist and whispered into her ear, "I thought you'd like this. At the far end is a room full of junk. With a bit of work, it could be a studio." She had turned to face him. He was so close that their lips touched; Jasper was not one to miss an opportunity to claim her mouth.

The kitchen swing door creaked when she pushed it open. The four staff were sitting around the kitchen table having afternoon tea.

Robert jumped up. "Lady Carmichael. Lord Carmichael said you were resting."

"Where's Jasper?"

"He left."

"Did he say where he was going?"

"I'm afraid not."

Margot, she thought.

Chapter Three

When Robert handed Kate the letter, she was watching Wes Clayton's team of carpet fitters working in the library. Apparently, Jasper had ordered the carpet some time ago. He knew her tastes, and the carpet was very similar to the one at Isaacs House.

With the letter in her hand, Kate walked into the orangery for some privacy. She was curious as the envelope was of good quality paper with a coat of arms in the top left-hand corner.

Lady Carmichael (Lady Landon),
I assume you are unaware of your link to the Landon family and the problems with the Landon Trust Fund.

Link? I have no link, Kate thought.

It follows, therefore, that you don't know that you are a Landon.
One summer, a beautiful teenage girl met a handsome, rich teenage boy. They spent the summer together. Young love. The girl fell pregnant. The boy's parents were very annoyed, to put it mildly; they had plans for their son that didn't include marrying a working-class girl. They wanted the pregnancy terminated, but their son wouldn't hear of it. So, they paid an evil man to marry the girl, and every month this evil man

received a cheque for the child's upbringing. The child's mother died; some say of a broken heart. The boy went off the rails: drugs, alcohol. He was killed in a car accident.

I do hope that you're putting two and two together. Just in case, I'll give you another clue.

Think back to a school prize-giving. Lady Isabel Landon gave a small speech before presenting the prizes. You were the last to receive your prizes of book tokens, one for Maths and one for English. You were an exceptionally bright child. Lady Isabel hugged you, and tears ran down her cheeks. Lord Landon had to release you from her grasp. When Reynolds, your father, heard about it, you were locked in the attic until the Landons left. They never returned.

I hope that I've convinced you that your father was Henry Landon Junior. DNA comparison would confirm your Landon heritage, but, alas, there are no living relatives to compare it with. Lord Charles Landon is not a Landon. Your great-grandmother had an affair—but that's a story for another time.

Now, back to the trust fund. It had been in decline for years, jumping from one crisis to another, but your grandfather, Lord Henry Landon, Chairman of the Landon Trust Fund, kept it going. Your grandfather was a caring man with a conscience; he did the right thing. However, since your uncle has become chairman, the fund is teetering on collapse. It needs a new chairman. A true Landon with Landon values.

The Landon Trust Fund is like no other, and one wonders how it came into being. It wouldn't be possible today. No one knows when the fund first began. There was a convenient fire in the Landon main office, and all the records were destroyed except the names of the investors and *the value of the diamonds they had entrusted to the Landons. One imagines that there must be a vault somewhere with these diamonds in.*

You see, Lord Henry valued these diamonds, and the investors were paid a yearly dividend. Of course, the dividend went up or down according to the diamond market. No one bothered to question Lord Henry's payments; after all, he was one of them, a lord and a member of high society. This would never happen today.

I have misgivings about how the fund was run. I suspect Lord Henry traded the diamonds. I'll leave it to your imagination with whom he traded them. All I'll say is that River's End House was very important to him.

The cavalier attitude of the diamond-addicted investors is coming back to bite them. When the police start to investigate the fund, these investors will be looking for someone to take the blame. Your uncle is already manoeuvring out of the firing line. Next in line is the last surviving Landon, and that is you.

However, the discovery of the Landon diamonds would save the fund, and you, from prison.

The letter was unsigned.

Kate folded it and stuffed it into the pocket of her long cardigan before slowly walking to the kitchen to make tea. The letter had perturbed her. She doubted its contents. She wasn't related to the Landons.

Deep in thought, she had just poured her tea when two arms snaked around her waist and soft kisses caressed her neck.

"You smell divine."

"I thought you were diamond hunting."

"I decided that I needed you more."

"Jasper, don't lie."

He wasn't listening; the softness of her neck had his attention until she handed him the letter.

Chapter Four

Kate finished drinking her tea while Jasper absorbed the implications of the letter.

"This was once a grand house, when Lord and Lady Landon owned it. They only visited during the summer," she said in her calm manner. She turned to face him. "Who comes to Wellsbury for a summer holiday?"

A lord dealing in the diamond black market, thought Jasper. *Wellsbury is an ideal place.*

He thought of his father, Colin, a renowned diamond thief who'd used Wellsbury to hide diamonds at the home of Hannah and Jacob Isaacs. Colin had rescued them from the Germans during World War Two.

"Their staff arrived about a month before them to get the house ready," Kate continued. "They stayed for about two months. Garden parties, evening balls for the great and good."

"You sound bitter, Kate."

"It wasn't a happy time for me. I was never allowed anywhere near this place. Reynolds punished me if I so much as looked at it. I was locked in my bedroom or under the stairs. Things changed when my mother died. He would rant and rave about the Landons. I never understood why until an end-of-term prize-giving."

Jasper held her hands. "Have you heard the gossip?"

"I don't listen to gossip."

Jasper studied his wife's expression. She had the same nervous look as when she woke from a nightmare. She was in turmoil. She had lost her home, and now this.

Kate was lost in thoughts of Reynolds. *"Seems you might be worth a bob or two. The old woman wants her granddaughter."* His evil laugh echoed in her ears as her recurring nightmare flashed into her mind.

Jasper stared at her. Her eyes had glazed over, and he started to panic.

"Kate, say something. Listen to me."

She turned her head to meet his stare.

His voice was low and calm so as not to upset her. "The Landons never returned to Wellsbury, and this house fell into ruin. The current Lord Landon, Charles, couldn't wait to get rid of it. He's a gambler and needed money to pay his debts. But it was his elder brother Henry, your grandfather, who made the Landons very rich. People queued up to put money in the Landon Trust Fund."

"He's not my grandfather."

"Lord Henry Landon seemed to have an endless supply of diamonds that guaranteed all the fund's investments. It was said that he had a vault brimming with them. And the crown jewels, so to speak, were two red diamonds and flawless clear diamonds."

"Were the Carmichaels involved?"

"No. We were not good enough for the high and mighty Landons." Jasper's blue eyes never left her. "Rumour has it that Charles Landon has sold most of the diamonds to Pieter Von-Pitt, except the red diamonds. But I don't believe that. I think Von-Pitt and Charles can't find Henry's vault. That untrue rumour has made the Landon Trust Fund very unstable. The search is on to find another Henry Landon. A Landon that, like Henry, is good with money, trustworthy; a Landon that is respected."

Kate stood. "Don't look at me like that. I'm not a Landon."

"My spies tell me that there are powerful men looking into your past, Kate."

She glared into his eyes. "I'm not a Landon," she repeated.

"Kate, you knew your mother was Meredith Spencer's daughter, but you never knew who your father was," he retorted. "There was some speculation that your father was a university professor, but I don't believe that, and he certainly wasn't Reynolds."

"I don't understand why my father has become so important. I've lived this long without knowing."

"It's important because the Landon Trust Fund is teetering on collapse. Trustees are looking for Lord Henry Landon's blood heir."

"And you think it's me?"

"It all fits, Kate. There's a reason Reynolds wouldn't allow you anywhere near the Landons, and there's a reason Lady Isabel Landon hugged you and cried. Have a DNA test."

"I don't see how that will prove anything. If you're right, all my blood relatives are dead."

* * *

Listening from the utility room was Robert. The staff quarters were above the kitchen, and the creaking kitchen door had piqued his curiosity. He watched Jasper take Kate's teacup out of her hand and run his index finger along her hairline.

"My love," Robert heard Jasper say, "you are a Landon. The love child of Henry Junior and Laura

Spencer, and that puts you in danger. Certain people will want you dead."

Chapter Five

The idea that she might be the Landons' missing heir filled Kate with dread. How she longed for her beach and sea.

"We have to be ahead of the game," Jasper had told her. He was convinced that Von-Pitt and Lord Charles Landon were up to no good and that they intended to use Kate to find the Landon diamonds and stabilise the fund. "Before we can go forward, I need to know if you and Lord Charles are related."

Charles Landon was the younger brother of Lord Henry Landon and had taken over the Landon Trust Fund. Charles was the apple of his mother's eye, whereas his father ignored him; this had led to speculation that Charles wasn't a Landon. However, this didn't prevent him from inheriting the Landon fortune and company.

"Jasper, I'm not a Landon. This is all nonsense."

But Jasper had kissed her and used his persuasive charm to convince her to send a DNA sample to a private lab for comparison with Lord Charles Landon's sample. How he had obtained a sample of Charles's DNA, Kate didn't want to know.

* * *

A week later, as Kate and Jasper were finishing breakfast, Robert walked in carrying the post on a silver tray. Kate eagerly watched as Jasper tore the end of a plain white envelope.

His eyes scanned the enclosed A4 sheet. "It's not a match," he said in a disbelieving voice. He dropped the paper onto the table. "It doesn't mean you're not a Landon, though. There is a rumour that old Lady Landon had an affair with the gamekeeper. She was left alone in the mansion for long periods. Her husband and eldest son were too busy making their fortune."

"How do you know that?"

"I'm a member of the Gentlemen's Club—a perk of being a lord. The old men have long memories and are full of gossip."

Kate's attention returned to the DNA results.

"Don't read too much into them," Jasper said. "All it means is that you're not related to Lord Charles Landon."

"There's not a Landon alive that my DNA can be compared with."

"There're historical records. I'm thinking of photographs or portraits. How do you fancy a trip to the Landon mansion?"

* * *

It was one o'clock in the morning when Jasper and Kate pulled into the Landon estate.

"Sold." Kate read the sign at the front of the property. "Did you know it was for sale?"

"Yes."

"You didn't say."

"I didn't know it was sold."

"What about staff?"

"He sacked them. Couldn't afford to pay them."

"You seem to know a lot."

"I've told you, it's a perk of being a lord."

Even in the dark, the mansion looked an imposing building.

"It looks big."

"The Landons were very rich. The estate is massive. Puts the Carmichael estate to shame. Even in this derelict state it will be worth a mill or two."

Jasper expertly opened a side door at the back of the mansion. Kate thought it best not to ask how he knew how to unlock the door. She waited while he searched for the electric control box.

"That's a bit of luck," he commented as the lights flicked on. "I want photos of the portraits."

Kate followed him to the stairs. Her eyes were everywhere, overwhelmed by the dust and cobweb-strewn extravagance of her surrounds.

"Kate, keep up," demanded Jasper. "You start at the bottom, while I start at the top. We have to be quick. Get the whole portrait, including the name."

"What?"

"Take the bloody photos."

"This is a waste of time."

Jasper stopped and stared at her.

"We should be searching for journals," she continued. "Lady Isabel's. I'm guessing bedroom. Probably in her desk." Her iPhone flashed on a portrait. "Secret compartment." She stopped and stared at an unnamed portrait. She felt she knew this man.

Reaching the top of the stairs, Kate called, "Jasper."

"In here."

She opened a bedroom door. Jasper was sitting at a desk, flicking through a notebook.

He handed it to Kate. "It was in this secret drawer. She recorded everything from the moment her son met your mother."

The colour drained out of Kate's face as she flicked through the notebook.

"My love, your father was Henry Landon Junior. There's no doubt about it." He pulled her into his arms and kissed her hair. "Come, we have to go."

"What are these?" she asked, picking up a pile of old notebooks, letters and photograph albums.

"No use. Put them back in the desk."

"Not likely," came her terse reply.

* * *

Kate was sitting in the Range Rover, looking at her watch. *Where are you, Jasper?* she thought.

The driver's door opened, and Jasper leapt in. "Feast your eyes on these," he said as he eased himself into the driver's seat.

Kate slipped her hand into a cotton bag.

"Careful," he said. "I don't want to lose any."

"I don't know a thing about diamonds but I'm guessing these must be valuable."

"I've got to examine them in daylight, but every bone in my body is telling me they're flawless."

"You've stolen them."

"My love, they're yours."

"Just because I fit your Landon timeline doesn't mean I'm a Landon. Have you thought that Henry Junior might have fathered other children?"

"Lady Isabel Landon knew who you were."

The Range Rover moved towards the entrance of the estate.

"You'd better give me the idiot's guide to diamonds, or should I ask Harry?"

Jasper glanced at his wife. *Why, after all this time, does she want to know about diamonds?*

An uncomfortable silence filled the cabin.

"No. I'll do it," he said. "It's best if we keep this between us."

Chapter Six

The loud shrill from River's End House's front doorbell echoed through the foyer.

Robert opened the door to a group of people.

"Pieter Von-Pitt and associates to see Lady Carmichael."

"You're not welcome here," bellowed Jasper as he marched out of his diamond office.

Von-Pitt stepped inside the foyer with his associates behind him.

Kate stood in the doorway to her library. She had been sorting what was left of her books that had survived the storm; her well-worn jeans rested on her hips, her white blouse was open to her cleavage.

Jasper stared at his wife's tousled hair and the sexy position of her jeans. Desire stirred. He walked over to her and sensually kissed her full lips. A pink glow flushed her cheeks.

Von-Pitt recoiled in disgust, then bustled forward. "Lady Carmichael, I presume. Let me introduce myself and my associates." He pointed to himself and to each associate in turn. "Pieter Von-Pitt; Tony Rice, a Canadian, top security expert; Lord Landon; Margot; and of course you know Joanne."

What's she doing here? Kate thought. *She's trouble.*

A sly grin stretched across Joanne's lips as her eyes lecherously wandered over Jasper. His jeans were tight, and his white t-shirt hugged his toned chest.

However, it wasn't Joanne that bothered Kate—she could handle Joanne. But she wasn't as confident about Tony Rice. Unfortunately, her recollection of Tony was an unhappy one.

She had never mentioned Tony to Jasper, even though Jasper had questioned her about her uni years. He would never believe that she had never had sex with Tony when he found out that they had studied together. She had promised Tony that he would have his wish at the after-exam party, but she never went to the after-exam party; she disappeared to London and her new job. The last she had heard of Tony was that he had gone to Canada with May, his uni fuck-buddy.

Out the corner of her eye, she caught Jasper staring at Tony. Jasper wouldn't miss the lust in Tony's eyes. She and Jasper moved closer to the Von-Pitt party.

Kate smiled and pushed her hair back with her glasses. "Mr Von-Pitt, you should have phoned. It's Sunday, and it's a day I keep to myself."

Kate's sharp, cold voice and stiff body surprised Jasper. This was not how she normally greeted guests. In the past, she had been civil to adversaries—Gypsy came to mind, a giant of a man, a drug dealer who had tried to take over the shopping centre and fuck her.

"I'm in Wellsbury tomorrow," Kate said. "Ring the office."

"Lady Carmichael, all we want is a moment of your time."

Jasper watched in horror as Kate scowled, clenched her fists and stepped towards Von-Pitt.

Jasper quickly moved, slipping his arm across her shoulders. "Pieter, my wife has a lot to deal with. The shopping centre demands her undivided attention, and she's trying to come to terms with the loss of her beach house."

"There's rumours that there's a hostile bid."

"You shouldn't listen to rumours, Mr Von-Pitt," Kate said tersely.

"You're in debt, Lady Carmichael. Too many empty units."

Jasper could feel Kate's temper rising in her tense body. He moved his hand to her waist, gripping her side. A heavy, angry tension swirled around the foyer.

"Mr Von-Pitt, I'm not sure why you've taken it upon yourself to interrupt my Sunday, but it clearly wasn't to say hello. If you think that you're going to sweet-talk me into selling the centre, think again." Kate's firm, aristocratic voice echoed.

"I've heard that so many times, Lady Carmichael, and I've always won."

"Not this time."

Von-Pitt stared at Kate. She didn't flinch.

Suddenly, he laughed, turned and walked out of the foyer.

Jasper waited until their people carrier was on the main road, then he followed Kate into her library.

"Kate." He stopped as his bare feet sank into the thick-pile carpet. He hadn't been in the library since Wes and his team had finished. Flames leapt from the logs in the inglenook fireplace. A small oak desk nestled by the window as if it belonged there, and a small worktable was opposite the bookshelves. A large, leather couch, similar to the one they'd had at Isaacs House, caught his eye. A couple of her paintings leaned against the desk. The room already felt like Kate.

"Kate," he continued, "you don't mess with a man like Von-Pitt. He's got spies everywhere, people who are on his payroll."

"What did you expect me to do: just roll over?" *Wrong word*, she thought.

"Did you roll over for Tony Rice?"

"No."

"A uni fuck-buddy? You have never admitted who had your cherry."

Kate cringed; he knew that phrase would rile her.

Here goes, she thought. *Another part of my life he doesn't know about.* "Whatever you think you know about my uni years, forget it. I should have told you, but there was so much gossip about me, I just let you believe what you wanted." She paused and looked into his eyes. "The thought of having a testosterone-fuelled student inside me repulsed me. Yes, I experienced groping and fondling; my breasts attracted men like bees to a honeypot. I stopped going to student parties, preferring to study, but Tony Rice pursued me during lectures, dinner time, teatime. He wore me down until I agreed to let him study with me."

"He fucked you."

"Don't you dare judge me! How many women have you fucked? I'm sure Joanne will remind me that I was never enough."

"You've always been enough; I just couldn't accept it."

An angry silence ensued.

"Eric was the first to penetrate me. He was too drunk to realise. I remember the pain as he thrust deep inside me. I cried. I wonder how many women lost their virginity pinned to the alley wall next to the George." She paused, gathering her thoughts. "You knew I lost Eric's baby... I was like most of the women in Wellsbury that wanted you to fuck them, only I didn't show it." Kate slumped onto the new couch. She wasn't up to arguing with Jasper.

"What about Rice?" His temper was rising.

"Rice means nothing to me. Not then and not now."

"Why is he fucking here then?"

"I promised him after the exam party, but I didn't go; instead, I caught a train to London and my new job."

"You expect me to fucking believe that he's here because you owe him a fuck?"

"I owe him nothing."

The door slammed as Jasper stormed out.

Chapter Seven

Von-Pitt had employed Tony Rice's Canadian security company instead of using a local company expressly because Tony Rice had been at uni with the young Kate Reynolds. Von-Pitt had become impatient with him when he refused to talk about Lady Kate Carmichael, née Reynolds. Her mother was Laura Spencer, daughter of the infamous lawyer Meredith, but Von-Pitt was interested in knowing who her father was, as it certainly wasn't that evil bastard Reynolds. Now that he had met Lady Carmichael, Von-Pitt was convinced she had aristocratic blood flowing through her veins.

Von-Pitt had left his associates at Jasper's Wellsbury hotel; he had a date with the elderly members of the Gentlemen's Club. Once a month, the older members of the club met for lunch to reminisce. On this occasion, Pieter Von-Pitt had tempted many more of them to attend with a free three-course lunch and an open bar. The dining room hummed with friendly banter and happy, satisfied men.

Von-Pitt leaned on the bar and called the old-timers to attention; it was time for them to earn their whisky and rich food.

"Gentlemen, some of you are wondering why I'm lavishing food and whisky on you." The room hushed. "I would like information on Lady Kate Carmichael, Lord Jasper Carmichael's wife." Von-Pitt placed a small voice recorder on the bar.

You could hear a pin drop.

After a brief silence, a distinguished-looking man walked to the bar. "I've drunk three malts and eaten the roast beef." His hand reached inside his expensive jacket, and from a leather wallet that had seen better days, he dropped a fifty-pound note on the bar. Then, he turned and left the room.

One by one, the members walked towards Von-Pitt and dropped fifty-pound notes on the bar. Von-Pitt was taken aback; they were shielding Kate Carmichael, or her father. Why?

The last member hesitated as he dropped his fifty pounds onto the bar. "If you'd asked about Jasper, they wouldn't have stopped talking, but Kate is off-limits."

"She owns half of Wellsbury. She won't sell," Von-Pitt anxiously said, eager to make the old-timer talk.

"Well, that's Kate's prerogative."

"It's ripe for development. She's holding the place back. No one will talk to me."

"Like I said, if you'd asked about Jasper, we wouldn't have stopped talking."

"What is she, some kind of princess?"

"A queen," the man said as he walked through the door.

An irritated Von-Pitt collected his money and stormed outside. His fat face glowed as he fought to control his temper.

A scruffy-looking man sidled up to him. "Thousand pound will buy the lowdown on Laura Spencer."

* * *

In a downmarket backstreet pub, Von-Pitt listened to this mangy individual as he guzzled the whisky

Von-Pitt had bought. After three large glasses, his tongue loosened.

"Every year, from June to September, a rich, aristocratic family visited their Wellsbury summer residence: River's End House."

That's the house Jasper has just bought, Von-Pitt thought.

"The family arrived in a silver Rolls Royce with a crest on the front, and an entourage of people and servants. They never mixed with the ordinary people, only people that arrived in black Bentleys.

"Things changed when Lord and Lady Landon were having a banquet and the flower arranger let them down. They looked locally for a flower shop. Reynolds, Kate's adopted father, was running a successful flower business at the time. He jumped at the chance to mix with the aristocratic Landons. Reynolds was introduced to their son and his friend, Laura Spencer. She was a beauty. Kate has some of her features. Reynolds fell in love with Laura, but she didn't notice him. She was besotted with young Landon.

"When the young Landon fathered Laura's child, the family looked for a scapegoat. Reynolds was only too happy to marry Laura and accept the hefty dowry.

"Meredith Spencer, Laura's father, knew the Landons, as he had represented them in many court cases. He was a favourite of the family as he never lost in a court of law. Many companies that had disagreements with the Landons settled out of court when Meredith represented them. However, Meredith reacted badly when he discovered that the apple of his eye was having a Landon baby and that, without consulting him, they had decided to marry her off to Reynolds. His mind must have been clouded by anger, as he disowned his daughter and cut ties with the Landon family."

Von-Pitt was eager to know more about Kate Carmichael's father. He waved at the barman to bring another bottle of whisky and laid another wad of money on the table that separated him from the informant.

"Rumour had it that a university professor had fathered Kate—a story spread by the Landons to take the heat off the family. But young Landon, heir to the Landon fortune, took to drink and drugs when he was denied the woman he loved. He was killed in a road accident, drunk."

An evil grin spread across Von-Pitt's face. At last, he had dirt on Lady Carmichael. "How would you like to earn another hundred or two?"

The scruffy man was all ears as Von-Pitt explained what he had to do.

A burner phone was pushed towards him.

"Use this when you have something."

Chapter Eight

Pieter Von-Pitt was sitting in the window seat inside the coffee shop opposite the shopping centre main office. His spies had told him that Kate arrived at the office before seven o'clock.

Her old Evoque pulled up and parked in her allocated parking space. Wes Clayton's brother, Jack, the owner of Clayton's Cars, arrived in a new Evoque before Kate had opened the office. After a brief chat, Jack followed Kate into the office. Half an hour later, they both left: Kate walked towards the arcade and Harry's diamond store, and Jack drove off in the old Evoque.

Von-Pitt pondered on why Kate was getting rid of her old Evoque, a car that she had refused to sell. It was part of the Kate brand, like blue jeans and a white fitted blouse. Was she about to change? For years she had been quite happy living a reclusive life in a beach house, ignoring the shopping centre and her property portfolio.

Suddenly, a silver Range Rover pulled in next to Kate's car. Jasper stepped out, pulled down on his jacket sleeves and gazed around in that superior manner of his.

Von-Pitt quickly moved away from the window; he didn't want Jasper to see him.

Jasper gazed approvingly at Kate's new Evoque. He smiled when she appeared next to him.

Von-Pitt couldn't hear what they were saying, but he cringed when Jasper looped his arm across her shoulders and they began to walk towards the farmers' market. Curiosity got the better of Von-Pitt, so much so that he followed them.

Godfrey Clayton, the farmers' market representative, was waiting. Von-Pitt noticed that Godfrey was doing all the talking. He swore under his breath as Godfrey pointed at the empty units opposite the market. Von-Pitt knew all about the empty units; they were part of his scheme.

His phone beeped. It was his contact in Carmichael Properties. Kate had closed the shopping centre office for the day.

Von-Pitt inwardly cursed. What was she up to? He had lost interest in Jasper; it was Kate that bothered him.

He suddenly noticed that she was writing in a small notebook. He wondered if she had stumbled across his empty units scam. He reached for his phone.

Von-Pitt was not one for small talk. "Has she found out about our scam?"

"Don't know," came the nervous reply. *"She's closed the office and changed the access code. I can't check what she's been up to."*

"Have you made copies?"

"Ye-es," he stuttered. *"They're in the office."*

Von-Pitt took a deep breath.

"No one thought she'd change the door code."

Von-Pitt wasn't listening. His face was the shade of beetroot; his gut was churning. His grip on his phone tightened as he hurried into the market square to find Kate and Jasper.

Once a week, the market square welcomed the arty types: dancers, musicians, theatre groups, artists. It was very popular with people wanting a free day out. The square had more than its share of bistros, cafés and restaurants where people could try food from all over the world.

Von-Pitt's heart was racing and he was short of breath; he pulled his tie away from his collar. He wanted to shout and throw his phone, but the market square was filling up and he didn't want to draw attention to himself.

He couldn't see Kate, but he spotted Jasper carrying a tray of drinks. There she was. Kate looked into Jasper's eyes and smiled, slipping her notebook into the bag that was slung across her shoulders.

Kate filled Von-Pitt's mind. Who was this woman? What was she writing in that notebook? Why had she dismissed the staff and changed the door code? He had to find someone who had known her before the beach house.

Von-Pitt had seen enough. He was so close to taking over the shopping centre, he couldn't lose it now. Kate's accountants had told him that the shopping centre was approaching bankruptcy and that the once-a-week market was keeping it solvent. She might have blue blood flowing through her veins, but she would need more than that to save the shopping centre.

Chapter Nine

Kate felt uneasy after Jasper left. She hadn't wanted him to leave her, but he had reassuringly said that she was being silly, she had been away from people for too long.

As she sat alone in her office, collecting the shopping centre paperwork to take back to River's End House, she began to think about the number of empty units. She was convinced that the numbers in the weekly reports didn't marry up with what she had seen that day. She had a lot to think about and do while Jasper was away, but the top priority was the shopping centre's finances.

The rain started to pour down as Kate loaded the documents and her computer into her new Evoque. She had felt sad when Jack Clayton drove away in her trusted Evoque that had never let her down; her life was changing against her better judgement. She missed the beach and sea; she missed painting and her books. She smiled as a thought occurred: she no longer missed sex; Jasper had made sure of that.

She was still smiling, thinking about car sex, as she nipped back into the office to collect the paperwork that she had left, but a loud noise like a building collapsing made her leave via the back.

She gingerly took a step out from the secluded rear entrance. A white van had careered into the back doors of one of the units and managed to set off the water sprinklers. Angry men, dripping with water, were running about and shouting.

Kate was briefly mesmerised by the ensuing chaos until Von-Pitt appeared. *What the hell is he doing here?* A slow smile crept across her face as she realised that the sprinklers had made an excellent job of wetting him through.

His anger echoed, and suddenly, men came running to help.

While Von-Pitt was preoccupied, Kate took the opportunity to see what was going on. To her surprise, the rear doors of the unit next to the white van were open. She was even more surprised to see a large microscope and computer were being fitted on the far wall. She wandered inside to find the back of the unit had been partitioned from the front. She racked her brain, trying to think of a planning application.

Her mind was focused on the alterations as she stepped outside; she wasn't prepared to see a Range Rover reversed into the open doors of the next unit.

She cast her eyes around, looking for the men who had been working around the units, and when she looked inside the next one, she was taken aback to see that it had also been partitioned. The rear section looked like a meeting room. In the centre was a newish wooden table with four wooden chairs, and on the table were two holdall-type bags and a large attaché case.

Her eyes welled at what she might find inside. Fear sped through her as her trembling hand hovered over a holdall. She glanced inside the bag, and there they were: bricks wrapped in white paper. One had been slit open, revealing the white powder.

She stepped back, her body shaking. Tears ran down her cheeks as she thought of her dead son. "Oliver," she murmured.

She found herself leaning on the open hatch of the Range Rover, her mind lingering on the day Oliver died. Jasper had also been hurting; he had tried to comfort her, but she was inconsolable. Jasper had wanted revenge, and he had had it the only way he knew—and that was what she must do now.

Kate searched for an accelerant and matches. Tucked away in the back of the Range Rover was a can of petrol, and on the table was a box of matches next to a packet of cigars, a bottle of malt and four tumblers.

In a trance, she poured the petrol over the drugs. She picked up the attaché case, then she walked outside, throwing several burning matches onto the petrol that had trickled onto the concrete floor.

Kate detoured her way back to her shopping centre office; she didn't want to be caught carrying the attaché case.

In the safety of her office, she flicked it open. Stacked in neat bundles were fifty-pound notes and, to her surprise, a bag of uncut diamonds.

She opened her old floor-mounted safe and tried to jam the case inside. It was too big. In a rush, she emptied the case and stuffed the money inside. She then turned to her wall-mounted safe and put the remainder of the money in there, with the bag of diamonds. With the money secured, she walked to the storeroom and hid the attaché case.

She hastily collected the rest of her paperwork and left the office.

It was while setting the alarm that the hairs on the back of her neck twitched and a cold shiver trickled down her spine. She momentarily froze as a frightening thought flashed through her mind: she had been caught stealing drug money.

As she reached the car door, the hood of her rain jacket was pulled and she hit the ground with a thud. Pain shot through her back and into her head.

She tried to move, but a kick landed in her kidneys.

"Get the documents," ordered a familiar voice.

Her hand fumbled in her jacket pocket for the office alarm remote. She pressed any button. All hell was let lose as the security lights flooded the area, including her car, and the office alarm went off.

There was a screech of tyres as a car stopped.

Chapter Ten

Kate didn't want to open her eyes. She wasn't in her bed. This bed was small, there was that unmistakeable hospital smell, and there was an annoying monitor beeping. In the distance, she could hear Jasper's angry voice.

"Robert, go back to the house and get the bedroom ready."

"Sir."

"Lock all the doors."

"Of course."

His demons must be rising, she thought.

"Mother can hear you, you know. You're not helping."

Harry. What's going on? I've got to stop this.

She tried to shout, but her throat hurt. She opened her mouth, but no sound came out.

* * *

"We had her, but bloody Jasper suddenly appeared." A frustrated Tony Rice stood. "You told me he was going to London." He glared at Von-Pitt accusingly.

"Jasper is his own man. He does what he wants and when." Von-Pitt's voice was uncharacteristically calm.

"Jasper's the problem."

"Margot will have him."

"I wish I had your confidence in Margot."

Von-Pitt put his head into his hands. He wanted to shout, but it would do no good; they had lost the chance of kidnapping Kate. Tony Rice wanted to fuck her, but he wanted the Landon diamonds. Jasper could be a problem. Could he rely on Margot's seductive power to get Jasper away from Kate, or should he eliminate him? Now would be the ideal time; Jasper wouldn't be expecting a killer to be roaming the hospital corridors.

Von-Pitt picked up his phone.

"Yes," snapped the man.

"Carmichael's at the hospital."

"It'll cost."

"Just do it."

* * *

Von-Pitt's assassin entered Jasper's private hospital just as dawn was breaking. He followed the signs to "inpatients", where he anticipated Kate would be. Catlike, he walked along the corridor. To his surprise, all the doors to the rooms were open. Beds were made, waiting for patients. There was no sign of Lady Carmichael.

Minutes later, he was sitting in his BMW X7. "She's not here," he said into his phone.

"Find out where she's gone," an irritable Von-Pitt answered. He didn't like early-morning bad news.

"The place is deserted."

Von-Pitt's anger assaulted the assassin's ear. *"Find her! No kill, no money."*

Von-Pitt flung his phone across his bedroom. "Fuck, fuck, fuck," his angry voice boomed.

Chapter Eleven

River's End House buzzed with activity; every fire was lit, even in the empty rooms. The house had to be warm for Kate. The doctor had reluctantly discharged her, even though the brain scan was clear. Jasper had carried her to the car, and Harry had driven them to River's End.

It was two o'clock when Jasper slipped out of the kitchen. Kate was asleep. There was no moon to shine his way to the boathouse. He opened the boathouse side door and stepped inside. A small yacht was loosely tied to the decking.

"You're late," said a gruff voice as the body attached to it jumped off the yacht. "The tide's turning. I don't want to be stuck here."

"Kate was attacked."

"Haven't got time for that." He pulled a cotton bag from his pocket. "Uncut."

Jasper looked at the uncut diamonds in his palm.

"No need to tell you that they're hot."

"How many?"

"Can you cut them?"

Jasper nodded. "Can they be traced?"

"I'm not your mate Lord Blackthorn. He's double-dealing. Joined that secret diamond club. He's pushing for papers to guarantee the diamonds' origin."

Jasper stared at the smuggler's face.

"Didn't know, did ya? Too trusting, that's your problem."

Jasper put the diamonds in the deep pocket of his jacket. "Will Blackthorn get his way?"

"Nah. Paperwork cuts into profits. Money always wins."

"There will be more diamonds?"

"This is not a good time for me."

"You'll manage."

"How is she?" the smuggler said, jumping onto the yacht and untying the rope.

"Got a headache and bruised body. Doctor says lots of rest."

The yacht's engine fired and it moved out of the boathouse.

"Watch your back. Von-Pitt's on manoeuvres."

* * *

Kate woke alone. Her head was throbbing; she needed more painkillers. She tried to stand, lost her balance and fell back onto the bed.

Where's Jasper? she thought.

She used furniture to aid her as she staggered to the bedroom window. She leaned on a chest of drawers for support as she gazed into the night sky, thankful that the window was slightly open and letting the cool night air in to revive her.

A dark shadow, jogging towards the house, caught her attention.

Jasper, she thought.

With a warm robe slung over her shoulders, Kate slowly walked downstairs using the banister for support. While the kettle was boiling, she found the painkillers and took two. She managed to make a cup of tea before her head began to spin.

The utility outside door creaked as Jasper returned. He stopped in his tracks when he saw her. "Kate. What's wrong?"

The creaking of the utility door woke Robert. Taking one stair at a time, he carefully and quietly negotiated his way downstairs.

"I needed painkillers. You weren't there," Kate said.

Jasper put his arm around her shoulders. "You should have rung for Robert."

"Where were you?"

"I needed to think. Stretch my legs," he lied.

Kate guessed he was lying; even with her spinning head, she noticed he hadn't removed his coat.

That's where the diamonds are.

"Come." He held out his hand. "Back to bed."

"Throw some wood on the library fire. I'll sleep by the fire."

Jasper was concerned. Her body language suggested that she was in pain; bed was obviously the best place for her. "You'll be better in bed. Your tablets are due."

"I've taken them."

"The doctor said not to take too many."

"Fuck the doctor. He hasn't got this head."

Jasper took a step back.

Robert, who had been listening, sensed that tension was building. *Lady Carmichael doesn't need a domestic*, he thought. He opened the door between the kitchen and utility.

"Everything alright, sir?"

Jasper felt awkward; he shouldn't have left her. "Lady Carmichael would like an early breakfast."

"Anything in particular?"

"Toast would be fine," he said.

"Butter and marmalade, my lady?"

"Please."

Chapter Twelve

River's End House shuddered as a helicopter came in to land. Jasper gathered the uncut diamonds and crammed them into his overfull safe, then hurried from his office to greet Lord Blackthorn.

"How's Kate? Nasty business," Lord Blackthorn said as he bustled past Jasper.

Before Jasper could answer, Lord Blackthorn had opened the library door. A pale-looking Kate was sitting staring at her desk. She closed the new MacBook that Jasper had insisted she have. Her right hand reached for a steaming cup of tea.

"Kate, my dear, how do you feel?"

Before she could answer, Lord Blackthorn began looking over the papers that covered her desk. His hand flicked over the paper she was trying to read.

"Shopping centre work, Kate? I'd thought you would be resting."

Jasper's eyes never left her as he walked towards the desk.

"You should put your foot down, Jasper, make Kate do as she is told. That's the way to treat women."

Kate's face reddened as she seethed under her breath.

Jasper tensed. He moved to her side and placed his hand on her shoulder, giving it a gentle squeeze.

A disapproving scowl descended upon Lord Blackthorn's face. "Come along, I haven't come here to discuss your domestic arrangements. Von-Pitt's bulging at the seams. I want to get our business over before he arrives."

* * *

Kate reopened her laptop, still seething from Lord Blackthorn's comment, and tried to upload the shopping centre accounts. But it was a waste of time; the reoccurring dizziness returned. She closed the laptop, slumped back into the chair and closed her eyes.

"My lady." Robert's voice was soft and gentle.

"I'm not asleep, Robert."

"Lord Carmichael is arguing with the Von-Pitt party."

"Party?"

"Mr Von-Pitt, Lord Landon, Mr Rice and the two ladies, Joanne and Margot."

Kate stood and immediately lost her balance. Robert caught her arm.

"You're not well. I shouldn't have told you."

Kate gripped his arm as she moved out of the library towards the living room. "A cup of tea would be nice, Robert."

Robert opened the living room door, and Kate slowly walked in.

Silence.

* * *

The rain pounded the bedroom window. Jasper's fingers slowly trailed along her spine. Kate lay naked across his chest.

"Jasper," she murmured.

"Shh. Sleep." His hand stroked her hair.

"I can't remember."

I can, he thought. *You walked into a fierce argument with Von-Pitt. You were very pale and unsteady. Robert stood at the door, staring at you. Then you swayed. It all happened so quickly. I pushed Von-Pitt out of the way and caught you before you reached the floor.*

* * *

Tony Rice, Lord Landon, Joanne and Margot sat in Von-Pitt's hotel room.

"Did you see how he ran to that bitch?" said Margot. "What the fuck has she got?"

"She's got something you haven't got, and neither has Joanne," answered Tony Rice as he filled his glass with Von-Pitt's Macallan.

"I thought she was a ghost," said a nervous Lord Landon.

"Shut the fuck up, Landon," snapped Tony.

"Normal service will be resumed as soon as she's well," said Von-Pitt.

"You lot have no idea what awaits you." They all turned to Joanne. "He... Jasper will want revenge. No one—I repeat, *no one*—does that to his beloved." She hesitated before continuing. "He's murdered for her. Max Wilson roughed her up, ripped her blouse, exposing her tits. Max Wilson could look after himself; he was found face down in the swimming pool."

"That doesn't mean Jasper did it," retorted Von-Pitt.

"Think what you like, Von-Pitt." Joanne stood and put on her jacket. "The Wilson brothers were killed in a car accident after they threatened her. Drunk driving."

"Where are you going?" asked Margot.

"I'm having nothing to do with you lot now this has happened. I told you to leave her alone." She met Von-Pitt's eyes. "Your trouble is you can't wait."

Von-Pitt's eyes bulged with anger. "You like my money. You don't get that by waiting."

"I owe you nothing. I've paid you back." Her hand rested on the door handle. "Leave her alone and you all will live longer."

Von-Pitt's quick temper burst. "I will have the shopping centre and all her land. Wellsbury will be mine. My headquarters. Where people once called 'Carmichael's' they will call 'Von-Pitt's'. The Carmichaels are dead."

Chapter Thirteen

Kate leaned on the tiled shower wall, letting the warm water wet her hair and revive her body. She had been lying in bed for a week; she was bored.

Dressed in a pair of oversized navy joggers, a long-sleeved white t-shirt and a long knitted waistcoat, she wandered into the kitchen. The staff were having their mid-morning break. Kate smiled, grabbed her warm jacket, slipped on her wellington boots and walked outside.

She stood and closed her eyes. As the damp air settled on her face, she concentrated on breathing. She imagined she was walking along the tide line at the beach house. The wet sand squelched between her toes as the warm sea covered her bare feet; the familiar smell of salt filled her nose.

Her eyes opened. *Was that the sound of waves crashing onto rocks?*

Without thinking, she set off in search of the sound of the sea.

An hour later, she was sitting on a rock, letting her mind drift to the rhythmic motion of the waves. The sound penetrated every bone; the smell revitalised all her senses. Kate was home.

Slowly, his arm touched her shoulders, gently coaxing her into his warm body.

She turned; their lips were close.

"You didn't tell me about this little slice of heaven," she said.

"I wanted to surprise you with a studio. Not as big as the one that Bruce built, but big enough for you to paint, read or listen to the sea."

"And love." Her finger traced his hairline. "Don't compete with Bruce. I would be happy with a shed."

"My wife is not painting in a shed."

"I'm your lover."

Their lips brushed.

"Come." He gripped her hand and swiftly walked towards the waiting Range Rover.

"You brought the Range Rover?" said a surprised Kate.

"Kate, you're teasing me. Those green eyes are on fire. I want you. Not on a windy, cold beach or on the back seat." He turned her so she was leaning on the passenger door. "But in a comfortable, warm bed." His voice faded as their lips met. The kiss deepened. Her fingers threaded through his silky hair. Desire raged, and Jasper's hand groped for the rear passenger door.

The sound of a hovering helicopter broke the spell.

* * *

Lord Blackthorn was sitting in the living room, sipping a malt. His angry eyes flared when Jasper joined him. "My God, man, can't you control yourself? You're married to her, for God's sake."

"What do you want?"

"Well, I don't want to fuck your wife."

With three steps, Jasper had him by the collar, pulling him off the settee. Lord Blackthorn's face turned bright red and he started coughing. Jasper threw him back onto the cushions.

"What do you want?" Jasper repeated.

Lord Blackthorn gulped his malt. "That temper of yours will be your undoing." His coughing subsided. "What's so fucking special about her?"

Jasper stepped towards him.

"Okay, okay. What do you know about stolen, uncut diamonds? Possibly Russian."

"Nothing."

"Von-Pitt's convinced that you're the fence. That's why I'm here."

"Taking orders from Von-Pitt."

"Some of my associates are listening to him."

"Fools."

"There's a lot going on. My associates are pushing for documentation that would guarantee the diamonds' origin."

"That's your problem, not mine."

"Put your feelers out. Find out what your criminal friends know about uncut diamonds and the Guarantee of Origin document."

"My business is legit. I source diamonds for rich clients and Harry's shop. I have paperwork."

"You're irresponsible. Diamonds flow through your hands without you even knowing. You can't get an accountant. How can you be legit?"

"I don't need one, I have Kate."

"Is she up to it?"

Jasper's temper flared; he didn't like being questioned about Kate. "She's recovering from an attempted mugging. My guess is Von-Pitt's involved. He wants Wellsbury, and Kate is in the way. Then there's the Landon connection. The City has the Landon Trust Fund under investigation. If it's proved that Kate is a Landon, there's a possibility she could save the fund… but that would give her more power, and Von-Pitt wouldn't like that."

Lord Blackthorn loosened his collar; he had suddenly become very hot.

* * *

Lord Blackthorn leaned against the helicopter's closed door. The pilot was waiting anxiously for the go-ahead to leave, but Lord Blackthorn had his phone firmly pressed against his ear.

"Carmichael knows. You've got to lay off Kate."

"As soon as Rice finishes with the new security measures, she's toast."

"How long will it take?"

"The bits are out of stock, so we're in the hands of the Chinese."

"In the meantime?"

"We watch her. All you must do is keep him away from Wellsbury."

"He won't leave her until she's better."

"You'll know when she's better; he'll be fucking her."

"She's very pale. She looks ill."

"What about the uncut diamonds?"

"He claims he knows nothing about them."

"He's lying."

"Jasper covers his tracks."

"Uncover them. That house is the cover for Carmichael's diamond dealings, just as it was for Lord Henry Landon's. Use your initiative. Have them watched. I have a yacht watching them."

"He won't leave Kate."

"I have every faith in Margot. She'll take him away from her."

"You don't have any idea. If Kate's not by his side, he'll be the diamond king all over again."

Chapter Fourteen

From the library, Jasper watched Lord Blackthorn talking into his phone. He guessed he was talking to Von-Pitt.

The helicopter blades finally began to turn as Lord Blackthorn fastened his safety belt.

Kate slid up to Jasper, slipping her hands under his t-shirt. "Who was he talking to? Any guesses?"

Jasper smiled as her fingers ran under his waistband. "I'm guessing Von-Pitt."

She rested her head on his back. "He's becoming a pain in the arse."

Jasper laughed. "Such language, Lady Carmichael!"

The helicopter took off.

"I'm Kate. Just Kate."

"You're mine."

"Can we be just Kate and Jasper? Lovers for one night."

He wrapped his arms around her so that her head rested on his chest. "Kate, what's wrong?"

"I have this feeling that we will have to battle to stay together."

"Nothing will part us. They have tried before." He kissed her hair.

"They have always wanted you, but this time it's me they want."

"Who are 'they'?"

"The forces of greed, envy, jealousy. It was always about diamonds. But not this time."

"Who are they this time?"

"Von-Pitt, Tony Rice, Margot."

Her hand caressed his chest. "Just one night, Jasper. No diamonds. No Lady Carmichael. Us alone. Jasper and Kate."

Jasper moved to close and lock the library door while Kate covered the floor in front of the blazing fire with cushions.

"You're not recovered," Jasper said.

"I can't let them walk all over me. Attack is the best form of defence." Kate slowly removed her clothes, one by one. She stood before him in a white lace bra and panties. His favourite.

He wanted to ask her questions, but they would have to wait. Kate in white lace always stirred him. He wanted her and she wanted him, and that was all that mattered.

She slowly removed his t-shirt, her soft lips kissing their way to his mouth. Their tongues danced as their bodies melted together. His hands deftly unclipped her bra, releasing her full breasts.

He sighed. "Mine." He feasted on her breasts.

Her head fell back and her hands massaged his head. Her orgasm was building. His lips meandered to her panties.

Her hands rested on his head as her panties fell to the floor. "Jasper," she cried as she climaxed for the first time.

With practised ease, he lowered her onto the cushions. Kate quickly removed his clothes. They lay skin to skin, enjoying the delights of each other's bodies.

He gripped her hips as he lowered her onto him. Her head fell back again as they moved together. She moaned in that delightful way he had missed so much as her second orgasm ripped through her.

"Kate, my love," he whispered as he moved on top of her. His fingers caressed her face.

She wrapped her legs around his waist. He hesitated.

"Don't stop."

"Kate, I—"

"Don't leave me like this."

She was wet and warm when he slipped back inside her. She sighed, and her hands threaded through his hair as he moved. A gentle thrust, and she cried his name. He felt her quiver. His thrusts became erratic as her third orgasm claimed her body.

Their legs entwined as their bodies moulded together.

* * *

Kate slowly opened her eyes as the library fire warmed her aching body. She felt at ease; even the aches didn't dampen her contentment.

The library door opened, and Jasper walked in carrying a breakfast tray. He smiled. "Happy?"

"Very," she calmly replied while looking for her clothes. "I can't find—"

"Oh. I put them on the fire."

"You burnt my panties?"

"They were torn!" He grinned. "But I..." He slowly pulled a clean pair from his pocket and dangled them just out of her reach.

"Jasper!"

Dangle, reach; dangle, reach; dangle, reach. Jasper's laughter rebounded around the room as he caught her arm and drew her into a passionate kiss.

"That wasn't funny."

"No? But your kiss gave you away, my love." He kissed her forehead.

"What did it tell you?"
"You love me. You want me."
"That will never change."
"You won't be needing these just yet."
The clean panties fell to the carpet.

Chapter Fifteen

It was two o'clock in the morning when Jasper awoke, alone. Kate's clothes, which he had folded into a neat pile, were missing.

He wandered over to her desk while dressing. Papers were scattered all over the top. A spreadsheet flicked up on the laptop screen. The heading was clear: Diamond Store One. Various rows had been highlighted in red. He looked at the legend; red referred to "unexplained". The diamond shop was in debt, very close to bankruptcy; a quick glance at the red row at bottom of the sheet confirmed this.

He found her standing looking out of the orangery's new bifold doors. The orangery had been refurbished; the old, cracked glass and aluminium frame were unsafe. Jasper would have demolished it but for Kate.

He slipped his arms around her waist. "Come back."

"I can't sleep."

"I'm not thinking of sleeping."

She turned so that their lips met. "I can't find where Harry's getting the money from."

"We'll sort it in the morning."

"That will be too late. It'll be an electronic transaction. The transfer might be overnight. It may have already happened."

"Open the bank account."

"It won't let me; the passwords have changed."

"Come."

He took her hand and went into the diamond office. He rapidly typed on his computer keyboard and the diamond shop bank account filled the screen.

Kate stared at it. "It's empty. Who else has access?"

"Me and Harry. He froze me out a few weeks ago, but I have the overriding authority."

"Does he know?" she said, mesmerised by the account while easing herself onto his lap. "Can you cancel the account?"

"That's a bit drastic," he said as he nuzzled her neck.

"Jasper, concentrate."

"I am." He flicked to another screen.

Enter administrator password.

Freeze account.

"You're the administrator?"

"Couldn't let Harry be in charge. His head is always in the clouds."

* * *

Kate looked at her laptop clock. *Nine thirty*, she thought. *Harry will be here soon.*

The library door bounced open.

"Were you party to the bank account closure?" snapped an angry Harry.

"It's not closed, just paused."

"I suppose you'd been fucking, and he persuaded you."

Harry's words angered Kate, but experience had taught her not to respond in anger. "Harry, calm down."

"How can I be calm? My diamond business has been finished by my parents."

"The account's empty, Harry. Account number—"

"I know. I was expecting funds."

"Who from?"

"Does it matter?"

"Well, it does."

Harry dipped his head.

"Von-Pitt?" she said. As silence ensued, Kate stared deeply into his eyes. "Harry, answer me."

"All right, yes. Von-Pitt. I don't know how he found out." He slumped onto the couch and held his head in his hands. "I'm falling to pieces since Lizzy left me."

Kate stepped towards him.

"I know we weren't married, but it hurts like hell."

Kate sat next to him and nestled his head on her shoulder.

"Is this how you felt when Dad left?"

"The pain does fade... but the memory lingers."

"Tell me," said Harry.

"My first memory of emotional pain was when I discovered that Jasper had been unfaithful. I hid the pain and carried on." She paused as the pain surfaced. "When he left me for diamonds, my heart broke. But I had Clare and Malcolm to lean on; they kept me going, as did Bruce. Then I experienced the heart-shattering pain of losing Oliver.

"My life with your dad hasn't been easy. We have argued and separated, but our love always resurfaced and was stronger." Her hand caressed his hair. "I never dreamt that the love I would feel for him would be so consuming."

"I've caused you pain, too. Look at the mess the shop's in."

"You've lost the woman you love. The pain will run its course, and in the meantime, you must lean on me and your dad. Don't neglect Little Jasper and Lucy; show them that you love them."

Jasper had been standing in the library doorway, listening. A lump lodged in his throat when Kate confessed to the pain he had caused.

"Now," Kate said, "I think a cup of tea is called for."

Harry looked into his mother's eyes. "What is it with tea?"

"There's no problem that tea can't solve."

* * *

Kate had almost forgotten about the diamond shop when Jasper said, "It's bankrupt. Had to call in favours. Von-Pitt is a major shareholder."

"Fucking Von-Pitt. Major shareholder in what?"

"NRJ Bank."

The atmosphere in the library suddenly charged as Kate tried to control her temper. "Let me think…" She started to pace. "I haven't found any indication that the business is bankrupt." She gazed at the papers strewn across her desk. "Close the shop and reopen with a new owner: me. How much does it owe?"

"My informant told me that Von-Pitt is spreading rumours that a large injection of cash would save it."

"Am I reading this right? Von-Pitt has manufactured this so he can get his hands on the diamond shop?"

"He is backing you into a corner, Kate. Let Harry declare his diamond shop bankrupt; Von-Pitt already suspects that you're the money behind it."

"No one knows that."

"I never charge for the diamonds I source. Harry's bespoke diamond jewellery does not cover costs."

"How much does the shop need?" Her voice faded as she realised that pouring money into the shop would be wasted.

"Harry hasn't inherited our business sense."

Kate sat quietly, staring into space. "I could re-structure the shopping centre business to include the diamond shop." She paused as she mentally juggled her plan. "I will become the owner of the diamond shop, the whole business will be rebranded. A name from the past: Carmichael's."

"How long have you been hatching this plan?" asked Jasper sharply.

Kate continued as if he hadn't spoken. "I'll come to London with you."

"I'm going to the diamond festival," he snapped.

"I know. I'll visit my solicitors to draw up the papers. I'll include the diamond arm. The shop will continue to sell jewellery, but a state-of-the-art laboratory will be included so Harry can create his bespoke pieces."

Moments passed as Kate and Jasper stared at each other.

"You'll need money, Kate."

"My Cayman Islands account can act as collateral."

"I don't like it."

"I think with a bit of jiggery-pokery, I could make this work." Her mind flashed back to when the shopping centre had had cash flow problems and she had used money she had found in the old Victorian buildings. Zak's money. What was left of that money was still hidden in the Isaacs House library.

"Your solicitors will never agree to such a dubious proposal."

Kate's angry glare shot through him. "My solicitors do as I tell them," she curtly replied.

Jasper was taken aback. "You'll be overstretched," he replied sternly.

"Is that what you think?"

"Kate, do you realise the power you will have? Harry's well respected in the diamond world; having you in control will reflect badly on him."

"How does it reflect on him if Von-Pitt bails him out? You seem to forget that I already have power—I own the shopping centre. Or do you mean I will have power in your diamond world?"

Chapter Sixteen

It was late when Jasper and Kate left Wellsbury for London, and Jasper was irritable with Kate. First, she had insisted on talking at length to Wes Clayton and Robert about various works on the house. Then, she had spent a considerable time discussing her proposal with her solicitors, who had expressed reservations about her scheme. However, she'd managed to arrange a meeting for the next day. Jasper floored the Range Rover and they sped down the motorway to London. His Carmichael-temper scowl was fixed upon his face.

A new day dawned, and Kate and Jasper went their separate ways.

Lord Jasper Carmichael confidently strode through the doors to the Gentlemen's Club and to the member's lounge. As a lord, he was automatically a member. He was dressed in a designer, three-piece, grey suit, white shirt and tie. Handmade Italian loafers graced his feet. His brushed hair kissed his shirt collar, and his rimless spectacles hid the intensity of his blue eyes.

"The meeting is upstairs," said a member without looking up from *The Times*.

Jasper took the stairs two at a time, and he didn't knock on the meeting room door; he went straight in.

The committee members turned to face him.

"What do you want?" snapped Lord Ambrose, the chairman, whose dislike of the Carmichaels stretched back to Jasper's grandfather.

Somewhere, locked away in the club's basement, was a secret file on Jasper's grandfather and his wartime activities that had made him very rich. Lord Ambrose took his role of chairman very seriously, protecting its secrets at all costs; Jasper, being a Carmichael, could not be trusted and consequently wasn't privy to the secrets.

"Leave!" shouted the chairman, pointing to the door.

"He wants something," said the man on Lord Ambrose's right.

Jasper turned to Lord Devon, who as a young man, had graced the gossip columns with his friendship with the much older Lady Landon, Lord Henry's wife.

"I do," said Jasper. "But not for me, for Kate."

He had the attention of all the committee members.

"What have you done?" said Lord Ambrose.

"It's what Von-Pitt has done."

You could hear a pin drop. Jasper looked at each committee member in turn. They looked nervous and moved their eyes away from him. He sensed that Von-Pitt had already been to the club.

Jasper slid his fingers into his waistcoat's breast pocket, then rested a small, white cotton bag in his palm. "I would like to know if Von-Pitt has been here. I'm willing to pay for such information." He emptied the contents of the bag into his palm. Five flawless diamonds glistened.

The committee members were mesmerised as Jasper moved them around his palm. He had suspected for some time that the Gentlemen's Club was involved with diamonds.

"You can't bribe us with diamonds," snapped an angry Lord Ambrose.

"I don't intend to bribe. I'm willing to donate to the club—in return for any information that concerns my wife."

He's playing with words, thought Lord Ambrose as he moved his eyes up and down Jasper. Ambrose was struck by how much he resembled his grandfather's portrait. Jasper was a shrewd businessman and an excellent diamond dealer, just like his grandfather. However, he had one weakness that his grandfather never had: the love of a woman. Jasper's love for Kate was legendary and had already been written in the Carmichael secret files. What she saw in him was a complete mystery. Some said theirs was a sexual marriage… he did have a reputation. Ambrose wondered if Jasper realised whose blood was flowing through her veins.

"Von-Pitt has already tried to bribe us with a roast dinner and as much whisky as we liked. He wanted information on Lady Carmichael. We all gave him fifty quid and left. Mind you, if he'd wanted to know about you, we wouldn't have stopped talking."

"She gets more like her grandmother every day," said Lord Devon absentmindedly.

"Shut up," snapped Lord Ambrose.

"I mean Isabel, Lady Isabel Landon, her grandmother," Lord Devon whispered.

Jasper stared at Lord Devon. There were rumours that, as a young man, he had been besotted with the older Lady Landon.

Jasper slowly slid the diamonds back into the bag.

"We don't want your Carmichael diamonds," said Lord Ambrose.

"If you change your mind, I'll be at the diamond festival tomorrow—with Kate."

Lord Devon's eyes lit up.

* * *

Outside the club, a scruffy individual held a phone to his ear. "Carmichael is just leaving."

"Find out what he's up to."

"They are going to the diamond festival. He's booked a limousine."

* * *

Kate opened the wardrobe. Her mind wasn't on the array of overpriced dresses that Jasper had insisted she have; her thoughts hovered around their lack of communication. He hadn't bothered to ask about her meeting with the solicitors; he seemed to be preoccupied with his own affairs.

Her fingers wandered through the hangers until a light-purple dress caught her eye. She held it against her. She favoured the V-neck and the way the fabric flowed over her hips to just below her knee.

Impatiently, she rummaged through her underwear drawer. Jasper always bought her expensive lingerie. She tugged a corset (or was it a basque?) from the back of the drawer, slipped her body into it and stared at herself in the long mirror on the back of the wardrobe door. She didn't care what it was called, it fit her like a glove. She ran her hands admiringly over the white lace to the suspenders.

She felt desirable and sexy as she slipped into a pair of light-purple heels and turned to the dress that hung on a closed wardrobe door.

"My God, Kate, you look stunning."

Two arms snaked around her waist, sending waves of nervous butterflies through her. Soft lips brushed her neck.

"No flirting," he said in a sexy voice as he closed the clasp of a diamond-encrusted necklace. "Harry requested that you wear it." He placed the matching diamond earrings on the dressing table.

Her head fell to one side as his warm kisses reached her shoulder.

"I hope you're wet."

She could feel his arousal pressing into her hip. "Jasper, we are going out. I don't want a 'we've just had sex' look."

"You'll be the envy of the festival."

Chapter Seventeen

Two hours later, they arrived at the glitzy hotel where the diamond festival was being held. Jasper's hand rested on the small of Kate's back as they walked into the foyer.

"It's happening," she whispered so only he could hear. "There're all looking. They know why we're late."

Jasper stopped and arranged her necklace. "It's you, Kate. You look divine. Your aristocratic genes are showing. They recognise class when they see it." His lips touched her ear. "The women are jealous that we have just fucked; the men are wishing they had fucked you." His arm moved to her waist and pulled her into him so their lips touched. "Everything will be fine. I'll do Harry's business, then we'll leave."

The hubbub of the main hall faded into silence as they entered. The crowd openly gawped at Lady Carmichael.

Jasper's hand tightened on her waist. "You know something, Lady Carmichael?" he whispered.

She looked into his eyes.

"I love you."

She smiled.

"Carmichael!" shouted Lord Blackthorn as he bustled towards them. He leaned into Kate, planting a kiss upon her cheek. "Glad you've come. Kate, my dear, gorgeous as ever. That necklace is exquisite. Harry's, no doubt." He guided Jasper and Kate to an alcove.

"Ah. The Landon red diamonds," commented Jasper.

"I'm in a bit of a mess. I need your expertise on my latest shipment, Jasper."

"Send them to River's End; I'll look at them when I'm back."

"I could do with an evaluation today."

"No chance. Kate is priority."

Lord Blackthorn pulled Jasper to one side while Kate stood admiring the red diamonds. "There's no doubt about it," Blackthorn said. "My sources confirm that she is Lord Henry's granddaughter—I shouldn't tell you this—what's left of the Landon empire is hers. Charles Landon is hopping mad, and he's being egged on by Von-Pitt. Charles wants the Landon diamonds."

"I thought those diamonds were Landon's?" said Jasper, nodding his head to the red diamonds protected by a glass dome.

"They are supposed to be."

"You don't think they are?"

"I don't believe anything Charles Landon tells me. I've got enough on my plate with all the security."

"Where's Tony Rice?"

"He's too expensive… Security on the cheap? That's me. Haven't a clue what I've been doing, but the installers have done a good job fitting cameras, lasers, pressure sensors and more besides."

Lord Blackthorn waited for a response from Jasper.

"We're here for Harry's diamond store."

It wasn't what he expected. "Rumour has it Harry's selling."

"Now, where have you heard that?"

Blackthorn touched the side of his nose. As he loosened the top button of his collar, Jasper noted that his neck had turned bright red. Jasper guessed that they were being watched.

Is Lord Blackthorn in Von-Pitt's pay? he wondered.

"With Kate here, I hope you'll be a good boy," Blackthorn said as he moved to rejoin the festival.

Jasper grinned. "Of course."

"What's wrong with Blackthorn?" Kate asked as she looped her arm through Jasper's.

"He's panicking that I'll steal the red diamonds," he whispered in her ear.

"They are very beautiful."

Jasper smiled and leaned into her, pointing at the diamonds. "They're very rare. Pure reds can cost a million a carat. See how rich you are?"

"I'm not a Landon, Jasper."

"You certainly weren't a couple of hours ago." He grinned as his hand gave her bottom a gentle squeeze. All the time he was talking, his eyes roamed, looking for the security. "Come," he said, "let's get Harry some diamonds."

Jasper rested his hand on the small of her back as they walked around the main room. Kate felt his body tense as they approached a glass door with two armed guards standing in front of it. Within, Kate could see a brightly lit showroom with glass-topped displays. People were milling around; she assumed that they were looking at diamonds. More armed guards were on patrol, watching the prospective buyers.

A small, round man approached the glass doors, and the armed guards opened them. The small, round man acted as though he was expecting Jasper to give him a friendly hug; he looked crestfallen when Jasper didn't respond. He briefly turned his attention to Kate, giving her a respectful bow.

They followed him into a small, windowless office that only had room for a desk and two plastic seats. When Jasper refused the offer of a malt, the small man's face reddened, and he began to look nervous.

Kate glanced at her husband and was surprised to see an angry scowl covering his face.

The small man pressed a buzzer, and a door behind the desk slid open, revealing a cupboard-like room with racks of glitzing diamonds. The small man lifted a tray from one of the racks and placed it on top of the desk.

Jasper worked his way through the tray, examining the diamonds with his eyeglass.

"Don't mess with me, Claude," he finally said in a low but menacing voice.

That's the first time he has called the man by name, Kate thought. *Why?*

"Jasper, my friend."

"I'm not your friend." Jasper abruptly stood.

"Sit, sit. Let's talk."

Jasper leaned on the desk, his palms down. "Talking's over." His cold eyes pierced Claude. "You owe me."

Kate couldn't take her eyes off her husband; his body had tensed, but his unusual calm voice made the words more threatening.

"Your price is too high," Claude said through gritted teeth.

With the speed of a cat, Jasper gripped Claude by his collar and pulled him across the desk. Claude coughed, trying to breathe. Jasper released him, and he sank back into his chair, rubbing his throat as he gasped for air.

"Your wife." Claude pointed at Kate.

"I wanted her to see the double-crossing bastard that's sent men to watch her. Now you know what will fucking happen if I ever see any of your men sniffing around again." Jasper's voice had lost its calm tone.

A red-faced Claude opened his desk's front drawer. He pushed a white cotton bag towards Jasper. "The rest will follow," he croaked.

Jasper emptied the bag on to the desk and held each diamond in turn to his eyeglass. The bag was then securely zipped into Jasper's inside pocket.

"He will fucking get you for this, and your bitch."

"He hasn't fucking seen anything yet. You all need reminding who's the diamond king." Jasper snatched Kate's hand and marched out of the room.

Chapter Eighteen

Jasper tightly held Kate's hand as they silently walked to a small restaurant. The owner greeted Jasper and showed them to a table in a dark corner. They sat in silence, supposedly reading the menu, but Kate couldn't take her eyes from the powerful man opposite: her husband, best friend, lover and diamond king.

"Kate, have you decided?" said Jasper, looking over the top of the menu. "Kate?"

She met his gaze. "I'm sorry. Chicken. If you're having red wine, that's fine."

Jasper put his menu onto the table. "Stop thinking about Claude."

"He wants revenge. It was in his eyes."

"He wouldn't dare. You know what I'm capable of."

An uneasy silence settled between them.

"He asked for my help. He knew the cost. It was payback time."

"Who's the 'he' Claude referred to?"

"He's just walked through the door."

A cold shiver shot down Kate's back as she recognised Von-Pitt's voice from across the room.

"They're all here," Jasper continued in a hushed tone. "Lord Blackthorn, Von-Pitt, Lord Landon, Tony Rice and Margot."

"I don't want to know. I want to know about those shady dealers and what to expect."

Jasper waited until the waiter had poured their wine. "I sent a message. Von-Pitt and Blackthorn will be under no illusion who the diamond king is."

"Message?"

He reached for her hands across the table. "I let things drift while we were apart." He paused and gazed into her eyes. "The diamond king is back now you are by my side."

Kate shuddered. "Is there another way?"

He lifted her fingers to his lips. "Not for me. But you can try any way you like."

After the waiter had finished serving their food, Kate said, "I'm not sure I understand."

Jasper smiled. "My love, your innocence may fool many, but not me."

An elderly gentleman stopped by their table. "I thought it was you. This must be your charming wife."

The gentleman smiled at Kate and kissed her hand.

"Lord Ambrose, what a surprise. And Lord Devon." Jasper shook the offered hands, and Lord Ambrose slipped a piece of paper into Jasper's palm.

"Did you enjoy the festival?" asked Lord Devon, whose love-struck eyes were fixed on Kate.

"Too glitzy for me," remarked Kate.

"Kate avoids bright lights and lots of people."

"Just like…" Lord Devon's words petered away.

"Come, Henry, the ladies await," Ambrose said.

Lord Devon took Kate's hand and kissed it again. "An absolute pleasure to meet you."

After they had left, Kate asked, "Who were they? Ambrose and Devon. Really?"

Jasper swallowed his laugh. "They're in charge of the Gentlemen's Club."

The waiter brought Kate a coffee and Jasper a port.

"How do you feel?" Jasper asked as they finished their drinks.

"Good."

He held out his hand. "A romantic walk to the penthouse?"

Chapter Nineteen

Sleep evaded Kate after Jasper kissed her and told her not to worry. She knew where he was going. Her body filled with fear as she anxiously waited for his return.

* * *

Dressed all in black, Jasper slipped out of the service entrance of the apartment block. He jogged to the hotel that had hosted the diamond festival, avoiding the city's cameras. Rough sleepers littered doorways, benches and pavements.

He made his way to the rear of the hotel and the kitchen door. He was relying on the staff being in too much of a hurry to leave to bother checking if the door was secured. Luck was with him. He stepped inside, leaving the kitchen door as he had found it.

The hotel was deadly quiet. Too quiet for Jasper's liking; a cold shiver passed along his spine, making him hesitate. He pushed the warning to the back of his mind and walked, catlike, towards the swing doors that opened into the hotel. His eyes fell immediately onto the glass dome sheltering the red diamonds, still in the alcove, just as he had expected.

Lord Blackthorn would have spent as little as possible on security, but it would need electricity. Earlier that day, at the festival, Jasper had noticed some men working in a narrow passageway next to the diamond alcove. There was a curtain hiding the passageway now; he looked behind it and saw a mass of wires leading to the mains. He levered himself into the passageway and, with the light from his iPhone, found the mains switch.

Jasper momentarily hesitated as he tried to work out if he would have sufficient time to throw the switch, manoeuvre out of the passageway and snatch the red diamonds. Every bone in his body was telling him it was a trap. Everything had been too easy: kitchen door open, no sounds, power box too easy to find. But he had inherited the Carmichaels' addiction to danger and the adrenaline rush that followed.

He who hesitates is lost, he thought.

As soon as he turned off the power, he felt the adrenaline begin to flow. He raced into the alcove, lifted the glass dome that protected the red diamonds, scooped them into a plastic bag and stuffed them into his pocket. He ran into the kitchen and out through the door. He didn't stop when he heard voices and running footsteps. His life now depended on his body maintaining the adrenaline surge.

Men were suddenly running towards him. Jasper turned and sprinted in the opposite direction. He had to get to the penthouse before Blackthorn's men. He didn't look behind him; thoughts of Kate pushed his body to breaking point.

His pursuers' footsteps faded; he had outrun them.

* * *

The penthouse door bounced open, and Jasper collapsed onto the carpet, gasping for breath. The veins throbbed in his temples and neck as sweat dripped off him.

"Kate," he croaked.

Kate appeared, dressed in a flimsy nightdress; even in his exhausted state, sexual desire stirred.

Between them, they managed to get him into the bedroom. Kate snatched the black clothes off his sweat-soaked body and hid them and his trainers between the sheets. Jasper climbed into the bed, and a now naked Kate joined him. She wiped the sweat from his face with a sheet.

"Pretend we are having sex," he gasped.

"What?"

With a loud thud, the penthouse door fell to the floor.

Pains shot through Jasper's body as he eased himself on top of Kate.

"Carmichael! I know you're here," bellowed Lord Blackthorn. He marched into the bedroom.

"Get the fuck out!" Jasper shouted.

Lord Blackthorn grabbed the corner of the white top sheet and tried to pull it off Jasper. Von-Pitt, Tony Rice and Lord Charles Landon, who had followed Lord Blackthorn into the room, were staring at Kate, but Jasper had skilfully moved the sheet to hide her nakedness. Von-Pitt lustfully sniggered as he adjusted his trousers.

The pain left Jasper as anger surged through him, watching the man lust after his wife. Naked, he strode towards them. Jasper was close enough that he could feel their warm breaths.

They all left the bedroom, except Von-Pitt who, in defiance, continued to stroke his crotch.

"Take your fucking eyes off my wife." Jasper's clenched fists were white as he stood before Von-Pitt, shaking with rage.

Lord Blackthorn took a moment to weigh up Jasper's outburst. Jasper was flushed, his blue eyes had a glazed appearance, his hair was damp and his body had a slight perspiration sheen. Blackthorn cast his eyes to Jasper's manhood; there was no doubt he was aroused. But Von-Pitt had made his intention perfectly clear: he wanted to fuck Kate. Jasper had killed for less.

"Now, now, Jasper. Calm down. We mean Kate no harm. Get dressed and come to the station. I have one or two questions," said Lord Blackthorn, trying to defuse the situation.

Von-Pitt, who had never witnessed the Carmichael rage, took the opportunity to step back.

"Am I under arrest?"

"No. You're not under arrest," Blackthorn answered. "But you're a person of interest in a robbery. A diamond robbery."

The room fell silent except for a man trying to mend the door.

Jasper moved his eyes to the sound. *Blackthorn was well organised; he even had a door fitter standing by. But does he have a warrant?* "Have you got a warrant?" he asked, trying to control his voice.

Lord Blackthorn's eyes wandered around the room as his face developed a pink tinge. "You bastard. You know no judge would sign one; you still have friends in high places."

Blackthorn wasn't going to admit that the warrant had been refused because Kate would be present. The judge wouldn't consider tainting Kate's Landon credentials. That was when Blackthorn had realised how important Kate was to saving the Landon Trust Fund and the many high-ranking people who had their money wrapped up in it.

"It was the Landon red diamonds that were stolen," Blackthorn continued. "The robbery had all the hallmarks of your father, Colin Carmichael. He was never caught, but we were so close to catching his son."

"I don't know what you mean."

Blackthorn knew when he was beaten, but there would be other opportunities to catch Jasper. He started to walk towards the door, then suddenly turned and said, "There's not a thief in London that would have walked into that hotel. It was surrounded. But that wouldn't have bothered Colin Carmichael. He relished in the odds against him. Like father, like son, Jasper. Like father, like son."

Blackthorn's words faded as he walked through the door.

Chapter Twenty

Lord Blackthorn pushed open the door to the Gentlemen's Club just as Big Ben chimed six o'clock.

"Good morning, my lord," greeted the elderly night manager.

"Anyone here?" Lord Blackthorn curtly said.

"No, my lord. Been quiet all night."

Lord Blackthorn hadn't the patience for polite chit-chat. "Sign them in." He pointed to Tony Rice and Von-Pitt. "Is the committee room locked?"

The surprised man answered, "No."

Von-Pitt, Lord Landon and Tony Rice followed the lord up the stairs to the committee room.

"Why are we here?" demanded Von-Pitt as Blackthorn opened the wooden doors of a wall cupboard.

Four crystal whisky glasses were placed on the long committee table. Blackthorn filled the glasses with Macallan, unaware that Lord Ambrose had installed a secret camera in the room, which was activated by a switch in the night office. The night manager had not only phoned Lord Ambrose but had switched the camera on.

Lord Blackthorn stood gazing out of the dirty windows, sipping his malt.

"Well?" said the impatient Von-Pitt. "We could have gone to the lounge and had breakfast."

"Too many eyes and ears, and we have a lot to agree upon," replied the thoughtful lord.

"Carmichael's guilty. He was in a state, hot and sweaty," snapped the impatient Von-Pitt.

"I think I would have been hot and sweaty too if I was going to fuck her," added Tony Rice.

Lord Blackthorn ignored Rice's comment. "How do we prove it? 'Hot and sweaty' won't stand up in a court of law. We can't search the penthouse; we didn't catch him red-handed."

"You've lost my diamonds," commented Lord Landon.

Lord Blackthorn returned to the table and glares at Lord Landon. "But there're not your diamonds."

The men were silent as they waited for Lord Blackthorn to continue.

"Let's get something straight: Lady Kate Carmichael was brought up by an evil man, Reynolds, but he wasn't her father."

"We know this," snapped Von-Pitt."

"I want you to remember it."

"Her mother, Laura Spencer, had a summer affair with Henry Landon Junior. There's no doubt that Kate is their love child. The Landons paid Reynolds to marry Laura and bring up the child."

"DNA proof?" asked Lord Landon.

"No. We do have a timeline and photographs; she was born nine months after that summer. Also, it was common knowledge round and about Wellsbury that the Landons had made some sort of agreement with Reynolds. However, Lady Isabel Landon had wanted the baby. She kept a journal of the whole episode. But it's missing, along with her notebooks."

"How do you know?" questioned Von-Pitt.

"I know because I'm the one who went to look for them… before the new owner got his hands on them."

"I'm the new owner," answered Von-Pitt.

"Exactly."

"Are you convinced that she's Henry Junior's child?" asked a red-faced Lord Landon, his mind whirling with what this meant for him and his gambling debts.

"There's no doubt in my mind."

"That means Carmichael will get his hands on the diamonds," said Von-Pitt.

"Kate's no bloody lady; I knew her at uni," said Tony Rice.

"But you never fucked her." Lord Blackthorn's eyes pierced into Tony Rice. "You knew Kate Reynolds, not Kate Carmichael. Remember what I said? The young Kate was brought up living with Reynolds, but despite him she shone at school and at uni. The Landons paid Reynolds to look after her, but he never did. Age has served her well; so much so that her aristocratic genes are there for all to see."

"But there's no DNA evidence," said Von-Pitt.

"And what do you intend? Take on Carmichael? You've witnessed just a flash of his temper; I've seen him in full flow. You go after Kate, and he'll come for you. Any of you."

* * *

Jasper's eyes shot open. He was alone in bed. The French doors to the balcony were open, and the early morning breeze wafted the full-length net curtains. Kate was standing gazing at the river with both hands wrapped around a mug of tea.

He sidled up to her and wrapped his arms around her.

She leaned into him. "They nearly caught you."

"But they didn't."

"Why, Jasper? Why?"

"Because I can."

"Try again."

He sighed. "If the diamonds are genuine, they are part of the Landon collection, which guarantees the investments of hundreds of people—ordinary people's pensions, income. The diamonds were supposed to be locked in a vault. This means Von-Pitt and his entourage have found the vault."

"Not necessarily," she countered. "Lord Henry may have kept them in a safe to show prospective investors. Lord Charles can't sell them because word would get around and there would be a run on the fund. What better way to prove to the financial world that the Landon Trust Fund is sound than to display part of the diamond collection?"

"You thought of all this?"

"It's not rocket science."

He twirled her round and removed the mug from her hands, carefully placing it on a small bistro table. "I want to kiss you."

Their lips touched.

"Out here in front of Blackthorn's spies?"

"I don't care a flying fuck."

"Neither do I."

Chapter Twenty-One

Jasper was sitting in the passenger seat of the Range Rover with his eyes tightly closed; the chase from the diamond festival to the penthouse had exhausted him. He drifted in and out of a doze as they purred along the motorway towards Wellsbury.

Kate was the better driver. She slowed the car before braking and she kept to the speed limits. If it wasn't for her, he would be in jail. He peered at her. The diamond festival had changed something inside her; she looked more confident, more Landon.

Her finger touched speed dial.

"Robert, we'll be there in an hour. Organise a meal. Something warm. Chicken. Lots of vegetables."

"His Lordship?"

"Chicken as well."

"Very well."

"I need a report from Wes."

"On your desk."

She uncharacteristically ended the call without saying thank you.

Jasper wasn't sure how long he'd been asleep for when he opened his eyes at Kate's ringing phone. The name Wes flashed.

"Kate."

"What news?"

"I'm just leaving Landon Hall."

They suddenly had Jasper's attention.

"Lord Charlie's been up to his old tricks. He needs money urgently. He's selling the Landon library."

"I thought Von-Pitt had bought Landon Hall."

"Money hasn't changed hands."

"I'm not interested in the library."

"Well, you should be. Lord Henry invested in first editions. Mint condition. Some have never been opened."

There was a moment's silence as Kate gathered her thoughts.

"I've nowhere to put them."

"That room next to your library can house the first editions. The rest in the Spencer library."

"How did you hear about the Landon library?" asked Jasper indignantly.

"Wondered where you were, Jasper. Been up to your old tricks, too, I hear. Now, Kate, what about this library?"

"Okay," she said. "Can we meet tonight?"

"See you later."

Wes ended the call.

* * *

They were sitting at a small bistro table in the orangery, eating a chicken roast. It wasn't Jasper's favourite meal, but he hadn't the inclination to make a scene; he had a lot on his mind after Wes's call. Every time he thought of the sale of the Landon library, his gut churned. He had tried to talk to Kate, but her replies were unusually monosyllabic.

Unbeknownst to either Kate or Jasper, Wes had phoned the staff, warning them of a brewing Carmichael argument. He had recognised

Jasper's resentful tone after he mentioned that Jasper had been up to his old tricks. Word of the red diamond robbery had travelled at breakneck speed through the diamond community. Jasper was the main suspect, and Kate had covered for him, making her his accomplice.

"Kate, we must talk about the Landon library."

"I'm still thinking." Her voice had mellowed.

Jasper stared deeply into her eyes, looking for any trace of a brewing temper. He decided to gamble that she would listen; he had to tell her what he suspected.

"It's a trap," he blurted. Before she could reply, he continued: "A true Landon would never let the family library be sold." He waited for her to deny that she was a Landon. "It's too convenient. Von-Pitt knows that Wes has your ear; he knows about your love of books and that you have a sense of family duty. If you buy it, you'll be admitting that you're a Landon, but more importantly, you'll be leaving a trail to your Cayman bank. He has spies everywhere. He's just waiting for you to make a mistake."

"You think Von-Pitt's behind this. I was wondering."

Her calm reply surprised him.

"If you want it, let me buy it," he said.

"What with? Diamonds?"

Jasper held out his hand. Now was the time for her to know. "Come."

He punched the code into the small keypad that opened his diamond office. The palm of a hand flashed, and a second door opened into Jasper's inner sanctum. Kate blinked as bright lights came on automatically.

"Come."

Jasper walked to a photograph of Kate on his yacht that hung on the opposite wall. The photo brought back happy memories of when he took her sailing. He lifted the photograph off the wall, and a small panel in the wall slid to one side, revealing a handle and a dial. At each correct number there was a click.

Jasper pulled on the handle, and the metal door opened onto several rows of drawers. "Grandfather's collection was hidden in that warehouse," he said. "Colin's diamonds were in that dilapidated artist studio at the beach house. This is *my* diamond hoard." He held out his hand. "Pull a drawer open."

"I know what's in them," she curtly replied.

Jasper decided to ignore her sudden change in tone. "But have you seen their beauty? I'm addicted to them as I am to you."

Jasper pulled drawers open: yellow diamonds, pink diamonds, clear diamonds sparkled, mesmerising Kate.

"This was Lord Henry's vault."

"You said—"

"I know what I said, Kate, but things have changed. You need to know." He put his hands on her shoulders and stared into her green eyes. "You covered for me; you hid the red diamonds. Lord Blackthorn will assume you are part of my empire. You stepped into my diamond world."

"I couldn't let you go to prison."

His finger stroked her cheek. "I know. You've always had my back."

Their eyes locked.

"They were waiting for me. I was overconfident. I took no notice of the signs."

"Are they all stolen?"

"Yes. Like Lord Henry, I operate from the cave and the boathouse."

Jasper opened a deep drawer. "These are for Harry."

"But you bought from that dealer."

"He owed me. His diamonds are legit." He pulled her into his arms and kissed her hair. "This is my legacy to our son and then to Little Jasper."

"I don't know if I can cope with all this."

"I love you, Kate. You're my soulmate. I would never leave you for a pair of big tits and an arse." He rested her head on his shoulder. "I'll deal with the Landon library; I'll pay Lord Charlie's debt—if there is one. I know his casino haunts and their bosses. The Landon library will be yours." His hand caressed her hair. "There's more."

"More? What do you mean?"

"You need to know my associates; you will need to memorise so many things, including the codes for here. If anything happens to me, you must take over the Carmichael legacy for Harry and Little Jasper."

"What happens if I go first?"

"I will have nothing to live for. Except diamonds."

* * *

The grandfather clock in the foyer struck three times. Kate hadn't slept a wink; her mind was playing ping pong with doubt about being involved in Jasper's murky diamond world. It went against everything she stood for. But Jasper trusted her, he needed her by his side. But diamonds had caused her so much pain, broken their marriage. And she'd had to accept that all her hopes that Harry would become an academic had been trashed when he was overcome with diamond fever. Could she, after all this time, lock her hatred for diamonds into the depths of her mind?

She threw on some clothes, tiptoed downstairs and stood in front of Jasper's diamond office door.

She desperately wanted to talk to him, to hear his reassuring words. Doubt had taken over her mind. She put her head in her hands and suddenly felt the need to feel the sea lapping over her feet, the wind on her cheeks, the taste of salt on her lips.

* * *

The intercom in Jasper's office buzzed.

"Sir, Lady Carmichael has just left."

Jasper switched on his private security monitor. A dark figure was walking towards the sea.

"Go back to bed, Robert. I'll sort it."

He locked up the office and prepared to follow her into the night.

Jasper stood in darkness at the edge of the beach, staring into the night sky and waiting for the moon to appear. Finally, his heart stirred as he caught a glimpse of her standing at the water's edge.

The desire to hold her and kiss her was overwhelming. He started to jog towards her.

As he approached, she turned and smiled. His kiss was intense as they moulded together.

"I'll be your diamond queen."

His finger traced her hairline as their eyes danced.

"Come."

Kate smiled; his husky voice was full of meaning that filled her with desire. He wrapped his arms around her as they strolled towards the sand dunes.

Chapter Twenty-Two

Von-Pitt and Tony Rice were standing at the spot where Kate had watched Oliver's ashes drift towards the sea.

"This place is crying out for development," Tony Rice said thoughtfully.

Von-Pitt turned to face where the café had once stood. "River's End Marina Leisure Complex will extend to the road."

"You can't call it that."

"I'll call it what I fuckin' like."

"It suggests it's part of River's End House."

"So?"

"River's End House is Carmichael's."

Von-Pitt turned back to face the river. "It'll all be mine. Can't you just see the yachts owned by the rich and famous moored along the riverbank all the way to River's End House?"

"It'll cost."

"Money will be no object once I have Carmichael's diamonds."

"You're assuming."

"I'm assuming nothing," Von-Pitt snapped. "His grandfather had a hoard of diamonds that were officially never found—but my gut tells me Jasper had them." He paused. "And then there's Colin's diamonds."

"Colin had nothing."

"Colin Carmichael was a diamond thief—he thrived on robbing diamonds; he could value a diamond just by looking at it. And you're trying to tell me he never left them to Jasper, his only son?" Von-Pitt paused again to take in the view. "Jasper has more diamonds than you've ever dreamed of, and she's in on it."

* * *

Robert knocked on Kate's library door. He eased the door open, mindful that she had instructed him not to disturb her.

He coughed. "A Mr Rice to see you."

Kate looked over the top of her reading glasses just as Tony Rice pushed Robert to one side. Kate's annoyance showed; she had been studying the books from Harry's diamond shop. She pushed her reading glasses into her hair and stared.

Tony Rice noted her cold expression.

Robert coughed again. "Tea? And Ruby's just taken a batch of biscuits from the oven." The staff were aware of Kate's weakness for hot tea and biscuits.

Kate smiled and, momentarily, the coldness disappeared from her eyes. She nodded. "Probably Mr Rice would like coffee."

"Nothing for Mr Rice." Tony's sharp voice surprised both Robert and Kate.

"What can I do for you?" Kate asked.

Tony stared at her, his mind whirling with the possibility of spending time in her bed. "I really wanted to see Jasper."

Kate thought, *That's a lie.* "I can't help you."

Tony thought, *That's a lie.* He placed a blurry photo on her desk. "This was taken at night from one of my security yachts."

Why has he got a security yacht photographing the beach? Kate thought.

"You look confused."

"I am. Why is one of your security yachts photographing the beach? This photo means nothing."

"This is why I wanted to see Jasper." He paused to study Kate's face. "To put it bluntly, we believe Jasper's involved with diamond smuggling. That he's up to his old tricks." His eyes intently watched Kate; any movement in her expression would confirm Von-Pitt's theory that Kate was involved. "That he's fencing illegal diamonds."

Kate slowly moved her cold eyes to meet his gaze. Her calm, measured voice didn't miss a beat. "Over the years, Jasper's been accused of many things. None of the accusations could be proved. So, can you prove yours?"

Tony pulled another photo from his pocket and placed it next to the first one. "My tech team can work wonders with photos."

Kate's eyes drifted to the photo of her and Jasper entwined in a passionate kiss. Her temper started to boil.

"That's you." He paused, his eyes focused on her face. "And you… stood for a long time staring out to sea. I'm guessing you were thinking; Jasper had done something you didn't like. And then, just like magic, he appeared." His index finger touched the enhanced photo.

"You have no right to—"

"I have every right. He's a criminal. I'm going to be the man that finally puts him where he belongs." He placed his palms onto the desk. "You refused me. You owe me. I thought that *I* wasn't good enough, but you married the bloody diamond king."

"There was nothing between us."

"Only because you didn't want it. But I'm going to have you, Kate, and prove that I'm the better man. You're going to look at me like you look at him."

* * *

Jasper's phone had blipped during his bartering session with the diamond smuggler.

"Answer that fuckin' thing," demanded the smuggler.

Jasper looked at the message. It was from Robert.

Tony Rice is here.

He opened the security camera app. A worried look descended upon his face as he watched the exchange between Kate and Tony.

"Trouble?" asked the smuggler.

"In a way."

"The yacht that patrols—"

"You've seen it?"

"What do you think?"

"Tony Rice."

"Who is this Tony Rice?"

"An associate of Von-Pitt." *And he wants what's mine.*

* * *

Kate shivered when Jasper's cold, naked body joined her in bed.

"Tell me," he said in a soft voice.

"Tony Rice came."

"He wants what's mine."

"There's a yacht recording our every move. He's after you. Building a case."

"What will they video? A kiss? Your legs wrapped around me as I move inside you?"

"You don't care?"

"Of course, I care."

Jasper sighed as Kate moved to rest her head on his chest.

"Lord Ambrose phoned," she said absentmindedly as Jasper's fingers meandered along her spine. Her words started to drift; she murmured, "He's convinced that I'm a Landon."

"Later, Kate. Later."

Chapter Twenty-Three

"Why must we keep meeting here?" grumbled Tony Rice, pulling his coat around his body.

Von-Pitt momentarily stopped recording the view from the old riverside café. "Can't you take the cold wind? I thought you Canadians were winterproof." He began to walk towards the riverside path. "There's a lot of land here, more than you see from here. But from the sky—"

"It belongs to Kate Carmichael," interrupted an angry Tony Rice.

"Don't you think I know that?"

"She'll never sell."

"She'll do as she's fuckin' told," snapped Von-Pitt.

"Her son's ashes sailed to the sea from here."

"I know about Oliver."

"Then you'll sympathise—"

"I'll sympathise fuckin' nothing."

Von-Pitt set a fast pace along the path. He stopped at the neglected spot that was once Kate's thinking spot. "She used to sit on that bench," he said. "From here, you get an uninterrupted view of the two rivers."

Tony Rice looked at the rotting remains of a bench. "Why am I here?"

"When will the security system be finished at Landon Hall?"

"I'm waiting for chips. There's a shortage."

Von-Pitt stamped his feet. "I'm moving the drug operation to Landon Hall."

"Without security? You're mad."

"The American Landons are taking an interest in the trust fund. I don't want them poking their noses in my diamonds or drugs businesses. Move the diamonds today. I don't want them at my London or Wellsbury outlets."

"You're mad. They will be easy pickings for Carmichael."

"That's why we're here. Only the two of us know. Carmichael mustn't find out."

The two men stared at the water.

The silence was broken by Tony Rice. "Nothing changed at River's End House."

"You mean you got nothing from Kate? Not even the promise of a fuck?"

"She didn't know where he was."

Von-Pitt turned to face him. "And you believed her? You're a bigger fool than I thought."

Tony's temper began to boil; he didn't like being called a fool, particularly not by the likes of Von-Pitt.

"Lord Blackthorn brings him diamonds," Von-Pitt said. "Carmichael doesn't go to London."

"So?"

"My spies inform me that those fools at the Gentlemen's Club know about the American Landons wanting to take over the Landon Trust Fund."

"I'm sure Kate doesn't know."

"She will know, and so will Carmichael. Lords Ambrose and Devon were seen with their butler at Euston. Train to Wellsbury."

"That doesn't mean that—"

"It means that they will not be staying at a hotel. Ambrose only uses his own butler."

"You assume they will be staying at River's End House? They hate Carmichael."

"Those two conniving old bastards are up to their lordly necks in diamonds; they need Carmichael to get them out of the shit. If they are prepared to go hat in hand to him, then what else are they capable of? There's a reason that old Carmichael was never allowed in the Gentlemen's Club. He was a very rich and powerful man with links to the government." Von-Pitt turned to look at Tony. "Old Carmichael was Jasper's grandfather."

"I know."

"What if Lord Henry Landon wasn't the saint that we were all led to believe? What if his fortune and the trust fund were financed by illicit diamonds, and the Gentlemen's Club covered it up?"

Von-Pitt turned to walk back to the car park. "I'll control the Americans; I don't want them to know about my diamonds or Landon Hall. You keep Carmichael at River's End House; I don't want him sniffing about while the Americans are here. It's vital they don't meet Kate."

"There's no proof she's a Landon," Tony said.

"Proof, man? For fuck's sake, you don't need proof. Just look at the Landon portraits. Isabel Landon isn't dead; she's walking around Wellsbury."

Chapter Twenty-Four

"Jasper, I'm not a Landon!" Kate's angry voice echoed around her library. She was oblivious to the staff standing just inside the door.

"Whether you like it or not," Jasper retorted, "there are a lot of people who think you are. These American Landons smell rich pickings from the Landon Trust Fund, and you, my love, are standing in their way."

"I have enough on my plate already."

"You won't have a plate if you don't claim your birthright."

Robert coughed.

Jasper turned. "Ah, Robert. Sorry to drop this on you all, but we're expecting guests that I didn't anticipate. Lord Ambrose, Lord Devon and a butler. Ruby, show these old lords what a home-made dinner is. Elsie and Robert, organise the sleeping arrangements. Ben, light a fire in the far bedroom."

"The far bedroom, sir?"

"It's the only bedroom with a small room next door for the butler." Jasper turned to face Kate. "I really need you on this."

"You haven't said why they are coming. The staff should know." Kate's voice had returned to its usual calm tone.

"Lord Ambrose didn't explain, but he sounded upset on the phone. I suspect it's something to do with diamonds. There's a lot going on."

"Lady Carmichael, we haven't the food."

"Make a list. I'll be with you in a minute."

Jasper pulled Kate into his side and kissed her hair. "Thank you," he whispered.

The day passed quickly. Ben lit all the open fires; doors were opened so the heat could circulate through the house. Jasper took a large spanner and a hammer to the radiator in the far bedroom and, with the help of brute force, made hot water begin to flow through it. Elsie and Robert were in their element, making the house ready to receive Their Lordships. Kate spent her time in the kitchen, giving Ruby her support and helping prepare food.

Wes Clayton arrived with the food order.

"Got visitors, then," Wes said to Kate while he unloaded the food. "How many are you feeding? A football team?"

Kate reluctantly answered, "Lord Ambrose, Lord Devon and their butler."

"Just the night, then."

"Haven't got that far yet."

"Where's Jasper?"

"He was attacking a stubborn radiator."

Wes walked over to the oven. "Chicken dinner?"

"Lady Carmichael's favourite," Ruby said with some pride. She enjoyed cooking for Kate.

Wes picked up a warm biscuit and blew on it. "Makes a good biscuit, does our Ruby." His eyes followed Kate as she inspected the fresh vegetables. "Just fetched them from Hope's Farm. Only the best, Kate."

Kate wasn't listening; she had too much on her mind. Why was Jasper insisting she was a Landon? And why were Their Lordships visiting? Was there a link?

* * *

By the time Their Lordships had arrived, River's End House was warm, including their bedrooms. The dining table was laid in a manner that would meet with Their Lordships' approval, thanks to Robert, and the beds had been made with the new linen Elsie had insisted they needed "just in case"—this was one of her "just in case" occasions. After the fires had been lit, Ben had disappeared to chop more wood for his depleted store. Jasper had organised the wine; crystal decanters were filled with whisky, brandy, sherry and port. Kate hadn't known that they had crystal glassware or that they had such a selection of wines and spirits. *There must be a wine cellar*, she thought.

"I must say, Jasper, you have the makings of an excellent home." Lord Ambrose smiled as he sat relaxing in one of their overstuffed living room chairs. The warmth from the roaring fire filled every corner of the room.

"Kate, you must congratulate your cook. Excellent food and wine," said Lord Devon. "The apple pie was delicious."

"Now, Jasper, shall we get down to business?" Lord Ambrose's voice had suddenly become businesslike.

Kate stood. "I'll leave you to your business. I have shopping centre paperwork that needs my attention."

Jasper nodded. Lord Ambrose stood and smiled, and Lord Devon was very quiet with a worried look upon his face.

* * *

Instead of dealing with the hundreds of emails, text messages and phone calls about a fire in one unit, another that had been vandalised and a third that had been flooded after a van careered into the rear doors—not to mention Harry's diamond shop and Jasper's desire to involve her in his scheme after the red diamond robbery—Kate pushed it all to one side to study Lady Isabel's notebooks. She suspected Lords Ambrose and Devon wanted more than a diamond deal with Jasper; they wanted her to concede she was a Landon.

Hours later, the sound of the staff preparing breakfast broke her concentration.

The library door opened, and Jasper poked his head inside. "Could do with you in the living room."

Lord Devon smiled at her when she walked in carrying a folder. "You look tired, my dear."

"She's been up all night. That bloody shopping centre," answered Jasper.

I wouldn't have been up all night if Their Lordships weren't here, thought Kate.

She settled into one of the chairs opposite Their Lordships and, just like magic, Robert appeared carrying a tray with a teapot, a china cup and saucer, and a plate of toast. He placed it upon a small table next to her chair.

Lord Ambrose began to fidget.

He's worried, she thought.

"Kate," he began, "you should be aware that the board of the Landon Trust Fund has asked for your American cousins to take over."

"Why does this concern me?"

Their lordships looked disappointed by Kate's unexpected reply. Jasper stood, walked to the drinks stand and poured himself a large malt.

Not this early, Jasper, Kate thought as he took a sip.

"Kate," Jasper said, "everything points to Henry Landon Junior being your father. That makes Lord Henry Landon your grandfather. It follows that you are Lord Henry's heir."

"I know the circumstantial evidence, Jasper—"

"We can't let the Americans take over," interjected Lord Ambrose.

"I've been trying to trace Lord Henry's family," Kate said in her matter-of-fact tone, as if it was an everyday occurrence. The Lords Ambrose and Devon looked very uncomfortable. She pretended not to notice. "I have found only one reference to the Landons in an American newspaper. I'm assuming that the Landon mentioned is our Lord Henry."

Kate opened the folder and showed them the article.

The death of the Gentleman Godfather.

Henry Landon, known as the Gentleman Godfather, passed away yesterday with his family around him. He's survived by his wife, Sarah, and his three sons: Henry, Michael and baby Charles.

Henry made the family rich through the Landon casinos and Landon diamond trading. His eldest son, Henry, was destined to become the head of the family. However, a close family friend told The Chronicle *that the brothers argued about who their father wanted to succeed him after his death, Henry claiming that it was his right and his diamond dealing that had increased the family fortune.*

The argument was settled with a fist fight.
The next day, Henry left America.

"Where did you find this information?" asked Lord Ambrose. "We have all the Landon records except Lady Isabel's—she kept a diary. When I heard that Von-Pitt had bought Landon Hall, I sent Lord Blackthorn to retrieve the diaries, but they had gone. No sign of a break-in… but it wouldn't have been difficult for you, Jasper."

"I'm to blame," Kate interjected before Jasper could speak. "When the DNA tests proved to be inconclusive, I wanted to take pictures of the Landon portraits."

"All fake, I'm afraid, except for the ones of Lord Henry, Isabel and young Henry. Lord Henry had an artist copy the family portraits that hung in the American gallery."

"Fake?"

"Lord Henry was a brilliant con man," Lord Ambrose answered. "In many ways, he and Jasper are alike. Isabel was a society beauty, an English rose who fell in love with an American."

"Her family disowned her when she married Landon," said Lord Devon. "But it was a love match; they adored one another. He made them rich—a self-made man who became a lord."

"I think he was conscious of what Isabel had given up when she married him; he made her rich and gave her a title," said a thoughtful Lord Ambrose.

Jasper slipped into Kate's chair, one hand resting on her shoulder and the other gripping his whisky glass. "Are you saying that Lord Henry Landon was an American criminal?"

"We never asked where he got his diamonds. Just like people never ask you, Jasper. You make people rich; Lord Henry made us wealthy." Lord Ambrose stared at Jasper. "Do you think I could have one of those?" he asked, pointing at the decanter.

Jasper reluctantly moved to pour Lord Ambrose a malt.

Lord Ambrose continued: "How do you think Henry got away with an investment fund totally reliant on diamonds? No official records, and people in high places turned a blind eye so they could have a slice of the riches." He swallowed two gulps of whisky.

"Who are 'we', Lord Ambrose?" asked Jasper.

"'We' is the club. The club's history is in the basement, though nothing has really changed since it became the Gentlemen's Club. Diamonds are and always have been its business. I suppose we are a secret society. Members are accepted based on their diamond wealth—all except Carmichaels. Your grandfather was power mad; he wanted to control the government. Your father would have been an asset, but Colin Carmichael was his own man, he was not interested in power or riches."

You didn't know my father, thought Jasper, recalling the diamond hoard Colin had left him.

"You are blessed or cursed according to how one interprets your diamond activities, Jasper. One foot in the law-abiding world and the other in the criminal world. We know all about your past; we couldn't accept a murderer in the club. But Kate is the force that keeps you in the law."

You know nothing about me, thought Jasper.

Lord Devon hadn't been listening. "You are just like her," he said to Kate. "An English rose. We all know about the episode at the school prize-giving. How Isabel hugged you and cried. She knew you were her granddaughter."

"But Kate married a no-good Carmichael—for love," Lord Ambrose continued, ignoring his friend. "Your love for each other is legendary. You have given Kate a title and made the both of you rich."

"It's history repeating itself," said Lord Devon.

Chapter Twenty-Five

Jasper snuggled Kate into his side as they watched the taxi taking Their Lordships to the station disappear.

"Did you take their diamonds?"

"I agreed to sell the club's diamonds."

"I don't understand them," said Kate. "They behave as if this is the nineteenth century."

"As long as they get their money, it is the nineteenth century."

"It's only a matter of time before the fund is liquidated. As far as I'm concerned, the Americans and Von-Pitt are welcome to it."

Jasper kissed her neck. "I like the assertive you."

She smiled. "I have work to catch up on."

"Later, my English rose. Later."

Jasper was about to close the front door when a Rolls Royce turned into the driveway.

"Fuck. What does he want?"

"Me."

"What?" Jasper's voice was unusually loud.

"It's the shopping centre." Kate's words fell from her mouth at some speed. "I came across three damaged units. Von-Pitt was in one when a van delivering cannabis plants hit the rear doors, setting off the sprinklers. The next unit had a very large microscope set up on a workbench, and the last had drugs, money and diamonds. I set fire to the drugs and put the money and diamonds in the office safe."

A shocked Jasper turned Kate so he could look into her eyes. "When did this happen?"

"The day I was attacked." Her garbled words were soft, and Jasper could hardly hear her. "I don't know what got into me. I saw red and thought of Oliver."

The Rolls Royce stopped in front of the door, and Von-Pitt stepped out.

"Why didn't you tell me?" Jasper said through a forced smile.

"So much has happened."

"Jasper." Von-Pitt's voice boomed. "How nice of you to greet us at your front door."

Kate moved inside the house as Jasper shook Von-Pitt's hand. Jasper tried to smile, but Kate's words filled his thoughts. Then, another car arrived with Arthur, the chief constable, and Martin, the chief fire officer. And finally, the Von-Pitt "hangers-on": Lord Charles Landon, Tony Rice and Margot. Lord Blackthorn's helicopter landed in the field opposite the house.

A prearranged meeting, thought Jasper as he turned to the foyer.

Robert closed the door as Jasper led the party into the dining room, where Kate and Elsie were busy organising refreshments.

When the group was settled, Chief Constable Arthur broke the silence. "We're here about that incident at the shopping centre." His tone was very businesslike.

"It's in hand," answered Kate.

"What's that mean?" interjected Von-Pitt, eager to control the proceedings.

"It means that my solicitors and insurance company have all the relevant information." Kate turned to the chief fire officer. "Thank your men for all their good work, Martin. It's appreciated.

Martin nodded.

"That's it, Kate?" said Lord Blackthorn.

"What more is there to say? You are all familiar with the incident; I see no purpose in repeating it."

Von-Pitt stood, pushing his seat backwards. "You see no point? Drugs were set on fire! Money and diamonds are missing! And that's all you have to say."

"I understand that a considerable number of cannabis plants were destroyed, a load of cocaine as well. There was no mention of money and diamonds." Kate paused for effect. "Do you know more than the police and fire officers, Mr Von-Pitt?"

Von-Pitt went to answer her, but words failed to leave his gaping mouth.

Arthur coughed. "Now... Now, Kate, you mustn't read too much into my friend's words. We haven't mentioned the money or diamonds as it would have attracted too much attention."

Von-Pitt's temper was bubbling over. "You," he said, pointing at Kate, "were at the shopping centre. You must have been aware of what was going on. I put it to you, Lady Carmichael, that you set fire to the drugs and helped yourself to the money and diamonds."

A scowling Jasper leapt up. "You'd better retract those accusations."

Tony Rice's hand stretched to Von-Pitt's arm. "Calm down, my friend."

"Before this goes any further, we have no proof of anything," said Lord Blackthorn, who was worried about the direction of the conversation. "Von-Pitt must be given some leeway. He has had some bad luck recently with money and diamonds going missing. He's understandably upset."

"The point is, Jasper, the diamonds are uncut. Now, who do you think can cut those diamonds?" said Margot.

"Shut the fuck up!" shouted Von-Pitt.

But Margot had no intention of listening. "The same certain someone that meets a certain smuggler? I wonder if it's the same person that disposed of the two men who had been watching you…"

"What are you on about?" said Kate.

A red-faced Lord Blackthorn coughed. "We have had this house under surveillance for some time, particularly when Jasper stopped coming to London."

"You know the reason for that," snapped Jasper. "Kate was attacked, and I didn't want to leave her alone. Anyway, you have a helicopter."

"You've changed, Jasper," said Lord Blackthorn. "Can't put my finger on it. But I do know that uncut diamonds are going missing and red diamonds were stolen from the diamond festival."

Chapter Twenty-Six

"Let's walk," said Jasper.

Kate slipped her arms into her warm coat as a smiling Jasper stood in front of her and pulled it up around her neck.

A fresh breeze greeted them as Jasper closed the kitchen door. He looped his arm around her shoulders and guided her towards the boathouse.

Jasper opened the boathouse's rear door, and Kate stepped into a small room that faced the top of the boathouse's river doors. She glanced around at a large sofa, table and chairs. In one corner was a tea-making area.

She jumped when Jasper's hand suddenly covered her mouth, while his other hand motioned in the direction of the water below. Her eyes widened as she heard noises; they were not alone. Jasper put his finger over his lips, silently slipped off his shoes and crept to the edge of the room.

"Get the fuck out of my boathouse!" he shouted.

"Ah, Jasper, my old friend. I didnae know you had yourself a yacht."

Jasper gripped the wooden banister as he slowly walked down the stairs to the jetty where a small dinghy was loosely tied to a wooden post behind Jasper's yacht.

Fear filled the man and his eyes never left Jasper. He knew Jasper would be annoyed—he shouldn't be in the boathouse—but he had been given his orders. All he knew was that the meeting "hadn't gone to plan". He was to spy on Jasper and Kate and, if the opportunity arose, kill them.

The man stepped along the jetty, his hand resting on his back where his gun was hidden.

Jasper reached the bottom rung. "I've come about my diamonds. The uncut ones." He stopped and stared into the man's eyes. Beads of sweat had formed on the man's forehead. Jasper hovered his right foot over the wooden jetty, distracting the man.

"You can have"—the man's voice quivered as Jasper's foot landed on the jetty— "eighty per cent of the diamonds." He was beginning to lose his nerve now that he had lost the advantage of surprise. Jasper had a ruthless reputation with men who double-crossed him—like him.

He made his move; Jasper had anticipated it and fell onto the floor. Jasper rolled towards the man and knocked him off his feet. The gun flew into the air. Jasper jumped up and dived for the gun. He whipped around and, without a second thought, shot the man in the head.

Kate ran down the stairs to her husband. She flung her arms around his waist and rested her head on his chest.

"Who was he?"

"A diamond smuggler."

"You knew him?"

"I've had some dealings with him."

Jasper pulled Kate into him and kissed her hair. "Go back to the house while I clear up."

"I'm not going back without you, and I'm not staying here. I'm coming with you."

An hour later, Jasper had cleared up and put the dead body in the dinghy. "His yacht can't be far away," he said.

Jasper moved his yacht into the river, with the dinghy tied to the stern.

"When were you going to tell me about this?" She was standing by him on the bridge.

"I meant it to be a surprise."

"It's not very modern."

"I like the older design. It has all the tech I need… and a bedroom in the stern." He flashed his eyes at her and grinned.

"There it is!" said Kate, gesturing to a yacht anchored up ahead. "The tide's got it."

"Take the wheel and guide it as close as you can."

Jasper moved to the stern and tied the dinghy's rope around his waist. When Kate brought the boats alongside one another, he scrambled onto the other yacht. He lost his balance as the tide pulled the dinghy from him, but after many tries, he managed to tie it to the yacht's railing. He then started the yacht's engine and lifted the anchor slightly from the riverbed. The tide was strengthening as it began to drag the diamond smuggler's yacht away.

Adrenaline pumped through Jasper as he jumped back onto the deck of his yacht.

They sailed back to the boathouse in silence.

* * *

It was midnight when they tiptoed into the kitchen of River's End House. Jasper kissed Kate before hurrying into his diamond office, leaving her to mash her tea.

Kate wandered into her library, carefully holding a tray with her pot of tea and biscuits with one hand while opening the library door with the other. She placed the tray on a small side table before putting some small logs on the dying embers of the fire. Flames slowly snaked around the logs as the dried wood started to crackle.

She pulled a blanket around her shoulders and nestled in front of the growing flames. Her mind drifted to the day's events as she absentmindedly dunked her biscuits into the hot tea and became mesmerised by the flames.

She had witnessed adrenaline-high Jasper many times; she'd known what to expect. He had carried her up the stairs of the boathouse and thrown her onto the large couch. She had cried out as he forcibly penetrated her. He was oblivious to her pain as he thrust deep inside her until he orgasmed. He had lain atop of her, his heart pounding and sweat dripping from his forehead.

She had pushed him off her and searched for her trousers.

"Where are you going?" he'd asked.

She had stared at him, dressed only in her white blouse—he had fucked her just as if she was a whore.

He'd leapt off the couch and gripped her arm. "Talk to me. Why are you getting dressed like this?" His eyes never left her as he tried to recall what he had done. He tried to hold her, but she pushed away. "Kate, I'm sorry. I didn't mean…" he softly said. "Have I hurt you?" He cast his eyes to her naked legs and cupped her sex, but she jumped away.

"Are you bleeding?" he'd asked. "I've got to know."

He knows what he did, Kate thought. If she'd had her beach house, she would have left.

She refilled her teacup and threw more logs on the fire. Time and time again, circumstances seemed to be pushing her into sharing Jasper's diamond kingdom.

Today, she had been reminded how ruthless Jasper could be, not only to his adversaries but also to her. A rogue tear trickled down her cheek and dropped into her tea as she recalled when she had been kidnapped by his enemies to attend to his injuries and, as soon as he was able, he had shot the men and made her climb down the side of the yacht into a dinghy. He hadn't cared that she was frightened. There had been every chance that the dinghy would capsize—and it did. "It was us or them," he had said, but it wasn't his words that had perturbed her but his eyes, which had darkened and had taken on a murderous look.

It suddenly dawned on her that she must deal with Von-Pitt before Jasper went on a murderous rampage.

Chapter Twenty-Seven

Robert was standing at the kitchen door when Kate returned from her walk.

"Lady Carmichael, a Simon Cavendish to see you."

Kate slipped off her coat and held it longer than necessary on its hook. She was taken aback. Simon Cavendish was a partner at the firm known as Cavendish Law; her lawyers. She suddenly felt very nervous as she tried to think of the reason he would have travelled to see her in person. Surely an email or phone call would have sufficed.

Simon was standing gazing out of the orangery's new bifold doors.

"Simon."

He turned and gave her one of his beaming smiles. "I was just admiring the view. You have river and sea frontage." He walked towards her, still smiling—and Simon rarely smiled. "This is wonderful, Kate. I could feel your presence even though you were out."

Kate was immediately on her guard. Simon Cavendish never behaved like this.

"I was walking along the beach. Needed to clear my head." Kate held her hand out, and Simon followed her into her library.

"Your library?"

"It's the start of one. I don't have the time at the moment."

Robert appeared with Kate's tea tray and a coffee tray for Simon.

"Are you interested in the Landon library? It's causing a stir in the book world."

"Jasper is making enquires."

"Ah. Jasper."

"Will you stay for lunch?"

"I would love to, but Aaron's in court so I'm in charge of the office."

"You could have phoned or emailed, Simon."

His body tensed. "This is best said face-to-face." He sipped his coffee and looked into her eyes. "There's no easy way for me to say this, Kate. Your grandfather was Lord Henry Landon, Chairman of the Landon Trust Fund."

"And you know this, how?"

"We have in our possession photographs and various papers that confirm it. Isabel, your grandmother, wanted to bring you up, but Henry wouldn't hear of it— he had plans for his son that didn't include having a working-class girl as his daughter-in-law."

Kate stood and stared into the fire.

Simon put his hand into the inside pocket of his jacket. "Look at these."

Kate flicked through photographs of herself: at her beach house, walking around the shopping centre, hugging Little Jasper, kissing Jasper.

"These are recent."

"Your American Landon cousins are here. They have been watching you for some time."

* * *

"Robert, where's Kate? And who's in the helicopter?" asked Jasper.

"Lady Carmichael is in the library with Simon Cavendish."

Jasper froze. There was only one Simon Cavendish he knew, and he was the controlling partner at Cavendish Law.

"Are you alright, Lord Carmichael? You look as if you have seen a ghost," said Robert.

Jasper stared blankly at Robert. *Cavendish is Kate's lawyer*, he pondered. *Cavendish only takes on the richest of clients. Kate is not rich. So, why is she a client?* The penny dropped. *She's a Landon—and they look after their own.*

* * *

"I'm not interested in the Americans or the fund."

"But they are interested in you. You are Landon blood who just happens to own Wellsbury—a ready-made foothold in England," said Simon.

"I don't *own* Wellsbury, and I certainly don't want anything to do with the American..." She paused. "American gangsters."

"Von-Pitt is trying to control things. He's East Coast and he doesn't want the West Coast muscling in on his territory."

"Von-Pitt, Von-Pitt." She cursed.

"We've been accepted into the Gentlemen's Club."

"But you're not lords."

"Just a matter of time."

"What do you want from me?" Kate snapped.

"Jasper will protect you. But Jasper's diamonds are also interesting them. These people mean business; they will come all guns blazing. No more walking alone."

"Is Harry in danger?"

"They are not interested in Harry. If they have you, they will have him."

"You seem to know a lot."

"We have many clients from all walks of life."

Simon stood and delved into his inside pocket again. "These are the necessary papers covering your latest scheme to protect your son."

"I am his mother."

"His head is in the clouds."

"He's having a difficult time."

"Excuses. Kate, let Jasper have him. That will sort him out."

"What do you mean?"

"We know that Jasper's smuggling diamonds, even if you don't or won't admit it."

Kate started to feel uneasy. Did he know that she was involved?

Cavendish changed tack. "What do you see in Carmichael? Is it sex? He has a reputation. He should be locked up, but he's too useful to the rich."

"What do you want from me?" Kate repeated.

Simon stared into her cold, green eyes. "The jigsaw will be complete when you leave this place and join the Landons. Your life will be one of luxury: lying in the sun, playing tennis, cocktail parties. You get the idea."

"But that plastic life doesn't appeal to me."

"Well, my dear, you don't have much choice; we already control your money. I must admit, I was surprised by the amount."

Anger travelled through Kate. "The Landons never cared about me when I was struggling to live. A Carmichael rescued me. He bought my flower shop, gave me a job, introduced me into the finer side of life."

"Your husband is a murderer."

"Prove it."

The air in the library thickened.

"I'm not a Landon. I'm not a Spencer. I'm Kate Reynolds, who married a Carmichael. Our marriage doesn't fit into your narrow definition of what a marriage should be; our marriage is built on love."

Simon scowled. "Sex, you mean." He stood and walked towards the library door. "Think about what I've said. Give me a call when you're ready. I'll send the helicopter."

"I hope you've not upset my wife." Jasper's loud, bitter voice filled the foyer as Simon Cavendish walked out of the library.

"Jasper, I was beginning to think that you had given the yachts the slip."

"Yachts?" said a surprised Kate.

"My dear, there are so many vested interests waiting for Jasper to make a wrong move."

Jasper stepped towards his wife and glared at the expensive lawyer. "And what do you mean by that?"

"Stop these word games. Who are these vested interests?" demanded Kate.

Tension built as Kate and Jasper silently waited for Simon.

"Very well. Von-Pitt, Lord Blackthorn's people and Jasper's smuggling friends. That's all I'm prepared to say on the matter."

"Only three? That does surprise me," said Jasper as he slipped his arm around Kate's waist.

"Can't you contain yourself?" Simon said disapprovingly.

"There are many rumours spread about me, but there's only one that's true: my love for Kate. I don't care if she's a Landon; she has taken the Carmichael name and she shares my bed. She loves me."

Simon had his hand on the front door handle. Angrily, he turned. "What does she see in you? You're a handsome man that dresses exceptionally well, I'll grant you that." His face was reddening with every word. "But you are a womaniser, thief, murderer. If ever I have the honour of meeting you in court, I will take great pleasure in putting you behind bars."

Chapter Twenty-Eight

Von-Pitt had moved to Landon Hall and was now walking over the overgrown lawn where a helicopter was landing. He had no desire to meet the American Landons, but he was eager to know if Simon Cavendish had been successful in persuading Kate to accept her Landon birthright.

"I hear those bloody Cavendishes have been accepted into the Gentlemen's Club," Von-Pitt said as he walked into the house with Lord Blackthorn.

Lord Blackthorn made himself comfortable in a leather seat next to the blazing fire. Landon Hall was a cold place whatever the time of year.

Von-Pitt came straight to the point. "Is she coming to London?"

"Cavendish failed. Apparently, she made it clear that she isn't a Landon. But my loyal spies informed me that Cavendish accessed her Cayman Islands account and was shocked how much money was in it. But when he tried to access it again, Kate had blocked him. The bank told him that only Lady Carmichael could access it." Lord Blackthorn sipped a brandy.

"How much?" asked Von-Pitt.

"Cavendish wouldn't say. I think he didn't want to lose her business. But the interesting thing is, he reckons she's bankrolling Jasper, as well as Harry's diamond business."

"She can't be that rich."

"What we tend to forget is that Kate hasn't touched her money; Jasper's always paid the bills, and when she lived at the beach her outgoings were minimal."

Von-Pitt refilled the brandy bowls. "I have underestimated Lady Carmichael."

"Don't take it too hard, so have a lot of men. In the past, they just wanted to fuck her to get back at Jasper. It never entered anybody's head that she was the power behind Jasper's diamonds."

"Are you sure?"

Lord Blackthorn eased himself deeper into the leather chair that dated back to Lord Henry Landon's day. "As each day progresses, I'm more and more convinced that Lady Carmichael is up to her aristocratic neck in diamonds."

* * *

Kate stepped from the shower with a towel loosely tied around her body. She had been up all night giving Von-Pitt a dose of her medicine.

Jasper was lying on the bed, hands behind his head, feet crossed and smiling.

"What are you smiling at?"

"Can't a man smile at his wife?"

The towel dropped while Kate selected matching underwear from the drawers in her wardrobe. Jasper moved and leaned on the wardrobe door jamb.

"Jasper."

"I'm just making sure you dress to my approval."

Kate slipped on a white lace bra and panties, fitted white t-shirt and blue jeans.

"We could spend the day enjoying one another."

"What, and let those bastards walk all over us?"

"Somehow, I knew you would say that." Jasper longingly stared at his wife, but he knew that she was right. She had been working on that old laptop, the one she used when she was hacking. "I'll get Robert to bring tea and breakfast into the library."

"Jasper." Her lips touched his. "I'll make it up to you."

His hand reached to her bottom and pulled her into a sensual kiss. "You'd better."

* * *

Jasper was pouring her tea into the fine bone china cup when Kate joined him in the library.

"You're expanding your talents," she said teasingly.

"You have no idea. Now, tell me what you have been doing on that dinosaur of a laptop."

"I've locked all my bank accounts, including the Cayman Islands."

"How many accounts do you have?"

"Zurich, Wellsbury and… er…"

"Kate?"

"I had this awful feeling not to trust the Cavendishes, but having said that, they have proven to be very useful."

"Kate, what have you done?"

"I opened a bank account in the Channel Islands."

"Just like that?"

"Well, not just like that; I had to invest in the bank. Everything went smoothly when I mentioned I was Lady Carmichael."

"There's no bank that you could have invested in."

Kate fidgeted and blushed. "Car-Lan Bank."

Jasper stood and started to pace. "You own a fucking bank without telling me."

"We were having problems. I needed to hide investments and money. I had no one to discuss it with. So, I just did it." Kate paused while Jasper thought through what she had done. "It's paid my investment back several times over; I'm not mentioned on any of their paperwork; I'm not involved with the day-to-day running—"

"Kate, you don't just go out and buy a bank. You know nothing about banking or the people who run it. The bank was in debt."

"I know. It seemed a good investment."

"As far as I remember, it was rescued by a cash buyer."

"That's right."

"And you're telling me that was you?"

"Yes. It was a gamble. I arranged to meet the board in London. It was an all-day meeting; they had to make several phone calls."

"Did it occur to you that they were probably phoning their masters?"

"Yes. I had a feeling that they were being told what to do. However, I did review their balance sheet and who their creditors were."

"Did it occur to you that a person or persons in high places wanted you to own the bank?"

"I don't know anyone in a high place. I thought that it might be someone you know."

Jasper stared at his wife, a total innocent as far as banking was concerned. *So, who's behind this?* he thought. *Many years ago, Lady Isabel, Lord Henry's wife, owned a bank. She had friends in high places. Kate does resemble Lady Isabel Landon.* "And you did all this from that dinosaur laptop."

"It hasn't got built in WiFi... Do you remember that computer from the whizz kid who worked for us? Well, he still updates my gadgets."

"What gadgets?"

"I plug them into the laptop. They're untraceable."

Jasper slumped into a chair and put his head in his hands. *Now she's bloody using a dinosaur of a computer to operate her bank accounts. God help me.* "There's no bloody whisky."

"I have no need for it."

"I do."

There was a gentle tap on the library door, and Robert gingerly stepped in carrying a tray with a bottle of malt and glass.

"I thought this might be useful, sir."

Kate took the tray from Robert and mouthed, "Thank you."

* * *

Robert joined Elsie, Ruby and Ben in the kitchen. They all expectantly looked at him.

"They are not arguing," Robert said. "Jasper needs a drink, and Kate is as cool as cucumber."

"She's very good at hiding her true feelings," said Elsie.

"I suspect Lady Carmichael has been up to no good. She spends a lot of time in the library alone."

"How do you know?" asked a confused Ruby.

"I have a feeling," answered Robert. "I fear there's more to come."

Chapter Twenty-Nine

Lord Blackthorn had found himself in a golf cart being driven around the Landon estate by Von-Pitt. They stopped outside a large farm building that had been used for storing various pieces of farm machinery.

"There were tractors and God knows what in here. I sold the lot off. Tony Rice is project-managing the cannabis business." Von-Pitt stepped from the golf cart and walked briskly to the building. Lord Blackthorn was a little out of breath as Von-Pitt explained that they were going to use hydroponics to grow the plants. "I'm leaving it all to Tony; he seems to know what he's doing."

By the time they had reached the end of the tour, Blackthorn was panting.

"And this is where we pack the drugs for distribution. Over there is going to be the control centre."

"That shed?" gasped Lord Blackthorn.

"Look, I know you're not really interested and probably didn't understand what I was saying, but this operation will be a gold mine. Drugs are the way forward. Think about it on the way back to the hall."

Lord Blackthorn was delighted to see Tony Rice sitting in the driver's seat of a Range Rover. His delicate body couldn't stand another trip in the golf cart with Von-Pitt driving.

Two hours later, Lord Blackthorn was sitting in his helicopter on his way to River's End House. He hadn't mentioned the diamonds in his pocket or the attaché case in the helicopter. Von-Pitt was obsessed with his empire, and anyone that stood in his way would be eliminated. Drugs were just a part of his operation; he wanted to expand into money laundering as well taking Jasper's diamonds. The main operation was to be based at Landon Hall, with the headquarters being Wellsbury's Carmichael House. During the coming twelve months, Von-Pitt anticipated owning the shopping centre, which was going to be his main outlet for selling drugs, and all the land currently owned by Kate. He also anticipated taking over Lord Blackthorn's business with Jasper.

* * *

"Lord and Lady Carmichael are waiting for you in the library," Robert announced as Lord Blackthorn stepped into the foyer of River's End House.

As he waited for Robert to close the front door, Lord Blackthorn was struck by how calm the foyer seemed. But he did not loosen his grip on the black attaché case. "Unusual for them to be in the library," he commented, hoping Robert would be forthcoming with information.

Robert knocked on the library door and waited before entering.

How tactful of Robert, Lord Blackthorn thought, *to give them a moment to compose themselves. Don't want to interrupt a private moment.*

Kate was at her desk, and Jasper was standing in front of the blazing fire holding a very large malt.

"I could do with one of those," said Lord Blackthorn as he slumped onto the fireside couch and pulled a white envelope from his pocket.

Jasper handed him a malt and took the envelope to the side table. He put his drink next to the envelope and slipped on a pair of cotton gloves. Smiling, he picked up one of the five sparkling clear diamonds from the envelope and examined it with his eyeglass.

"Can they be traced?" asked Jasper.

"Don't insult me," replied Lord Blackthorn. He waited for Jasper's evaluation. "How much?"

"Don't accept anything below three mill for the large one. The others, about a mill each," said Jasper, opening the attaché case.

"It's all there. What we agreed. Five mill."

Blackthorn handed Jasper his empty glass for a refill. "I've been with Von-Pitt at Landon Hall. He's there with Tony Rice." Swig of malt.

Jasper waited for Lord Blackthorn to continue.

"Von-Pitt wants me to join his drug and diamond business." Swig of malt.

"The drug farm is well on the way. Rice is in charge. I didn't get to see his diamond vault, but the number of armed guards around the place made me think it isn't finished." Swig of malt.

"I didn't like it, Jasper. He intends to take over our business. We have an excellent arrangement: I move diamonds from organisation to organisation, get a good price; they know that they come from you." He swished his glass and drained the last of the malt.

"Carmichael House is going to be his headquarters, and the shopping centre his retail outlet. He didn't say what was going to happen to you two—but I can guess." Blackthorn carefully returned the empty glass to the side table. "You're being watched. I don't know if it's Von-Pitt or the Americans. Probably both."

Blackthorn replaced the diamond envelope in his inside jacket pocket and stood. "You should be in prison for what you've done, but you're more use to the people that matter 'out'. They won't take too kindly to Von-Pitt or the Americans trying to muscle in on our arrangement." He turned to face Kate. "You are a Landon, and they look after their own. You should have accepted Cavendish's offer, but there is a fair number on the committee that admire you for it."

He turned the door handle and stepped into the foyer. "Watch your back, Jasper."

Jasper opened the front door and saw the helicopter pilot stamp on his cigarette. "How much does he know?" asked Jasper, nodding towards the pilot.

"Don't worry about him," Blackthorn said. "I pay him well."

Chapter Thirty

Kate slipped her arms around Jasper's waist, and he pulled her into his side and kissed her hair as they watched the helicopter leave River's End House.

"Can he be trusted?" Kate asked.

"My gut tells me no. He's playing both sides."

Robert was hovering by the library door.

"Take the rest of the day off," Jasper said. "We are going for a long walk."

Before joining Jasper, Kate tidied the library and put the attaché case in her wall safe.

Once outside, she was surprised to find Jasper waiting in the old Land Rover Defender.

"You need the sea, and I need the boathouse," he said, pointing to the sacks of wood and a basket of food.

"Do you intend to be out all night?"

"If need be."

* * *

"This place is too cold," Kate said, rubbing her arms as Jasper was lighting the fire in the boathouse.

Jasper smiled and pushed the couch nearer the fire. Then, a loud screeching noise made her turn. Jasper was pulling on a concertina screen that separated the living area from the water below.

"Lord Henry thought of everything," she said. "I wonder who he entertained here… Not his wife."

Ten minutes later, they were walking along the beach. Jasper had his arm draped across Kate's shoulders.

"It's not *your* beach, but when the tide's out it's not too shabby."

"Do you see that boat?"

"Don't worry about it." He wrapped his arms around her and claimed her mouth. "Let's give them something to talk about."

"We have a lot to discuss."

"I don't want you involved."

"I'm already involved."

"I shall have to pay a visit to Landon Hall."

"That's what they want."

"Stop talking."

"What's that noise?"

"The boathouse." Jasper sprinted towards the dunes.

Kate's heart began to race. She looked out to sea as the contents of her stomach rose and her chest tightened. She reached into the inside pocket of her coat for a bottle of tablets she hadn't needed for a long time, then closed her eyes and let her mind drift into the sound and smell of the sea, waiting for the tightness to ease.

"Kate, what are you doing?" gasped Jasper.

She didn't answer, but her hand left the bottle in her pocket.

Jasper came up behind her, put his arms around her waist and rested his chin on her shoulder.

"Can you feel it?" she asked.

Jasper didn't answer.

"Close your eyes. Open your mind to the sound of the sea."

"Kate, my love, let's go back."

He wrapped his arms around her and guided her slowly towards the path through the sand dunes.

Just before the pathway, she stopped. "Here," she said. "The sea is so angry, but here the waves roll onto the beach as if something is slowing them. Maybe a sandbank."

Jasper stopped and stared. Kate had accidentally stumbled across the only safe spot to beach a dinghy.

* * *

The foyer clock struck 3 a.m. as Jasper sat alone in Kate's library. In his hand he nursed a large malt as he stared at the blazing fire. His plan for a night of love with Kate had ended abruptly with a loud noise. He had guessed that the noise came from the boathouse, and he wasn't wrong. From the top of the sand dunes, he'd spotted a yacht manoeuvring in the river. The sound of wood cracking could only have come from the boathouse doors. The oak doors were solidly built, but could they withstand being rammed? Inspection would have to wait till the morning. He hadn't mentioned it to Kate as he was concerned about her present mindset.

Jasper's thoughts were interrupted by the library door slowly creaking. Kate looked stunningly beautiful in the flickering firelight.

"Kiss me." Kate's hands ran through his soft hair as their passionate kiss deepened. "Love me."

"That's not a good idea. You need to rest."

"I need to feel you inside me."

He stared into her glowing eyes; his finger trailed her hairline. "Kate," he murmured.

"Don't make me wait, Jasper."

Chapter Thirty-One

It was early afternoon when Kate walked out onto the landing, her hair still wet from her long shower. Jasper had worked his magic, and she had slept. But she didn't feel refreshed.

A wave of nervous fear sped through her as angry American voices filtered into the foyer. She had been dreading that the American Landons would appear unannounced; she had researched them, and they had a reputation of being violent if they didn't get what they wanted.

Slowly and cautiously, she made her way down the stairs. Suddenly, she was poked in the back with something cold and hard, causing her to lose her balance and stumble. The poking continued, directing her to enter the dining room, where she saw a man standing with his hands gripping the back of a chair. He was a stranger, but Kate recognised his features from the portraits at Landon Hall.

"Look who I found sneaking down the stairs," growled a rough voice from behind her. "Sleeping beauty." He poked her again.

Kate's eyes quickly scanned the room. Jasper, Harry and Little Jasper were tied to chairs, and Lucy was sitting in her high chair, whimpering. Jasper's head was slumped onto his chest; blood was trickling onto his shirt.

The man that had been poking her with his gun started to poke Jasper. He took hold of his hair, pulling his head up so Kate could see his face. Jasper's eyes were closed and his face was covered in blood. The man let go of his hair, and Jasper's head slumped back onto his chest.

"Never believed the rumours… till now. I'm looking at a Landon," said the man whose hands were still on the back of a chair. "Jethro Landon, head of the Landon crime syndicate." He turned to the men standing behind him. "And these are my sons. Jacob runs New York, and Matthew, Miami." He paused. "And you, Lady Carmichael, will run London—even though you're not a thoroughbred, so to speak." He continued with some pride in his voice: "We American Landons only have Landon blood; yours is diluted with Spencer blood."

Kate was taken by surprise. *Does he mean that the American Landons inbreed?*

"You look surprised," Jethro said. "I'll explain. Landons marry cousins. We look after our own; we have our own clinic. I intend that your son and grandson will have children with American Landon women." He hesitated and looked into Kate's staring eyes before continuing. "Your granddaughter will marry one of my cousins."

Kate's stomach churned as she silently pondered her next move.

"When we leave, you, your son and grandson will come with us to California. Carmichael can stay here after I have taken his diamonds."

"What if I refuse to go with you?"

Jethro flung the chair across the room. "You will fucking do as you're told! Or… you'll watch as I destroy everything you love, including your beloved Jasper, son and grandchildren." He delighted in her shocked expression. "I'm sure you'll find appropriate resting places. Although the Carmichael mausoleum is a little overcrowded." He laughed, showing his gleaming white teeth.

Kate shuddered as she fought to keep her voice calm. "You don't frighten me. I've been threatened by men better than you."

Jethro stepped towards her, his eyes bulging in his red, angry face.

Kate swallowed hard. "I understand now why Henry Landon left America and married an English aristocrat; he didn't want to be part of your incestuous marriages." Her mouth filled with bile and her body quivered. Jethro was so close to her that she could feel his stale breath.

His fat paws pulled on the collar of her white blouse. "Don't think that your superior attitude will deter me. Henry fucked an English aristocrat, had a son with her. He liked the rich lifestyle and he made himself very rich with black-market diamonds."

You could hear a pin drop as an angry silence lingered.

Kate's soft, calm voice pierced the tension. "He came here every summer to deal diamonds with criminals. River's End House is perfectly situated for the smugglers. There were lavish balls and garden parties where, I've no doubt, the rich and famous mingled with criminals and exchanged diamonds—they all had an addiction. A trust fund was set up, an illegal, diamond trust fund—"

"That's e-fucking-nough!" Jethro shouted.

Kate stepped away to try and hide her shaking. But she couldn't let him win without a fight. "That brings me to my point." *Here goes*, she thought as she swallowed more bile. "One of your American companies will take over or merge with the Landon Trust Fund, and your highly paid lawyers will draw up the necessary papers to make sure that none of the investors lose out."

"Fuck you. Who the hell do you think you are?"

"Kate," Jasper croaked.

"No one tells me what to do, especially not a half-breed." He turned to his sons. "Take her to Carmichael's diamond office."

"Only Jasper's right eye will open the diamond office, and your brutes have managed to close it," Kate lied.

Jethro stormed over and lifted her by her collar. Their foreheads touched. "You'll bloody do as you're fucking told and open the fucking door."

Kate's legs gave way as she was dropped to the floor.

"Pick the bitch up."

At that moment, Jethro's phone rang.

"What the fuck do you want? I told you not to disturb me!" he bellowed.

Kate watched as the redness that covered his face dissolved into a pink then a ghostly white. Jethro stuffed the phone back into his pocket.

He pushed Kate out of his way. "Collect your shit; we're leaving."

"Now?" said one of his sons.

"Of course bloody now. We have a problem."

Jethro raced to Jasper and lifted his face by his hair. "You fucking Carmichaels, if you fell into a barrel of shit, you would come up smelling of fucking roses. But we haven't finished, Jasper. I'll be back. In the meantime, my friends will keep pouring the shit over you until you have nothing. No diamonds. No Kate. No Carmichael Castle estate."

Before the front door had closed behind the Landons, Kate raced into the bathroom and threw up the contents of her stomach into the toilet. Harry heard his mother throwing up in the bathroom, but selfish Jasper continually shouted her name.

Harry knew it would be a waste of breath trying to stop her from going to him, so he took Little Jasper and Lucy back to Isaacs House.

Chapter Thirty-Two

The American Landons had given Jasper a thorough working over. Kate lay with him in the bath, letting the warm water soothe his bruises while she cleaned the cuts. However, there wasn't much she could do for his swollen eyes. Kate had wanted him to go to the hospital but he had refused.

She gave him a sedative to help him sleep then wandered into the kitchen to mash a pot of tea. She was surprised to find the staff sitting around the kitchen table. She had forgotten that they must be as traumatised as she was.

"Lord Carmichael?" asked Robert.

"Sleeping."

Ben set her tea tray upon the table. Kate smiled and thought of Malcolm, who had always known when she needed a cup.

"Harry just phoned. Little Jasper and Lucy fell asleep in the car," Robert said.

"We were worried about you," said Elsie.

"Don't worry about me," said Kate. "I've been in many tight situations." *But not as tight as this*, she thought. "Only, Jasper was the one causing the problems then, but this time it's me." She turned to Ben. "Is the Focus ready to go?"

"Aye, tank's full. Checked the oil. Tyres okay."

"Where are you going, Lady Carmichael? It's not safe."

"The Americans' interest in Carmichael Castle is bugging me. Something is wrong. I've got to check."

"Can't it wait till the morning?" said Robert.

"I'm afraid not. Look in on Jasper. I'll be back for breakfast." She picked up a bottle of water from the fridge and walked out the door.

There were very few cars on the road to Carmichael Castle as Kate floored the Focus. She tried to concentrate on the road, but Jethro Landon and his comments about Carmichael Castle mausoleum and other parties ruining Jasper played on her mind. She had so many questions, particularly about his interest in the mausoleum.

Kate would have missed the turning to Carmichael Castle if bright lights flicking through the hedgerow hadn't caught her attention. She pulled off the road onto a gravel lay-by where she could see clearly the lights.

They are very close to the Carmichael mausoleum, she thought.

She carefully closed the car door behind her and began to walk towards the track that led to the mausoleum. As she got closer, the arc lights got brighter and she could see boxes being carried out of the mausoleum onto a farm trailer. She crept into the bushes and listened.

"This is the last," said a gruff voice.

"Follow the track to the hall." Kate's heart missed a beat as she recognised Tony Rice's voice.

"Where should I leave these?"

"Throw them inside."

"Don't you want to hide 'em?"

"No. I want the plods to find them."

The heavy mausoleum doors creaked as they were closed, and the diesel engine of a tractor fired. The tractor slowly moved onto the track that led away from the mausoleum.

"Be fuckin' careful!" shouted Rice. "We don't want to lose this load."

"We should use the fuckin' road," answered the unhappy gruff voice.

One by one, the lights on the building were switched off. Then, headlights lit Kate's hiding place, and she gingerly crouched into the undergrowth. Her heart began to race as the vehicle moved and turned towards the road. She waited and waited until an eerie silence settled.

Finally, gasping for breath and trembling, Kate stepped from her hiding place. She mentally debated her next move. If it wasn't for Tony Rice's presence, she would have returned home, but where Rice was, Von-Pitt wouldn't be far away.

Kate pulled on the mausoleum doors and nearly lost her balance when they opened. Her old fear of this dark, damp place kicked in as she carefully stepped onto the top step. With the light from her iPhone, she scanned the Carmichaels' resting place.

As she ventured onto the second step, she caught sight of two white packages. Pushing her fear to the back of her mind, she walked towards them. She was convinced that they contained drugs.

She scanned the rest of the mausoleum, looking for more evidence. Slowly, she walked to Colin Carmichael's sarcophagus. No one would guess that this was the final resting place of the notorious diamond thief. Colin's coffin was undisturbed.

Kate didn't like thinking on her feet, but she had to dispose of the drugs. She delved into her jacket pocket for her emergency plastic shopping bag.

With the drugs safely in her bag, Kate closed the mausoleum doors and quickly walked back to the Focus.

On her way home, she stopped at a deserted all-night petrol station and dropped the drugs into the skip.

Chapter Thirty-Three

Dawn was breaking when Kate stopped at the River's End House garage. To her surprise, Ben stepped out of the garage.

"Cutting it a bit fine," he said.

Kate tried to smile.

"Like that is it?"

"Worse," she said.

"I'll steam clean," he said, nodding at the dirty car.

"Jasper?"

"Elsie gave him another cup of that sleepy water. There're your nightclothes and breakfast waiting."

"Ben, you shouldn't have got involved."

"It's like this: you're in some kind of trouble—not of your own making, mind, you don't deserve it—so, we decided to give you a helping hand."

Kate planted a kiss on his cheek and smiled as he turned a shade of pink. "Don't tell Jasper."

As Kate and Ben entered the kitchen, Jasper burst in through the other door.

"Kate. Kate!" he called. He stopped in his tracks as his eyes met his wife's. "What are you doing? You know how I get when you're not there."

Kate planted a soft kiss on his dry lips.

"What's that supposed to be? You can do better than that."

But Kate was already walking out of the kitchen.

"Now where are you going?"

"Follow and you'll find out."

"I don't know what's got into you."

"Your morning coffee, sir?" said Robert, swallowing a smile at Jasper's discomfort.

"I don't want that," said an angry Jasper. "I want her."

* * *

Kate was tired; the warm bath was making her feel sleepy as it eased her aching body.

Suddenly, Jasper's angry voice boomed from the foyer. "What do you want?"

"It's Lady Carmichael we want a word with," said Arthur, the chief constable, whose voice travelled up to Kate in the master bathroom.

Kate's eyes shot open, and she pushed herself out of the warm, soothing water.

Jasper's temper was rising. There wasn't a muscle in his body that didn't hurt. He glared at Von-Pitt's followers: Tony Rice, Margot, Arthur and Lord Blackthorn, who were now all standing in his foyer. He needed Kate by his side.

Margot's lustful eyes settled on Jasper's open white shirt and jeans that rested on his hips. She moved to his side and slid her arm around his waist. "You're wasted on her," she whispered. "You need a woman that can satisfy you."

He flung her arm from him, pushed her away and walked into the dining room.

Von-Pitt caught up with her. "Well?"

"I need more time. I want him alone."

"Time's running out," he replied, then followed Jasper into the dining room. "I wish you'd buy more furniture," said Von-Pitt disapprovingly as he gazed around the room.

"You've got a seat; be thankful for that," snapped Jasper.

"But a hard dining chair. Really?"

"Think yourself lucky."

"Ah, Kate," said Lord Blackthorn.

Jasper hurriedly stepped to his wife and wrapped his arms around her.

"Better?" she whispered as she stretched to kiss his cheek.

"I am now," he replied in a calmer voice.

Von-Pitt pulled his chair closer to Margot's. "He's not interested in you. Look at him, only eyes for her."

"I just need more time."

"It's just run out."

"Kate," began Arthur. "We'd like to talk to you about last night."

Kate pulled a chair out from the dining table just as Robert set her tea tray down.

"You look tired, my dear," commented Lord Blackthorn pointedly, while Robert and Elsie served coffee and tea.

"What do you want, Arthur?" asked Kate impatiently as she sipped her morning tea.

"We've just returned from Carmichael Castle."

"What the…?" Jasper's anger had returned.

Arthur ignored Jasper's mini outburst. "We had it on good authority that the mausoleum was being used for drug storage."

"You'd better have evidence," snapped Jasper, holding his side.

Arthur dismissed Jasper's anger and fixed his eyes upon Kate. "Considering that Jasper was in no fit state to drive after the Landon beating, that leaves you."

In her typical calm voice she said, "I'm not following you, Arthur. What am I supposed to have done?"

"Let me spell it out. Last night, you drove to the mausoleum at Carmichael Castle and removed the drugs."

"To where?"

"We haven't got that far, my dear," interjected Lord Blackthorn with a slight grin.

"Well," Kate continued, "I hope you have evidence. I don't take kindly to being accused. My solicitors are a helicopter ride away."

"This is getting out of hand," said an irritated Lord Blackthorn. "We are not accusing you of anything."

"Stop beating around the bush," snapped Von-Pitt. "She was seen."

Kate moved her attention to Von-Pitt as an image of her throwing the drugs into the skip flashed into her mind.

Jasper asked, "And where was that exactly?"

"For goodness' sake," snapped Lord Blackthorn. "A car was spotted in a lay-by, but it wasn't the Evoque."

"For fuck's sake, she can drive any car!" shouted Von-Pitt, pushing his chair back with such force that it tipped over.

"This has gone far enough," said Kate as she emptied her teacup. "Solicitors. I'm tired of these continual accusations, Arthur. From now on, I want my solicitor present."

"I knew this would happen. Jasper, I want to talk diamonds," said an angry Lord Blackthorn.

"Give me another couple of days."

"This isn't over!" shouted Von-Pitt. "Five men have lost their lives."

Jasper and Kate looked at Arthur.

"You don't know?" said a surprised Arthur. "The yacht that rammed the boathouse doors sank."

"Talk to the Americans," answered Jasper.

"They are missing!" bellowed a red-faced Von-Pitt.

"Their plane never arrived in California," replied Arthur.

Chapter Thirty-Four

"Tell me again what you did with those cocaine bricks."

Kate was driving Jasper's Range Rover to Carmichael Castle. They had been arguing since Von-Pitt and his followers had left River's End House. Neither of them had slept in their bed: Kate in the library and Jasper in the living room.

Angry tension filled the car. Kate hadn't wanted to drive him to Carmichael Castle, but when his temper turned into the Carmichael rage, she let him have his own way.

"I've told you," she said. "I threw them in a service station skip."

"You shouldn't have gone. You were putting yourself in danger."

Silence.

Kate had no intention of repeating herself. Jasper couldn't accept that if she hadn't been at the mausoleum, the drugs would have been found and he would be facing a long prison term.

Suddenly, he thumped the fascia. "I'm fucking useless like this."

"Give yourself time to heal."

"How can I heal when I can't properly fuck you?"

"I thought you were pretty good the other night. Considering."

Silence.

As Kate turned into the road for Carmichael Castle, Jasper held his side.

"You're not up to this; you've probably got cracked ribs."

When they turned onto the mausoleum track, Jasper wrapped his arms around himself. Kate stopped the Range Rover close to the mausoleum doors.

"Kate, help me out of this bloody thing."

When his feet touched the ground, he cried out in pain. She leaned him against the closed rear door before giving him more painkillers.

They looked into each other's eyes.

Their anger started to melt. She touched her lips to his. He held her arm and pulled her close, so close that their lips trembled with anticipation. Her hand reached for his head as their mouths met.

* * *

Hiding in the undergrowth that surrounded the mausoleum stood Tony Rice and the tractor driver.

"That guy certainly knows how to kiss."

"Shut the fuck up," said Tony.

"She's putty in his hands."

Kate's hands were in Jasper's hair. His hands were on her backside, pulling her into him while their tongues danced.

Tony couldn't take his eyes from Kate as she melted into Jasper.

The tractor driver began to rub his crotch. "Fancy a night with her."

Jealousy was raging deep inside Tony. He abruptly turned and gripped the man's throat. "I've told you. Shut the fuck up."

* * *

"Come," said Jasper as they walked to the mausoleum.

Kate pulled the doors. "See, they're open."

Jasper stood on the top step and looked down to water lapping against the bottom step.

"What's wrong?" asked a concerned Kate.

"There's water."

"Water? Where's that from?" she asked as she joined him.

"The dam must have burst."

"What dam?"

"It's just a mound of earth Grandfather had built to stop water filling the bottom of the estate." Jasper turned and walked back to the car, talking into his phone. "Tiny, the mausoleum's flooded."

"Jasper, tell me about the water," Kate said as she followed him.

"When I was sorting some old papers, I came across a map of this section of the estate. Carmichael land was taking the water from the surrounding area, so Grandfather had a dam built to divert the water from the estate."

"You never said."

"Kate, you have never shown interest in the estate. Anyway, it's no big deal. The estate hasn't flooded for years. I suppose this heavy rain has just breached the dam."

Suddenly, an old pickup screeched to a halt by the Range Rover. Kate's eyes widened as a giant got out and walked towards them.

"Kate, this is Tiny, he looks after the grounds."

"Lady Carmichael." Tiny reached for Kate's hand and held it in his soft palm. "Absolute pleasure."

"Tiny," she hesitantly replied.

As she watched Tiny and Jasper walk to the side of the mausoleum, she couldn't help but think that Tiny's soft palms were not indicative of a man who worked with his hands.

Chapter Thirty-Five

Jasper was still in bed when Kate left for a sunrise walk. Robert was waiting when she returned.

"Lady Carmichael, Lord Carmichael asked me to tell you not to worry, he'll be back later."

"Did he say where he was going?"

"Not in so many words, but he left with a very tall, well-dressed man."

Kate's heart missed a beat.

"Lord Carmichael knew the man," Robert added.

"Did he have a name?"

Robert hesitated. "I believe Lord Carmichael referred to him as Tiny."

"Did Lord Carmichael mention Carmichael Castle?"

"No, my lady. But just before his visitor arrived, Lord Carmichael opened the diamond office."

"Thank you, Robert."

Kate walked into her library, thinking about the possibility that Jasper and Tiny were hiding their involvement with diamonds and using Carmichael Castle as cover. Had Jasper resurrected the diamond king?

* * *

Kate was taken by surprise when Harry joined her for breakfast. He leaned across her desk, helping himself to a slice of toast.

"He's gone, has he?" he said with his mouth full. "Saw him driving the Range Rover. Who's the man with him?"

Robert knocked on the door and brought more toast, coffee for Harry and a second pot of tea.

"I think it's a man called Tiny."

"A diamond friend, no doubt."

"Harry, why do you think the worst of your father?"

"My gut tells me he's itching to get away."

"Let's concentrate on the expansion of your business."

Harry sipped his coffee as he moved to the fire.

"I need your input," Kate added. She stretched the plan for the remodel of the three units that were involved with the drug fiasco on her desk.

"What do you think of your personal workshop?"

"I would like it bigger."

Kate scribbled on the plan. "Security will be a problem."

"Ask Dad, he knows how to break in."

"Harry."

"He's up to his old tricks."

Kate folded the plan and tucked it into the top drawer of her desk.

"Where does he get the diamonds from?"

"I met one of his contacts at the diamond festival."

"And?"

"It was all above board; paperwork changed hands and the diamonds were delivered here and to the shop."

"What about those Americans?"

"They wanted me to accept I'm a Landon." Kate paused and met Harry's eyes. "I'm not a Landon. I'm not going to California."

"I couldn't cope without you here. It would break Little Jasper's heart."

Kate joined him by the fire and leaned on his shoulder. "Drive me to the shopping centre and we can discuss the plan."

"Okay. I'll drop you back home on the way to pick up Little Jasper."

"Don't put yourself out; Robert can fetch me. I'll go to the gallery. In fact, we can take some paintings."

Kate opened the library door.

"What about Dad?"

"He said not to worry. So, I'm not."

* * *

It was unusual for Kate to be working late in the gallery, but she'd felt that she was on a roll. Harry had finally contributed to the conversion of the three units into a diamond workshop and store. Phone calls had been made, and a team of builders were starting next week.

The rear gallery door creaked open, and closed.

Kate didn't look up; she was expecting Robert. "Nearly finished," she said.

An eerie silence swept through the gallery.

Then, the hairs on the back of her neck rose.

"I've come to collect," Tony Rice said in a menacing voice.

She turned to face him. He was walking towards her.

"I'm expecting Jasper."

"Lover boy is at Carmichael Castle. I was told that the small bathroom was a favourite place of yours to fuck. I couldn't believe it." He paused and began to pace the gallery. "I won the uni sweepstake to have your cherry, but Miss Frigid disappeared. It's time to claim my prize."

Kate stepped back into a wall.

"That'll do nicely, you pinned against the wall."

He suddenly stopped pacing and launched himself at her. He gripped the top of her blouse and snatched it open, scattering the buttons across the gallery floor. He pushed her bra up, exposing her ample breasts. She tried to knee his crotch, but missed. His eyes darkened and an evil grin spread across his face. He gripped her breasts, making her flinch with pain.

The lights went out.

Suddenly, Tony was slammed into the wall. A hand was squashing his face into the wall and a knee was jabbing into his back.

Kate slowly turned and felt Jasper's evil eyes upon her. She could hear Tony trying to fight back, but it was useless. The last man that exposed her breasts ended up dead. She gulped when she heard the snapping of bone. The sound of clothes ripping followed, as Tony fell against the brick wall. Kate didn't need to see Jasper to know that his Carmichael demons were in control. She knew Tony was dead.

She could hear Jasper's heavy breathing as he struggled with the body.

When the lights came on, Kate fell to the floor. Through her tears, she collected her blouse buttons, then sat and waited, unsure what to do next.

The stillness in the gallery was broken by a thumping on the glass door. Kate leapt up and covered herself.

She was greeted by a very anxious Robert. "Lady Carmichael, are you alright?"

Kate nodded. "I'll double-check the back door is locked."

There was no sign of Jasper.

Chapter Thirty-Six

Jasper glanced at his car clock. The hour hand was on three and the minute hand rested on twelve. His demons were still swirling deep inside; he needed her, but he feared that she wouldn't want to see him.

He stepped out of the car and wandered down to the beach. Her beach. Staring out to sea, he watched the lights of passing boats. He would be out there sailing if she rejected him.

He let his thoughts drift to the time they had shared this beach, walking, arms wrapped around each other, along the water's edge after making love. He could hear her soft, reassuring voice as she calmed his Carmichael demons.

They had surfaced again when he saw Tony Rice walk into the rear entrance of the gallery. He had followed and watched as he ripped Kate's blouse open. No man did that to his wife; Kate was his and there were consequences if any man tried to rape her. He'd had to be quick; Tony Rice could handle himself. Jasper had wanted to stay with her, comfort her, but he had to get rid of the body.

With heavy legs and heart, he walked back to the Range Rover.

His hand trembled as he turned the kitchen door handle of River's End House. He stepped inside to a dimly lit kitchen where the staff were sitting around the table. Robert pointed to the orangery.

Jasper's beloved stood gazing into the breaking dawn.

She was holding her morning mug of tea between her hands. She didn't know how much more she could take of Jasper's demons; he was becoming more violent.

Jasper slowly walked up behind her and held his breath until he had the courage to murmur, "Kate."

The mug tumbled from her hand as she turned to face him. Her hand stretched to his head as their lips collided. Their kiss deepened.

"He was going to rape you; I just saw red."

She put her finger across his mouth. "I know." She passionately kissed him, hoping that it would quell his demons.

* * *

It was mid-afternoon when Jasper took the call from Arthur, the chief constable, asking if he and Inspector Paul Johnson could come to River's End House on a matter of some urgency.

Arthur didn't have time for pleasantries. He pushed past Jasper on his way to the living room. "Where's Kate?"

"Here," she answered in her calm voice.

She took Jasper's breath away. Her green eyes sparkled above her pink cheeks. She had been walking and the wind had ruffled her hair.

Robert was following her with a tray of tea and cake.

"Haven't got time for this," said Arthur, glancing at the tea.

"I always have afternoon tea."

Arthur ignored her. "Tony Rice was found dead."

Kate let his words hang as she stirred her tea. "I'm sorry to hear that."

"Joanne tells me he was infatuated with you. Stemmed back to the days you were at uni with him."

"He was under the misguided impression that I owed him a fuck."

Arthur stuttered; he had never heard Kate use that word. "What, er, do you say about that, Jasper?"

"I know all about Kate's sex life at uni."

"He wanted to fuck your wife. How do you feel about it?"

"Many men have desired that."

"You're very calm about it."

"That was the past. Kate's shares my bed now and no one else's."

"Where were you yesterday?"

"You know where I was. Carmichael Castle. There's a flooding problem."

"Kate?"

"At the shopping centre with Harry, finalising the alterations to three units. And then the gallery."

"We've been to the gallery. It was being cleaned."

"That's right," Kate said. "Wes Clayton rang. He had men with nothing to do and wanted to know if they could start a day early."

"What were you doing at the gallery?"

"Moving the painting I had brought over."

"There were also men there today working in a passage that leads to the back entrance."

"That's right. The lights had gone off, so I wanted the electrics checked."

A heavy, tense silence descended.

"I'll be clear. We suspect"—Arthur nodded at the inspector—"that you two had something to do with Tony's murder."

"Murder? You never said he was murdered," commented Kate.

"The pair of you have only answered my questions, you haven't asked any."

"Be careful, Arthur," Jasper said.

"I know; you'll have those expensive lawyers onto me."

"There was no ID. It looked like a mugging, but his neck was broken," added Inspector Johnson.

Arthur stood. "You two are involved in this. Tony was lying next to his Jaguar in the car park behind the gallery, and you heard nothing?"

"You never asked me if I heard anything," said Kate.

Arthur began to walk to the door. "You know what I think? Tony Rice roughed you up, and Jasper took his revenge. But this time, Jasper, Von-Pitt's after you—and he will get justice."

Suddenly, the front door flew open and loud shouting echoed around the foyer. Von-Pitt pushed Robert to one side and marched into the living room. His eyes scanned the room and settled on Kate.

Jasper moved like a cat and stopped in front of him.

"Get out of my fucking way!" Von-Pitt shouted as Jasper put his hands on his shoulders. Von-Pitt moved his head so he could see Kate. "I'm going to fucking destroy you. Fucking bitch. You may have fooled the Americans with your aristocratic manner, but you don't fool me. Everything you cherish, I will fucking destroy."

Jasper's temper began to stir. He pushed Von-Pitt towards the door, his angry eyes piercing into him. "You'll have to destroy me first."

"You fucking don't frighten me," Von-Pitt shouted as Jasper manhandled him to the front door, which Robert was holding open. He stumbled outside. "You're a dead man, Carmichael. You and that bitch."

Chapter Thirty-Seven

The Evoque stood, as it had many times, in the lane that led to her beach house, waiting for its mistress. If it could, it would have turned and watched her.

Kate was standing in the remains of the gully that had led to her beach. She was hurting; her world was starting to crumble. The cold sea lapped over her trainers, but she didn't notice. *What's happening?* she thought. *It's one thing after another.* Her beloved was lying in a hospital bed in a coma; Little Jasper was in the room next to him with his leg in plaster.

She should have been in the car with them, but she'd wanted her old Evoque back and it needed an MOT and service. Harry had dropped her off while they had continued to the shopping centre—but they never arrived. The truck came out of nowhere and hit the driver's side of Harry's BMW. Jasper had been sitting in the front next to Harry and, as usual, was not wearing a seat belt. But on this occasion, it saved his life; he was thrown from the car and his head hit the pavement.

The truck was embedded in the car. Harry, little Lucy and nanny Edith had needed to be cut free. Little Jasper had been sitting behind Jasper, strapped in the child seat that had saved his life. Kate blamed herself; the accident was meant for her but it had taken away her son and her granddaughter.

Memories of her boy flashed through her mind: the baby that never cried; the toddler that learnt to walk wobbling along a beach; the quiet child that never judged her, just loved her. How proud she had been when he went to university, how shattered when he told her that he wanted to follow in his father's diamond footsteps. But he'd still made her proud with his bespoke jewellery. She had been so happy for him when he found love with Lizzy and had Little Jasper and Lucy. He had cried on her shoulder when Lizzy left him. He was always there for her when his father left her; no matter how many times Jasper left, Harry was there to pick up the pieces.

Tears flooded from her eyes and dripped into the water. That inner strength she had would now have to show itself for all to see. Jasper was unconscious; he would need her when he woke. Little Jasper would need all her love as he recovered. All the business demands would have to be pushed to one side. She could control the shopping centre, but she wasn't so confident about Jasper's diamond business; his enemies would be manoeuvring to take control. However, her family took priority. She would mourn Harry and get the two Carmichaels back on their feet.

* * *

Days had merged into one as a dazed Kate organised her son and granddaughter's funeral. It was a small, private affair. Little Jasper had insisted on being there although he was in pain and the doctors didn't want him to attend. He stood by her side, holding her hand all through the burial service.

Jasper was still unconscious; the doctors were carefully monitoring his brain. She tried not to think of life without him.

Even though the funeral was private, elderly men in expensive suits attended. She had no idea who they were. By the time the event moved to River's End House, their presence was beginning to bother her. They never introduced themselves or spoke to anyone.

Her emotions were running high; she wanted to be alone with her own thoughts about Harry, and there was only one place for her when she felt like this: the beach.

Am I being selfish? she thought as she left the small gathering at River's End House.

She didn't see Tiny walking towards her.

He wanted to give her his personal condolences. He asked about Jasper and managed to slip into the conversation that the water from Landon Hall was being pumped onto the Carmichael estate.

Kate didn't want to know about the water. As far as she was concerned, the whole of the Carmichael estate could flood. But it would matter to Jasper; she would ask Ben to make a few enquires.

Chapter Thirty-Eight

Kate was at Isaacs House, moving Little Jasper's belongings to River's End House, when Ben arrived to help.

"A word, Kate," he quietly said. "It's bad."

What's bad? she thought.

"All of Landon Hall's water is being pumped onto Carmichael's. The mausoleum is flooded. It appears to be being pumped from land that Von-Pitt is building on. I took a look, there're still puddles inside these new buildings. I'm guessing, but it looks like Von-Pitt is setting up a drug farm of some sort."

She had completely forgotten she had asked Ben to see what was happening at Carmichael Castle. Her mind had been taken up with hospital visits, talking to doctors and preparing for Little Jasper's homecoming.

"I've got to do something, haven't I?" she said.

"If you don't, Von-Pitt will be up and running."

"We'll talk tonight. Check the Focus over."

* * *

Kate left Robert and Elsie to convert her book storage room into Little Jasper's downstairs bedroom while she went into Jasper's diamond office to look for remote-controlled explosives. Many years ago, Jasper had explained how to use them; she hoped that she could still remember.

Her plan was simple: she'd blow up the pump or stop it working. It was the best she could think of at short notice. Ben had been against the idea and tried to persuade her not to do it, but she pushed his doubts out of her mind as she parked the Focus in the gravel lay-by.

She heard the pump as soon as she began to walk towards Landon Hall. To her surprise, it was very close to the road, with the discharge pipe over the other side of the road. With the help of the moon, poking out from behind the clouds, she placed her first explosive on a dryish part of the pump.

Jasper's dam was higher than the road and was being used as a support for the discharge pipe. *The cheek of it*, she thought. *Taking advantage while Jasper's ill.* She placed her second explosive where the pipe connected to the pump. With a bit of luck, the pump explosive would stop the pump, but if it didn't, the pipe explosive would break the connection.

With the detonators in place, Kate quickly walked back to the car.

She pressed the remotes and waited.

There were two large bangs, and the noise from the pump stopped.

* * *

A trembling Kate staggered into the kitchen at River's End House. Robert, Elsie, Ruby and Ben were sitting around the kitchen table.

"Thank God, you're back," said an emotional Robert.

Elsie put her arms around her, Ruby poured hot water into a teapot, and Ben went outside.

"The Evoque is waiting," said Robert.

Kate looked surprised.

"The hospital phoned. Jasper opened his eyes and asked for you."

"There's no need to rush over there," added Elsie. "Apparently, he slipped back to sleep. The doctor said it was a good sign."

Kate slumped onto a stool and sipped her piping hot tea.

An hour later, she pulled a chair up to Jasper's bedside. She rested her head on his leg and took his hand in hers. Jasper moved his fingers.

"Jasper, my love," she whispered, then drifted into a restless sleep.

A hand gently squeezed her shoulder. "Lady Carmichael, I've brought you tea," said the night nurse.

Kate opened her eyes and smiled.

"The doctor's very hopeful that Lord Carmichael will make a good recovery. He'll be having another scan today to see if the bleeding has stopped and the swelling's going down. You look tired, Lady Carmichael. You should go home and sleep."

The hospital was coming to life when Kate left to join the morning traffic. She stopped at Isaacs House to check all was well. As she walked through the rooms, she shivered; there was a coldness there that she had never experienced—but there was something that she must do.

She went to her old office wall safe, removed Harry's individual diamond boxes and the small cotton bags of diamonds, and hid them with the remainder of Zak's cash and diamonds in the secret cupboard in the small library.

Little did she know that Isaacs House would soon be her home.

Chapter Thirty-Nine

Kate cursed as she dodged parked cars and a helicopter that were blocking her way to River's End House. She feared that an unwelcome party was waiting; she was tired and wasn't up to a battle with Von-Pitt and co.

Why can't they leave me alone?

Ben appeared from among the parked cars. "Robert's put them in the dining room and we're waiting for the heating engineer to come."

Kate nodded as if she was taking this in her stride, but deep inside, she was in turmoil.

She made her way to the dining room. They were all there waiting for her: Arthur with Inspector Johnson, Von-Pitt, Margot, Lord Charles Landon and Lord Blackthorn.

"Good God, Kate, you look like shit," exclaimed Lord Blackthorn.

"Thank you," she answered, sitting upon a chair while Robert set a breakfast tray before her.

"I'll get straight to the point, Kate," said Arthur in his stern voice. "Where were you last night?"

"Where do you think, Arthur?"

"You left the hospital over an hour ago."

"I stopped by Isaacs House."

"She's lying. She's meeting Carmichael's diamond thieves."

Kate pushed her chair from the table. "I don't like being called a liar." The harshness of her voice took everyone by surprise.

"Von-Pitt, shut the fuck up," snapped Lord Blackthorn. "Kate, have your tea and toast while I explain. Someone sabotaged the water pump at Landon Hall."

Before she could answer, Von-Pitt marched up to her. "My buildings are under a foot of water."

"Where's Jasper's groundsman?" asked Inspector Johnson.

"I don't know where he is. I don't know about your buildings," said Kate.

"We can't see Jasper. Apparently, under your orders," said a miffed Margot. "There's security everywhere. Family only."

Von-Pitt laughed. "She's the only family left. They're all dead."

"That's enough, Von-Pitt!" shouted Lord Blackthorn.

"Well, I demand to see him," said Margot, joining Von-Pitt to stand near Kate.

"Demand all you like; you aren't seeing him." They all turned to face Ben, who was walking towards Kate, swinging a baseball bat.

"Now, be nice people and fuck off."

"Who the fuck are you?" asked Von-Pitt.

Ben ignored him. "You're trespassing. No warrant. Lady Carmichael's lawyers will be in touch."

As if on cue, Arthur's phone rang. He didn't say a word. However, his face developed a beetroot colour. Then, all eyes turned to him when the room shook to the sound of a hovering helicopter.

Lord Blackthorn didn't wait to see who was in it. "I told you this was a bad idea and there would be consequences," he shouted as he stormed out of the room.

The helicopter landed and the engine cut. The dining room was so quiet that you could hear a pin drop as they nervously waited to see who was coming.

Mumbling drifted from the front door; footsteps echoed through the foyer.

Robert opened the dining room door. "Mr Simon Cavendish, Lord Ambrose and Lord Devon."

Kate stood to greet them as Lord Devon flung his arms around her.

"Oh, my dear."

"Henry. Behaviour," admonished Lord Ambrose with his stiff upper lip.

"It's all very exciting," said Lord Devon. "We were on our way to a meeting when the call came through to divert to here."

Simon was busy helping himself to the coffee that Elsie had put on the table.

"I would appreciate something a little stronger, my dear," said Lord Devon, scanning the room for a drinks cart.

Robert appeared with a tray of glasses with generous portions of malt. Ruby bustled in with a fresh pot of tea for Kate.

Without further ado, Simon began. "I can only imagine what your intentions are." He was staring at the intruders. "It will stop. You will leave my client alone."

"Who the hell are you to tell me what to do?" said an angry Von-Pitt.

"You want to fight me? Go ahead."

Lord Devon helped himself to another glass of malt and Lord Ambrose slapped his hand.

Simon ignored the wayward lords. He lifted his phone from his inside jacket pocket. "I'm here now, Phillip. Chief Constable, this is for you."

Arthur gingerly took the phone. He went bright red as he listened.

At the end of the call, Arthur cleared his throat and turned to face Von-Pitt. "This continual badgering of Lady Carmichael will stop. All future contact with Lady Carmichael with be through her solicitor. If any of you decide to ignore this, court proceedings will follow. Do you understand my instruction?"

A heavy silence descended.

"Inspector, show these people out," said the chief constable in his authoritative voice.

Von-Pitt couldn't resist whispering so only Kate could hear: "This isn't over."

When they had all left, Lord Ambrose took her hand. "Now, now, my dear, pay no attention to those people. Concentrate on Jasper and Little Jasper."

He patted her hand as Lord Devon whispered into her ear, "We look after our own."

"The order has been issued, Kate," Simon said.

"How can you do that, Simon?" said Kate, trying to understand what had just happened. "Who's Phillip?"

"When you have power, you can do whatever you like," answered Simon.

Lords Ambrose and Devon kissed her cheeks and followed Simon to the helicopter.

Robert closed the front door and returned to the dining room. "Lady Carmichael, the hospital just phoned. I'm quoting: 'the Carmichaels have kicked off'."

Kate buried her head in her hands. *Can this day get any worse?* she thought.

Chapter Forty

Heads turned when Kate parked her old Evoque in Jasper's director's space. She was surprised by the vocal crowd that surrounded the glass doors leading into the private hospital.

A casually dressed Kate pushed her way through the crowd. It wasn't until the hospital porter opened the door and greeted her as "Lady Carmichael" that the reporters shouted, "Lady Carmichael, a word!"

"What's going on?" she asked the porter.

"The meeting's upstairs," he answered.

"Meeting? What meeting?" said a miffed Kate, looking down at her blue jeans tucked into a pair of black leather boots.

"I shouldn't be telling you this, but Von-Pitt's here with Lizzie, a judge and Arthur, the chief constable. They are taking Little Jasper. He kicked off, and Lord Carmichael nearly fell out of bed."

Kate's temper was bubbling as she took the stairs two at a time.

The swing doors bounced open. The room went silent and all eyes turned to Kate. Her temper rose when she saw Arthur and Von-Pitt so close to her grandson. *I've had enough of this.* She lifted her phone and speed-dialled Simon.

"Now, now Kate. You don't know what this is about," said a very nervous Arthur.

Kate's angry green eyes pierced the man sitting at the head of the table. She marched up to him. "And you are?"

"Kate, this is Judge Jones. He deals with, er, children," said Arthur.

"Arthur, stop arse-licking!" bellowed an annoyed Von-Pitt. "We are taking Little Jasper away to be with his mother."

Lizzie suddenly rushed to Little Jasper and tried to grab his hand.

The swing doors crashed open. A tall man with dark, penetrating eyes stormed into the room. He marched up to the judge. "What the hell do you think you're doing?"

The judge went ghostly white, Arthur reddened, Von-Pitt stepped away and Lizzie let go of Little Jasper's hand.

The man turned and faced Von-Pitt. "You, get out of my sight."

Von-Pitt slinked out of the room.

"This child is the ward of Lady Carmichael. Do you understand, Judge Jones?"

The judge nodded.

"I can't hear you."

"Ye-yes, Mr Carrington."

Kate was given a cursory glance as Mr Carrington walked past her to the door.

Little Jasper wrapped his arms around Kate's legs. "Does that mean I'm staying with you, like Grandpop said?"

Kate kissed his hair. "I wouldn't have it any other way."

She felt Jasper's staring eyes and searched the room for him. He was in a wheelchair, just inside the room. A nurse was standing by his side.

Kate smiled and, with Little Jasper by her side, walked to her husband and planted a kiss upon his cheek.

Jasper didn't smile. He stared at his wife, thinking, *What the hell is Phillip Carrington interfering in Kate's life for?*

***

The doctors had wanted Jasper and Little Jasper to return to their hospital beds, but the two Carmichaels joined forces; Jasper discharged himself and signed for Little Jasper to leave. Kate didn't have a say in the matter. Fortunately, Little Jasper's room was ready, and Ben and Robert helped Jasper to the master bedroom.

Both Carmichaels wanted Kate to sleep with them. Jasper was very demanding, reminding her of his jealousy when Harry and Oliver were small. However, she held the ace: they were both tired and the doctor had given her sedatives to help the patients sleep.

Kate was in turmoil. The thought crossed her mind that these demanding Carmichaels would be the end of her. She loved them both dearly, but somehow, she had to survive. She needed Harry's clinical logic.

Kate was beyond exhaustion when she drove to her beach.

***

The wind was blowing off the sea as Kate stood at the water's edge and thought of Harry.

"I don't know why you stay with him; he just uses you," Harry's voice said in her head.

He had never approved of how Jasper treated her.

"He's going to leave you again. I know the signs. You've got to be strong now I'm not by your side."

How can I be strong, she thought, *when I'm desperate for sleep?*

Kate was alone with her thoughts as the sun slowly crept above the horizon. With a heavy heart, she left her beach with the realisation that her special, kind, thoughtful, loving son was gone forever. Her last memory of him was of a happy Harry looking forward to working with her on his new diamond store.

She drove home slowly.

A pair of angry blue eyes were fixed on the Evoque when it appeared in the River's End House driveway.

"Kate. Where the fuck have you been?" bellowed Jasper as she got out of the car. "You know I need you. Little Jasper's beside himself. He thinks you have left him."

"With my son."

Chapter Forty-One

Car headlights lit the alleyway to the Gentlemen's Club side door. Four people stepped from the car: Lord Blackthorn, Lord Charles Landon, Pieter Von-Pitt and Margot. The door to the club opened, and the party followed Lord Devon along the narrow passage.

"Did you feel that?" said Margot.

"Ha! You felt old Carmichael," answered Lord Devon.

"Shut up, Devon. We don't want any of your silly stories," said Lord Blackthorn.

Lord Devon turned and began to walk up the stairs. He stopped at the top and waited for the party. "It's not a silly story," he said as Lord Blackthorn joined him. "Many of the members claim to have seen him wandering about the club. Usually, when his grandson is mentioned."

"We haven't mentioned his bloody grandson."

"Yet."

A stream of light suddenly shone from an open door. Lord Ambrose stood with a straight back, impeccably dressed in a Savile Row suit. He turned and went back into the committee room.

On the large table, by four of the seats, were a notepad and pencil, a glass of malt and a bottle of Glenmorangie.

For the briefest of moments, Lord Ambrose exchanged a glance with Lord Devon that confirmed he had left the side door to the club open and the door to the committee room ajar. Lord Devon admired his friend's devious ways. Ambrose had gambled that Jasper was having the club watched; he wouldn't resist paying them a visit, even if he was in pain.

"Look here, Ambrose, what's going on?" said a miffed Lord Blackthorn as he emptied a glass of malt and refilled it. "Why all this cloak-and-dagger stuff? We only asked for a meeting."

"Discretion," Ambrose answered as the other members of the party made themselves comfortable.

"Who the bloody hell are we hiding from? Carmichael? He's still recovering."

"Having trouble fucking her," Von-Pitt added with a snigger.

Lord Ambrose stared at Lord Blackthorn. "You of all people should know not to underestimate Jasper."

* * *

The foyer clock struck eleven as Jasper closed the library door. He was more than disappointed she wouldn't be spending the night with him.

His phone blipped. A text.

Jasper, a plane will be landing. You need to be here. Somot going on at the Gentlemen's Club.

He hurried upstairs to change into his black jeans and hoodie. His gut churned; it had never let him down when trouble loomed.

Jasper had set a team to watch the club around the clock. He suspected that Harry's death wasn't an accident. If Kate had been in the car, as planned, the whole of his dynasty would have been wiped out. When Phillip Carrington had squashed Lizzie's attempt to take Little Jasper, he knew Kate was in trouble.

When Jasper landed in London, a car was waiting.

"Four of 'em went in," said Tiny, who was driving the car. "Lords Blackthorn and Landon, Von-Pitt, Margot."

"They are after Kate."

"How do you work that out?"

"Trust me."

* * *

Lord Ambrose inwardly cringed when Von-Pitt took centre stage. He readjusted his tie; he hated the man, but it must not show.

"I'd like to thank you for allowing my female associate into the building," said Von-Pitt in his best conciliatory voice.

Lord Blackthorn coughed. "We're here about the trust fund and diamonds." He was determined that Von-Pitt wouldn't take control. "Since Lord Henry departed and the American Landons mysteriously disappeared, the trust fund's performance has declined. Mr Von-Pitt would like to discuss a new arrangement."

"I don't make arrangements, Blackthorn. But you know that," said Lord Ambrose.

"But you haven't replaced Lord Landon. We can't keep going along like this. The club rules specifically state that a Landon must have control over the fund."

"The matter would have been resolved, but for an unforeseen accident."

"I really hope you're not referring to Carmichael."

"He's in a bad way," interrupted Von-Pitt.

"For your information"—Lord Ambrose moved his attention to Von-Pitt—"Lord Carmichael has been seen with Lady Carmichael. I would say he's on the mend."

"My people tell me they have stopped fucking and they are not speaking."

"I will remind all of you that they have lost a son and granddaughter," Lord Ambrose said. "They need time to grieve. Particularly Kate."

"So, we wait and lose clients for Kate?" snapped Lord Blackthorn.

"I don't know the arrangement you have with Mr Von-Pitt," Ambrose said. "But the Gentlemen's Club has no arrangement with anyone, and that includes Jasper Carmichael—even though he is an exceptional businessman and a gifted diamond expert, both of which he inherited from his grandfather and father."

"You favour him," said Von-Pitt.

"Jasper cut his business credentials buying and selling property all over the world, against some well-established businessmen."

"That's putting an acceptable slant on it," said Lord Blackthorn.

"The club has followed Jasper's business dealings, some above board and others that crossed the boundary into the criminal world."

"He's a criminal and a murderer," snapped Von-Pitt, rising from his seat.

Lord Ambrose ignored his outburst. "He is the best diamond dealer in the country. I once emptied a bag of diamonds in front of him. Some were fake and some were real. He sorted them into two piles, then he valued the real ones. He was spot on, including the valuations."

The room silenced.

"You see, Mr Von-Pitt, diamonds run through Carmichael's veins."

"You're protecting her," said a surprised Lord Blackthorn. "She's the Landon you need."

"There's no doubt in my mind that Kate Carmichael is Lady Isabel Landon's granddaughter."

"There's no DNA proof," offered a miffed Lord Charles Landon. "And there never will be now that American strain of the family is missing; there're no documents in Henry Landon's papers that mention his son's illegitimate child. I'm the last of the Landons."

Lord Ambrose slowly walked to the window. "Lord Henry Landon left a box of very important papers in trust with the club. One of the files—"

"Is about Kate Reynolds. Her mother and father," interjected Lord Blackthorn.

"Lord and Lady Landon fell to pieces when their son was killed. The papers were, if you like, a contingency plan for the worst. 'My worst fear is that the American family get their hands on my work.' This was written in Henry's hand on the opening page of Kate's file."

"You can't be serious, Ambrose. She's married to a Carmichael."

"His whore, more like," said Von-Pitt.

Lord Ambrose's temper snapped. "How dare you?"

"She married a criminal, a murderer. He's fucked his way around the world!" shouted Von-Pitt.

Lord Devon stared at his friend. Lord Ambrose had closed his eyes and was concentrating on his breathing, trying to quell his raging temper.

"We have no control over who we love." Lord Devon's voice was soft and calm. "Carmichaels don't love, according to Old Jasper Carmichael. The man that had two families, trying to father a Carmichael worthy of being called a Carmichael. He only met the child Jasper once and declared him 'a true Carmichael'. From then on, young

Jasper was hated by his family." He paused. "Sex calms Jasper's Carmichael temper; he needs a lot of sex when his temper is raging. As a child, Jasper was denied love; sex with Kate not only calms his temper but has introduced him to emotions he had never experienced."

"He can't love her!" shouted Margot. "He's mine; we share a common interest in diamonds."

"I'm afraid, my dear, Kate is the only woman he will share a bed with."

"What the fuck has she got that I haven't?"

"Like I said, we have no control over who we fall in love with, or the power of love."

"You're talking gibberish, old man," Von-Pitt said impatiently.

"When Lady Isabel Landon fell in love with an American gangster," Lord Devon continued, unfazed, "her aristocratic family disowned her. But they were in love; an all-consuming love. Diamonds gave her riches that her family could only dream of. A room full of people would quieten when Lady Isabel arrived; she was beautiful, her clear complexion and sparkling green eyes would captivate the crowd. Henry would slip his arm around her waist and plant a kiss on her cheek. Their eyes glowed with love. I know, Mr Von-Pitt, because I was a child when I feel head over heels in love with Isabel, myself. Whenever I see Kate Carmichael, I think of her." Lord Devon was quite emotional.

"You old fools, you risk the Gentlemen's Club for love?" shouted Von-Pitt. "I'm offering you a deal, here and now. No strings."

"But, Mr Von-Pitt, you don't understand," said Lord Ambrose. "If Kate were male, she would already be a member. It's only because she's female that she's not."

"I don't understand, Ambrose. You knew she's a Landon and did nothing," said Lord Blackthorn.

"I admit that I've lied about. Lord Landon. Kate didn't concern us; we never envisaged a situation where she would be needed. We have managed to run the trust fund without showing any red flags until…" He turned his gaze to Lord Charles Landon. "Charlie owed money. A lot of money."

Lord Blackthorn stood and pointed at Lord Ambrose. "You!" His loud voice echoed. "You let her marry Jasper Carmichael."

"At the time, the club wouldn't have anything to do with females."

"I suppose it's bloody acceptable now?"

"The committee has agreed."

"She doesn't want anything to do with the trust fund. In fact, anything Landon. She refused the Americans," said Lord Blackthorn.

* * *

As Jasper slipped through the open side door to the club, he realised that he had missed the bulk of the meeting—but any snippet of information would be useful. Silently, he moved up the passage to the stairs.

He was surprised to find that the committee room door was ajar. He intently listened to the discussion. It was obvious that Ambrose had a plan to get Kate to run the Landon Trust Fund.

As the meeting came to an end, he retreated into the shadows and waited for the party to leave. Then, as the lights were switched off, Jasper entered the room. With the help of his iPhone torch, he located the cabinet where Ambrose kept his supply of malt. Somewhere, hidden in this cabinet, Ambrose had a tape recorder.

Jasper smiled when he found a webcam. *The old bugger has updated his surveillance equipment.* He flipped open the side of the camera and removed the SD card. *Ambrose has probably had cameras installed all around the building.*

He poured a generous Glenmorangie into one of the unused glasses—it wasn't his favourite malt, but it would do—then slumped into Lord Ambrose's chair and sipped. It was obvious that Ambrose wanted him to know about the meeting, but why? The question stuck in his mind.

Jasper placed his empty glass onto the table and removed a small listening device from his inside pocket. He securely stuck it underneath the table before slowly leaving the room.

Chapter Forty-Two

The view from the window of the early morning train to London was a blur. Kate's mind overflowed with the upcoming meeting at the Gentlemen's Club. Lord Ambrose had forcefully reminded her of the consequences of her refusal to accept her Landon roots.

"You have a new responsibility now with the death of Harry. Little Jasper will need you. I'm sure you don't want to put him in danger; what would happen to him if you weren't around?" repeated in her mind. *"Jasper will leave you. It's just a matter of time. His addiction to diamonds will prevail."*

Lord Ambrose had shown the other side of his nature, and Kate didn't like it.

Her mind wandered to Jasper, who had gone on one of his diamond trips with them not talking. They hadn't had sex since he had returned from hospital. But he was unwell and irritable. Was this the reason for the lack of sex?

She looked at her Apple watch, another gadget that Jasper insisted she wore.

"Kate, you have a habit of leaving your phone," he had told her, and that was true, but now she could be contacted all the time. It was also true that sometimes she wanted to be alone and uncontactable. She missed the days of walking along her beach, the only sound the lapping of the sea around her feet—her phone left on the table in the beach house. She intended to forget

her new watch, too, but at the moment, it was a useful gadget.

The train slowly pulled into Euston. Kate gathered her leather messenger bag and leather jacket, and joined the crowd as they raced towards the exit.

She was about to join the taxi queue when Lord Ambrose's butler appeared and directed her to the Rolls Royce.

* * *

At the window seat of the café opposite the alley that led to the side door of the Gentlemen's Club, a man sat, wearing a well-worn cap disguising his salt-and-pepper hair. A pair of black-rimmed glasses hid his piercing blue eyes.

His spy in the club had alerted him to a very important meeting, but thoughts of Kate broke his concentration. He should have told her where he was going but, for some reason, he couldn't.

Jasper Carmichael pressed the earpiece into his ear and listened to the talk in the club's committee room.

"She's on her way," announced Lord Ambrose.

Jasper's heart missed a beat. *Kate*, he thought.

He was imagining the committee taking their seats around the table when the Rolls Royce pulled into the alleyway. Lord Devon opened the car door, and his wife walked into the Gentlemen's Club. A security guard appeared at the end of the alley and another stood by the side door.

A very important meeting indeed, thought Jasper.

* * *

Lady Kate Carmichael walked into the committee room and looked at each member in turn. The only ones that she recognised, apart from Lords Ambrose and Devon, were Lord Blackthorn and the Cavendish brothers.

Lord Devon stood by the seat opposite Lord Ambrose and helped Kate remove her jacket. She pulled a folder from her bag, sat down and opened the top two buttons of her fitted, white blouse. Her hands flipped her greying hair so it rested on her shoulders, then she settled her green eyes on Lord Ambrose.

"Before we start, Kate. Where's Jasper?"

"I don't know, Lord Blackthorn."

"Oh, come on."

"Jasper has always operated on a need-to-know basis. I don't need to know."

"Lord Blackthorn, that's enough," snapped an annoyed Lord Ambrose.

There was a brief silence while Lord Ambrose gathered his thoughts.

"Lady Carmichael," he began, "may I introduce you to the club's committee. Today is a momentous day for us. We can't wait for you to head the Landon Trust Fund."

The group around the table nodded as Kate flipped through the papers in the folder.

She cleared her throat. "As far as I'm concerned, the fund should be dissolved, taken over." Kate's voice was stern and businesslike.

* * *

Jasper rose from his seat in the café and hurried to the alleyway. He stood opposite the guard, who gave him a dismissive glance.

Jasper concentrated on Kate's business voice. He had heard this tone many times; it meant trouble was brewing.

* * *

The room hummed with the members' discontent. Lord Ambrose was humming and hawing; Kate's comments had thrown him.

"I think a history lesson is called for," he said. "You're Lord Henry Landon's last surviving heir. The love child of his only son and Laura Spencer. I have documents to prove this. Lord Henry left private documents here for safekeeping."

"But he didn't leave *this* important document." She held it between her fingers. "The Deeds to the Gentlemen's Club."

* * *

Jasper began to fidget. *Where the hell did she get that from?* he thought.

Then, the night they broke into Landon Hall flashed into his mind. He had left her in Lady Isabel's bedroom. It must have been amongst her papers.

Kate, you should have told me. You're playing with fire.

* * *

"This is a copy." She stood and dropped it front of the Cavendish brothers.

A brief silence ensued as they examined the document.

"It's Lord Henry's signature," said Simon Cavendish as he passed the paper to Lord Ambrose.

"As the last surviving heir to Lord Henry Landon, I own the Gentlemen's Club," said Kate.

"We need the original before we can proceed." Lord Ambrose's temper was rising; this was his worst nightmare.

He'd known about the Deeds; they had searched everywhere for them. His hand rubbed his forehead as he cast his mind back to Lord Blackthorn's report on the Landon Hall search. No paperwork had been found in Lady Isabel's bedroom and they hadn't found any diamonds. The latter part had surprised him; he had been confident that Lord Landon would have left diamonds there.

"I believe there was a break-in at Landon Hall," he began, his dark eyes firmly fixed on Kate. "There were no diamonds." He paused and intently watched her for a flicker of recognition. "However, we didn't spend a lot of time in Lady Isabel's rooms. After all, why would a mere woman have such an important document?"

As Kate's temper boiled, she sat poker-faced, staring at Lord Ambrose. *You misogynistic bastard*, she thought.

* * *

Hold it together, Kate, Jasper thought. *He's trying to rattle you.*

* * *

Kate's voice was soft and calm. "Let's get back to what we know. I have the Deeds to this property. By your own statement, you're convinced that I'm Lord Henry Landon's last heir. Therefore, it follows that the Deeds are held by their rightful owner. I can only surmise how Lord Henry came to own the property… probably the club got into financial difficulties. Lord Henry loaned the club money, or diamonds. Whatever happened, it came at a price."

"You know nothing," blurted Lord Ambrose.

"Problems with the trust fund only began when Lord Charles Landon needed money. I'm guessing he was using the fund's money to pay his debts." Her eyes never left Lord Ambrose. "The club that you oversee is in financial difficulties due to its dependence on the Landon Trust Fund. Why else would you need Jasper's help? When you turned to the fund for financial help, like your predecessors had done, the coffers were empty. No cash. No diamonds.

The members glared at Lord Ambrose.

"Let us talk about your husband," he said.

* * *

Jasper's eavesdropping was abruptly ended by the squealing tyres of a large BMW turning into the alleyway. He quickly hid himself behind a skip.

Von-Pitt and three buzz-cut guards jumped out of the car and ran through the side entrance. Von-Pitt was on a mission. Jasper's gut churned; he was after Kate.

The alleyway guard had moved and was walking towards the BMW. Jasper swiftly moved behind him. He wrapped his arm around the guard's neck and pulled him to the ground. The door guard ran towards Jasper, but Jasper met him full on and quickly rendered him unconscious.

Moments later, Jasper and one of the guards crashed through the committee room doors just as Lord Ambrose was shouting "Get out!" to a red-faced Von-Pitt.

All eyes, except Kate's, turned to face Jasper and the guard rolling on the floor. Instead, she grabbed a bottle of malt from the table, turned and smashed one of the buzz-cut men over the head. The other guard pushed a chair to one side and angrily moved towards Kate, but he was greeted by Jasper's fist.

Jasper and Kate's eyes met. In an instant, she was in his arms being showered with kisses.

* * *

"What the fuck just happened?" said an angry Von-Pitt.

"Jasper Carmichael happened," said Lord Blackthorn.

Lord Ambrose sat with his head in his hands mumbling, "How did he know?"

"Pull yourself together, Ambrose. Whatever you've read about old Jasper, this Jasper Carmichael is a hundred times worse—or better, depending on your point of view."

"Did you see the way they kissed? True love," said a dreamy-eyed Lord Devon.

"For God's sake, Devon, shut the fuck up," said Lord Blackthorn.

"Without her, we're ruined," said Lord Ambrose. "She's a Landon, she should be head of the fund. All it needs is a loan."

"You don't know Kate," said Lord Blackthorn. "She would never be the head of a diamond fund, and that's what it is. It was formed and run by a criminal: Lord Henry Landon. I'll make a few calls and get the fund dissolved in some way. Let Jasper sort the club's diamond problems. And don't ask questions."

"You're giving in just like that?" snapped Von-Pitt.

"You don't get it, Von-Pitt. Jasper's red line has been stepped over. You better pray that she's calming him down, because if I know Jasper, he'll be after revenge."

"Red line? What fuckin' red line?" said a puzzled Von-Pitt.

"He means his wife, Mr Von-Pitt," offered Lord Devon.

Chapter Forty-Three

Jasper and Kate hadn't talked since leaving the club. Tiny had been waiting for them and whisked them away to a small airfield. Jasper had taken Kate's hand and hurried her to a light aircraft where he settled her into a rear seat and secured her seat belt.

"No escaping," he'd said, giving her a flash of the irresistible Carmichael smile.

He'd then moved to the pilot's seat as Tiny took the co-pilot's seat. She hadn't taken much notice of what was going on after that as her mind replayed the meeting at the Gentlemen's Club. Had she done the right thing, or should she have admitted that her grandfather was Lord Henry Landon?

However, all thoughts of the meeting disappeared as they circled the field opposite the front door of River's End House. Kate could clearly see the outline of a runway and outlines of roads, and there was an army of men with heavy machinery, working. A JCB was digging a trench in front of the house, and a team of men, with the help of a tractor, were planting trees.

Finally, they landed.

"I'll explain later," Jasper whispered as he offered his hand to lead her from the aircraft.

Kate did not take his hand. Instead, she stormed off the plane towards the house, at a loss to what was going on.

Jasper decided to give her some space and did not follow her.

Robert opened the front door as Kate stormed into the foyer. "My Lady, Lord Carmichael tried to call you just after you left for London." He followed Kate to her library. "It's going to be an airfield. The house will be screened by those trees and shrubs."

Elsie appeared carrying a tray of sandwiches and tea. "Ben's gone on the school run in your Evoque," she said, disgruntled.

The house phone rang, and Robert ran to answer it. Elsie put logs on the library fire as Kate slumped onto the couch.

"That was a garage in London confirming a delivery of Range Rovers," said Robert as he returned to the room.

"Does Lord Carmichael have any idea the upset this has caused?" said Elsie.

"He has no idea," said Kate. "This is typical Jasper."

"You seem to be taking it very well," said Elsie.

"Not really. I've had a bloody awful meeting and now this."

* * *

Little Jasper didn't want to go to bed; he continually talked about being accepted by the school's popular kids now they all knew about the airfield from their parents. Kate translated that as: she was the only person in Wellsbury who hadn't known. Apparently, the kids had gleefully told Little Jasper that his grandpop was expanding his diamond business—some said he was head of a criminal diamond gang.

"Don't believe what they say. When people can't find out about Grandfather's business, they make it up," she despondently replied.

"Gran, sometimes you spoil everything."

Kate smiled and kissed him goodnight.

What is Jasper doing? she thought as she headed back downstairs. His behaviour was upsetting her. She needed to be alone; she longed to feel the wind on her cheeks and the sea on her feet, but above all, she needed solace.

"I'm going for a walk," she said to the staff that were gathered around the kitchen table.

"Forgive me," said Robert, "but is that a good idea? Lord Carmichael gave strict orders."

Kate smiled. "I'll take full responsibility, Robert."

"It's spotting with rain."

"I won't notice," she replied, closing the kitchen door.

Kate emptied her mind as she slowly walked to the angry sea. By the time she reached the sand dunes, the sound of the crashing waves dominated her thoughts. Barefoot, she walked to the water's edge and closed her eyes.

* * *

The two men who had followed her stood in the dunes, watching.

"Boss," said one, whispering into his phone. "Lady Carmichael is standing staring out to sea."

* * *

Jasper inwardly cursed as he walked away from the diamond party that Margot had invited him to. He should have told Kate about it before he'd left, but the men he was there to meet had demanded complete secrecy. It would cost him; he knew Margot's price for arranging the meeting, but would it end his marriage?

"Boss," whispered the voice on the other end of the line. *"What do you want us to do?"*

"Leave her. If she walks into the sea, grab her." He thought that was unlikely as she had Little Jasper to care for.

* * *

By the time the phone call ended, Kate had disappeared.

The men waded into the sea shouting, "Lady Carmichael!"

There was no reply.

In desperation, they raced back to the house.

Lady Carmichael was gone.

Chapter Forty-Four

Lack of sleep was taking its toll on Kate. By the time she had returned from the school run, her patience had disappeared.

"Robert!" she uncharacteristically bellowed. "Find the man in charge of these earthworks."

"Right away. But you have the chief constable and Mr Von-Pitt waiting for you."

Kate stormed into the living room. "I haven't time for this, Arthur. I'll come to the station with my solicitor."

"I'm doing this as a courtesy," replied Arthur, thinking how tired Kate looked. Was Von-Pitt right? Had she been up all night? Had she set fire to Landon Hall?

Elsie appeared with a tea tray and helped Kate slip off her jacket.

Arthur waited until Kate had sipped her tea and made herself comfortable. He was briefly mesmerised by how thin she was; Harry's death had taken its toll.

"It's about Landon Hall and Lord Charles Landon," he began.

Butterflies swirled in Kate's stomach. "Talk to Mr Von-Pitt. Isn't he the new owner of the hall?"

"Lord Charles was involved in a mugging that went wrong. He fell, hit his head on the kerb. Cracked his skull."

"I'm sorry."

"This makes you the owner of Landon Hall."

"I thought Mr Von-Pitt had bought the hall."

"He paid Lord Charles's debts, but the sale of the hall was never finalised. That makes *you* the owner of the hall."

Both men watched Kate as she poured a second cup of tea.

"I don't see a problem," she said. "If Mr Von-Pitt has paid Lord Charles's debts, as far as I'm concerned, he owns the hall. The lawyers can sort it out."

"There was a fire at the hall," Arthur said.

Ruby bustled in with toast and another pot of tea. "You haven't eaten for days," she said by way of an explanation. "And Lord Carmichael's plane has landed."

"You were saying, Arthur," Kate said.

"Probably we should wait for Jasper."

"No. As the owner of Landon Hall, I should know. Is the hall burnt down?"

"It's nothing to concern yourself about. The fire was at the far end," said Von-Pitt.

What's he covering up? thought Kate.

The living room door bounced open and in stormed an angry Jasper with Lord Blackthorn at his shoulder and a smug-looking Margot close behind.

A penetrating silence descended.

Robert and Elsie raced in with a pot of fresh coffee and cake.

"Leave it," commanded Jasper. "Kate will see to it."

"Kate will not," Kate said.

"What about this fire?" asked Lord Blackthorn, looking for the drinks tray.

"Kate," snapped Jasper.

"Lady Carmichael knew nothing about it until a few minutes ago," said Arthur, taking control of the situation. "Mr Von-Pitt says it was at the far end of the hall."

Margot sidled up to Jasper, carrying his coffee. "It's how you like it," she said with a grin, and Von-Pitt smiled.

"Mr Von-Pitt had to involve Lady Carmichael as she is now the owner of Landon Hall; Lord Charles was recently killed during a mugging."

"Kate?" said Jasper, noticing that she had lost weight and looked very tired. They hadn't shared a bed since the accident. He was neglecting her.

"As it appears that I own the hall, the best course of action would be to wait until all the facts are revealed."

"What facts?" Jasper asked.

"Mr Von-Pitt paid Lord Charles Landon's debts on the hall, but apparently the sale of the property wasn't finalised."

"You calling me a liar?" snapped Von-Pitt.

"I'm saying the sale of the hall must be investigated along with the fire. It would be very foolish for any discussion to take place prior to that." Kate stood and went to leave.

"First you flood the property and now you've set fire to it," accused Von-Pitt.

Kate stopped and stepped towards him. "I'm becoming exceedingly tired of your accusations." She flipped the top button of her blouse and massaged her neck; her anger was rising. "I'll let this outburst go, as you're upset, but next time, be prepared for the full force of the law to descend on you. And Mr Von-Pitt, my pockets are deeper than yours."

"Are you threatening me?"

"I'm giving you notice that there will be consequences for your actions." From her jeans pocket, Kate pulled out her phone.

"You bitch!" shouted Von-Pitt.

"That's underhanded, Kate," said a surprised Arthur.

"Do you think that I would sit down and have a heart-to-heart with the pair of you? Never underestimate me, gentlemen."

"Lady Carmichael," Robert said hesitantly. "There's an estate agent asking for the keys to Isaacs House."

"Tell him to fuck off."

Robert's mouth opened and closed.

"Did Kate say what I think she said?" a surprised Lord Blackthorn asked Jasper. "It's time you two had a serious tête-à-tête."

"I think we may be past that," said Jasper as an angry Kate left the room. *She knows*, he thought.

"But you rescued her from the Gentlemen's Club," said Lord Blackthorn.

"That was before I…" Jasper's voice faded.

"Oh, come now, Jasper, she cannot know about your little misdemeanour," said a smiling Von-Pitt.

"Keep your fucking nose out of my marriage."

Chapter Forty-Five

Ruby poured Ben a mug of tea.

"Is he gone?" she asked.

"Four o'clock. He's gone again and she's wandering about the beach. If they don't talk soon, she'll move to Isaacs House."

"You mean, she'll leave him?"

"He's already left her."

* * *

Jasper was becoming more and more irritable. He couldn't bring himself to talk to Kate. He was guilty; he had fallen into Margot's trap: the promise of new diamond contacts if he fucked her.

He had arrived at a lunchtime meeting with Lord Blackthorn, Von-Pitt, Lord Ambrose and Lord Devon, with Margot, after spending the night together at Carmichael House penthouse.

Von-Pitt was all smiles as they walked in. Jasper was slowly slipping into his net.

The meeting was starting to bore Jasper when Eric Forrester and his wife were shown to a table by the head waiter. Jasper had met Eric only once and had been impressed by his work ethic. He owned a demolition company and was doing well now that his son, Julian, had joined him. However, Julian was a rake; he fucked rich older women.

"What do you think Forrester is doing here?" asked a curious Lord Blackthorn.

Jasper shrugged his shoulders; he was thinking the same thing.

Suddenly, the head waiter turned and scurried towards the main doors, which were being held open by the hotel receptionist. Then, stepping through the doors was Kate. Her cheeks were slightly flushed, her green eyes on fire as she flicked her hair, smiling. Jasper's designer trousers suddenly became uncomfortable. But when Forrester's son, Julian, walked in beside her, his hand touching the small of her back, jealousy surged through Jasper.

"What's going on, Jasper?" asked Lord Blackthorn.

"Kate's about to take herself a lover. How exciting," said a grinning Lord Devon.

"Shut the fuck up, you old fool," snapped Jasper, thinking, *Over my dead body.*

"You've only yourself to blame," retorted Lord Devon. "Kate's a very desirable woman, just like her grandmother. He left her alone, too; too busy making money with his diamonds. Sound familiar, Jasper?"

Jasper wasn't listening; he was racking his brain, trying to think why Kate would be having lunch with the Forresters. He watched Kate's every move, looking for any flicker of a sexual relationship with Julian.

Godfrey Clayton, the chairman of the shopping centre's farmers' market, suddenly appeared by Kate's side.

"Not now, Godfrey," Kate said.

"What about the farmers' market accounts?"

"I've had a lot on my mind."

"You have time for lunch."

"For your information, this is a working lunch."

"You're neglecting the shopping centre again."

"Breakfast tomorrow at River's End."

Godfrey took a step back.

"I'll be up around five; I like to walk to the sea." Kate paused. "Actually, I'm taking Little Jasper to the hospital first thing. Bring the accounts there."

The head waiter coughed. "Lady Carmichael, there's been an incident at the school. Little Jasper has been taken to hospital."

Kate moved her chair back.

The head waiter clicked his fingers, and a young waiter appeared. "Put Lady Carmichael's lunch in a box."

"I'll come with you," said Julian.

Kate half-smiled and flicked her hair. "That's not necessary."

"Come to dinner," said Eric Forrester.

"It's better if you come to me," she said, turning for the door. "I'll arrange something."

Jasper caught the arm of the head waiter. "What's happened?"

"Her grandson's been taken to hospital. Some incident at school."

"Do you know where Lady Carmichael and Julian Forrester have been?"

The head waiter leaned into Jasper. "Looking at her wrecked beach house."

Jasper felt a pang of hurt. *Kate wants her beach house. She's leaving me.*

Chapter Forty-Six

Kate sat watching the sunrise, with Jasper's thick coat keeping the morning coolness at bay. No matter how hard she tried, she couldn't relax her mind. She knew she was trying to do too much but she also knew she had to keep busy; if she stopped, she thought of Harry and tears were never far away. She needed Jasper to hold her, love her. But he was busy with Margot. She would have to make do with his coat.

Little Jasper was becoming a handful. He had been in a fight and cracked the plaster on his leg. The doctor had removed the plaster and rebandaged it. Little Jasper had taken it all in his stride and insisted on going back to school.

"Lady Carmichael." Robert's calm, reassuring voice broke her thoughts. "There's a Mr Godfrey Clayton to see you. Ruby's cooking breakfast."

"Has Jasper phoned?" she asked, walking back to the house.

"Apparently Lord Carmichael has returned to London."

* * *

It was a slow drive into Wellsbury as Kate joined the school run traffic.

Little Jasper climbed out of the Evoque using a walking stick for support. She had tried to talk him out of going to school, but he wouldn't hear of it.

Leaving the slow-moving traffic, Kate cut across the shopping centre's main car park to the rear entrance to her office. She didn't usually use this entrance, but she didn't want to bring attention to the fact that she was at the shopping centre.

She punched her code into the keypad, and the door slowly opened. She didn't bother switching on the lights or waiting for the door to close as she wasn't going to be long.

Two hands grabbed her waist and pinned her to the passageway wall. Warm, soft lips claimed her mouth.

"I've wanted to do that from the moment I met you."

It was Julian Forrester's voice. He had opened her jacket, and his fingers were slowly opening her blouse.

"Get your hands off me," she said, gripping his fingers, which were now touching her lace bra, and trying to push him away. She lifted her knee, but he dodged it.

"Now. Now," he said. "You'll love every minute. I like older women. Their bodies are soft and so responsive; their pussies are warm and wet." He lustfully squeezed her breasts.

"Stop. You're hurting me."

"Is that too hard? I'm told you like it rough."

She tried again to push him away.

"Where's your office?"

Suddenly, there was a loud knock on the outside door. Julian froze.

"Lady Carmichael, you in there? Are you okay?" shouted the security guard.

Julian pinched Kate's breast. "Tell him everything's fine."

Kate hesitated.

He slapped her face and increased his grip on her breast.

"I-I'm fine," she shouted.

They heard the guard walk away.

Julian started to pace up and down the passage. Kate carefully pulled her bra up over her breasts and closed her blouse.

He began to sweat and ran his hand through his hair. Suddenly, he faced her and gripped her neck. "This isn't over, bitch. You're worth a lot of money to me." His nose brushed her face. "Tell Jasper I'll be waiting." He let go of her neck and slapped her face again.

Julian opened the outside door just as two guards were running towards it. He pushed them to one side and got into his car.

Kate just heard the guard requesting the doctor, then she passed out.

* * *

Jasper wasn't in London; he was in Wellsbury, listening to Von-Pitt pontificate about South American diamond contacts—Jasper knew more South American diamond dealers than Von-Pitt had had hot dinners.

Kate came into his mind. He had fucked up big time; he'd always known the score if he fucked another woman, but he never thought Kate would leave him. He should have explained to her what he was doing but, as usual, he had ignored her. Maybe he deserved to lose her, after leaving her to grieve Harry and care for Little Jasper alone—and Julian was a younger man with a reputation for fucking older women.

He closed his eyes, and the image of Julian Forrester resting his hand on the small of Kate's back floated behind his eyelids.

His phone vibrated. A message from his surveillance team:

Lady Carmichael at office. Julian Forrester just ran out of office rear door. Doctor's car just arrived.

Jasper could feel his temper rising. *Forrester's fucking hurt her.*

He stared at Margot, but instead of her he saw Kate, naked, with her legs wrapped around him. He heard her cry out his name, felt her hands in his hair. Their mouths joined; he could taste her. She was his.

* * *

"Thank God, you're here," said Robert as he opened the front door. "It's Lady Carmichael. She's been attacked. She hasn't said a word since I fetched her from the hospital; the doctor insisted she have an X-ray and be examined."

Jasper was boiling inside. "Where is she?" *He's dead meat.*

"In the orangery, staring into space."

He entered the orangery as gently as he could, trying to control his demons. "Kate, my love, what's wrong?"

"Go away."

Kate's arms were wrapped around her. He put his hand on her shoulder.

"Don't touch me." Kate's voice quivered.

"Tell me," he said in his soft, caring voice.

"I can't bear anyone to speak to me... touch me... after..."

"After what, my love?" He took a step closer.

"No one will believe me." Her body started to shake.

"I will, Kate. And he must be on your security tape." He gingerly slipped his arm around her. "Come."

Robert opened the library door, and Jasper sat Kate on the couch in front of the fire. In the firelight, Jasper could see the bruises forming. He pulled her head onto his shoulder, then stroked and kissed her hair.

"I thought he was going rape me... I tried to fight him off." She sobbed.

He's a dead man.

"He attacked me in the passage... Pinned me against the wall. He, he grabbed my breasts. It hurt, but he didn't stop."

"Who? My love, who?"

"The security guard knocked on the door, and he stopped." Sob. "My breasts hurt; he was squeezing that hard... He slapped my face... He said I was worth a lot of money."

Jasper lifted her into his arms and carried her to their bedroom.

* * *

Jasper lay in the bath. "Come," he said, holding out his hand.

Kate stood still with her arms wrapped around her.

"Kate. It's me. I want to help you heal."

Slowly, she removed her clothes and stepped into the warm water. They lay for some time in silence; the only noise was the water as Jasper moved it over her.

"It was Julian Forrester," he said.

"How did you know?"

"I saw you with him yesterday. He has a reputation for fucking older, rich women."

"He didn't fuck me."

"He sexually assaulted you. That's rape in my book. Make no bones about it, if he could have got it up, he would have penetrated you. His DNA is probably all over your clothes. I can see bruises forming on your back." He soaped her breasts.

She flinched. "They hurt."

He lifted her out of the bath and wrapped her in a white towel.

"What did the doctor say?"

"He wanted me to stay in overnight. I couldn't do that; the papers would be all over it."

Chapter Forty-Seven

Jasper had left Kate asleep; he had an important appointment.

"I wondered when I'd see you." Julian was standing on the edge of his outdoor swimming pool. "I'm going to take her from you, old man," he confidently said.

"Go and find another older woman to use your charm on."

"That marina you used to own is full of them, but none as alluring as your wife."

"I'm asking nicely, Julian."

He laughed. "You see, your criminal background doesn't scare me. Kate has everything I ever dreamt of. Rich, sexy, soft skin, full tits, a warm, wet pussy."

Jasper clenched his fists.

"I see it this way, old man: I'll fuck her once a week and live like a king. I should thank you; you neglected her at just the right moment."

Jasper swallowed hard, trying to control his bubbling temper. "What do you want, Julian?" He began to move closer to him.

"I've got what I want: a sexy meal ticket. Seduction is my forte. You know, candles, soft music, red wine, Italian food. I'm an exceptional cook. Ply her with food and she'll be mine."

Jasper was so close to Julian that he could feel his breath. "Kate's very precious to me." *You overconfident little prick*.

"Rubbish. You fuck around."

"But there's only one Kate. You slapped her around, bruised her tits. You shouldn't have done that."

"Next time, I'll fuck her. All the way. It'll be a pleasure."

Jasper kneed Julian, making him lose his balance and drop into the pool. Julian, taken by surprise, gasped for breath. As he struggled, Jasper's hand held him under the water until he stopped moving.

* * *

It was early morning, and Kate was standing with the lapping waves covering her trainers. She was wrapped in Jasper's windproof coat. Robert had told her that Lord Carmichael had left early after receiving an urgent call but that he'd be back later.

Translated: he's gone to see Margot, Kate thought.

"Kate!" called Ben from the seat of the quadbike. "Arthur, the chief constable, is here asking about Lord Carmichael."

She nodded and climbed onto the back of the bike.

Kate found Arthur in the kitchen, tucking into a plate of bacon and eggs.

"I heard on the grapevine that you're an early riser," he said with his mouth full. "But not as early as Jasper. Where is he?"

"I'm not sure."

"When did he leave?" Arthur wiped his mouth with a piece of kitchen towel.

"I'm not sure," she repeated. "I must have been asleep. Is it important? It is Saturday; he's probably with Margot."

"No, I've checked."

He knows about Jasper and Margot. It must be common knowledge, she thought.

"His car is missing."

"Arthur, what are you getting at?"

"Young Forrester face down in his swimming pool. The two elderly ladies he had been servicing said he'd told them he wouldn't be seeing them for some time, until he had seduced a very important lady."

Kate sat silently, staring into space.

"Ring any bells, Kate? I'll jog your memory: Max Wilson was found dead in a swimming pool after he roughed you up."

"That was a long time ago. He put me in hospital."

"The doctor told me that he'd wanted you to stay in overnight, but you refused."

Silence.

"They say young Forrester couldn't take his eyes off you."

"I don't see the connection."

Arthur turned over a newspaper that was lying on the table, to show the headline: *Lady Carmichael Attacked*.

Kate went bright red.

"The connection is, Kate, what were you doing with him?"

"He's going—*was* going—to give me a quote on removing the beach house."

"Did Jasper know?"

"I haven't told him."

"Why not?"

"I was waiting until I'd decided."

"I'll tell you what I think: Jasper found out about you and Forrester and has made sure there is no you and Forrester."

Silence.

"They reckon Forrester was good in bed. He preyed on older, lonely women—fucked them a few times until he had their money, then moved on to the next one. That's why there's a family rift." He paused. "I see it this way: you were Forrester's next victim—rich, attractive. He may have even been thinking of marrying you, and Jasper wasn't going to have that. After all, Jasper has said many times: 'Kate's mine.'"

* * *

Jasper sat on a log that the storm had washed onto Kate's beach. He couldn't go home; Kate would recognise the Carmichael demons that were still swirling around inside him. He tried to think about the happy times they had spent on this beach, but Julian Forrester's words wouldn't leave his thoughts. *"Fuck her once a week… rich, sexy, soft skin, full tits, a warm, wet pussy."* He'd deserved to die after what he'd said about his Kate.

But that bastard wouldn't have got near her if Jasper had been with her instead of chasing Margot's fictitious diamond dealers. He had been well and truly played. They were all involved: Von-Pitt, the Lords Blackthorn, Ambrose and Devon. But why go to all the trouble of luring him into their web? He wished he hadn't fucked Margot; she was nothing special. Not like Kate.

He took six small bags of diamonds out of his jacket pocket. He had found them in Julian's desk drawer; Julian's laptop and address book were now in the Range Rover. Jasper studied the bags. Were they payment diamonds? But payment for what? Fucking Kate, maybe.

Suddenly, the penny dropped: it was Kate that Their Lordships were after. Blackmail was their goal; Kate wouldn't cope with people knowing she had a lover. Ambrose and Devon wanted revenge for her refusing to be a Landon, Lord Blackthorn would want information about Jasper, and Von-Pitt wanted Wellsbury.

Game on, he thought as he jogged back to the car.

Chapter Forty-Eight

Kate was staring out of the closed orangery doors when Jasper returned. He slipped his arms around her waist and nuzzled her neck.

"How are you feeling?" he asked.

"Arthur's been. He wanted to know where you were. They found Julian dead. He thinks you drowned him, like Max Wilson."

"Arthur can think what he likes. You're mine."

* * *

Jasper moved the hair away from her neck. He was snuggling her back.

"I know you're awake, Kate. Your breathing changed. You're mine, Kate."

"He must have followed me… I didn't know myself that I was going to the office; it was all last minute. He grabbed me in the passageway… He must have got in before the security door closed…"

"And?"

"He pinned me to the wall. I tried to stop him, but he was too strong."

"Details, Kate."

She hesitated. "He pushed my bra up." She choked up and tears tipped over the edges of her eyelids.

"And he squeezed your fucking tits," Jasper impatiently interrupted. "Did he fucking penetrate you?"

"Jasper, you're losing your temper."

He moved her so he could see her face. "Yes or no, Kate."

"No. You can see what he did."

Suddenly, the bedroom door flew open. Jasper pulled the sheet over Kate's naked body as Arthur, the chief constable, marched to their bed.

"Jasper Carmichael, I'm taking you in for questioning about the unexplained death of Julian Forrester."

"You're making a habit of breaking into my bedroom."

Von-Pitt pushed past Arthur, his evil eyes resting on Kate. A grinning Margot stood behind him, and the Lords Blackthorn, Ambrose and Devon stood in the doorway.

What the fuck? thought Jasper.

"You're going to prison this time, Carmichael. And know this: I put you there," said Von-Pitt.

"Shut up, Von-Pitt, I'm in charge here," said Arthur. "And take your eyes off Kate."

Jasper eased himself from the bed and threw Kate her silk robe.

"Before you ask, Kate, here's the warrant," said Arthur. "Not all the judiciary are in your pocket, Carmichael."

"Von-Pitt, get out while they put some clothes on," said Lord Blackthorn.

Jasper stood on Kate's side of the bed, holding a blanket up to protect her modesty.

"Oh, come on, Jasper. Let us all see," Von-Pitt said.

When Kate was covered by her robe, the blanket drifted to the carpet, and a naked Jasper stepped towards Von-Pitt and grabbed his neck.

Von-Pitt's face reddened as Jasper's grip slowly tightened.

"Kate, stop him!" shouted Arthur. Their Lordships and Margot had already disappeared onto the landing.

"You harm a fucking hair on her head, and I'll do you," Jasper said.

Von-Pitt's legs buckled as Jasper loosened his grip, and he fell to the floor, coughing.

"I suggest you stop this charade, Arthur," Kate calmly said. "Arrange a date when we can have our lawyers present."

"Don't listen to her; she's a bloody Landon," retorted Von-Pitt from the floor.

Kate moved her eyes to Von-Pitt, wondering why being a Landon mattered.

"Von-Pitt, for goodness' sake, keep your mouth shut," Lord Ambrose called impatiently from the landing.

"That bastard nearly strangled me, and she's not going to get him off," said Von-Pitt, rubbing his neck.

Jasper walked up to Kate, slipped his arm around her waist and pulled her into a passionate kiss. "They'll come for you," he whispered into her ear. "They're after the diamonds. Hide them and take over. I'll handle this lot."

"You can visit him, Kate, but there will be no bail. Jasper is a flight risk," said Arthur as he led Jasper and the rest of the party downstairs.

Chapter Forty-Nine

Kate was walking down the stairs after putting Little Jasper to bed when Robert opened the front door to a man dressed in an immaculate black suit and wearing a black trilby, which he handed to Robert.

He gazed at Kate. "Lady Carmichael," he said, sidestepping Robert. He strode to the foot of the stairs, holding his hand out. "I'm Phillip Carrington."

Kate's eyes quickly scanned this tall man with dark, penetrating eyes. He had an authoritarian air about him that was indicative of always being obeyed. "I'm sorry?" she said with surprise in her voice as she shook his hand.

"Carrington was your grandmother's name before she married Landon."

What now? she thought as she turned to Robert. "We'll go into my library." She turned back to Phillip. "Tea, coffee, whisky, brandy, sandwich?"

"I've eaten, but a brandy would be acceptable."

Phillip sat in one of the fireside chairs opposite Kate. She could feel his eyes scrutinising the room.

"This is your library?" he said with surprise in his voice as his eyes lingered on the empty shelves.

"What's left of my books are spread out on a table in another room. I don't seem to have the time to sort them."

"Your grandmother was Isabel Carrington," he abruptly began.

"I'm not a Carrington, Spencer or Landon."

"I've been warned about your negative attitude towards your heritage, but I can assure you that you are Isabel's granddaughter. I would like to compare your DNA with the Carrington DNA, if that will help to convince you."

Kate stood and stepped towards the drinks tray that Robert had set upon a side table. She poured two generous portions into the crystal brandy bowls. "You are very confident about my DNA," she said as she sat into her chair.

"Isabel confided to a family member who has recently died. There was a bundle of letters tied with a white ribbon. Isabel's letters are full of you. How proud she was, particularly of your examination results. There are a few photographs, too."

"I'm told that I favour my mother."

"Ah, yes, Laura Spencer and Isabel were similar. Blonde hair, kind, caring. You are all of these, except for one trait that I believe is inherited from your grandfather, Meredith Spencer."

"And that is?"

"Your hidden, steely determination."

Kate sipped her brandy and stared into the fire. An uncomfortable air began to float about the library.

"The Carringtons are a rich and powerful family, have been for centuries. We look after our own, Lady Carmichael. Although, having said that, we did push you to one side after you married Carmichael. Nonetheless, I was surprised that Lord Ambrose didn't mention that your grandmother was a Carrington. Ambrose can be quite vindictive when he doesn't get his own way… but I think you've already come to that conclusion." He swished his brandy around the bowl. "The family was pleased when you refused to get involved with that trust fund; you showed excellent judgement."

He stopped and stared into her green eyes. "Your husband should be behind bars, but a certain section of the"—he hesitated—"upper class suffer from diamond addiction, and your husband has an uncanny talent with diamonds. In the past, they have pulled strings to keep him from jail, but this time he's there because of you. They will build a case proving he murdered Julian Forrester—Julian was being paid to seduce you so you could be blackmailed."

He stopped and stared into her eyes, waiting for a flinch that would tell him she knew more than she was letting on. But Kate didn't flinch; she suspected he was setting a trap.

"The Gentlemen's Club," he continued, "had a good life while Landon controlled the trust fund. They would like those times to return. But if they can't have a trust fund, they'll be happy with Carmichael's diamonds, and so will those rogues, Lord Blackthorn and Von-Pitt." He crossed his legs. "You do have Carmichael's diamonds; you're the only one Jasper trusts. I can't imagine how much they are worth…"

Kate could feel his eyes staring deeply at her, but she didn't flinch.

Phillip began to fidget; he was becoming impatient with her. His informant had convinced him that she would be a pushover. The uncomfortable silence deepened.

"It's time that troublesome group was put in their place." From out of his pocket, Phillip dropped what looked like a USB stick onto the drinks table. "Those cocky bastards need to be shown who's boss. They have no idea how to manage money; that's why they need diamonds. All their banking arrangements are on this." He pointed to the gadget. "Do with it as you wish."

Phillip looked at his watch, stood and walked towards her. "You can contact me on this number." He placed a card in her hand.

Kate gave it a cursory glance. No name, just a mobile number. She followed him into the foyer, where Robert stood at the door, holding Phillip's hat.

"The family has discussed you and Carmichael at length," Phillip said. "The consensus is that you have made your bed and, consequently, you must lie on it. Carringtons don't love; the family is all that matters."

Translated, Kate thought, *money and power.*

"You are blessed with love, and your grandson and husband know it. Your love for Carmichael has never waned, and to be fair, he loves you. Much to the disgust of the family, Isabel fell head over heels for that American Landon. He idolised her, showered her with love and diamonds. Sound familiar, Lady Carmichael?"

Phillip smiled at Robert and took his hat from Robert's hand.

After he had left, Kate stood for several moments, staring at the closed door.

"You can go to bed, Robert. I'll check on Little Jasper. I have a lot to think about."

* * *

Kate knew she wouldn't sleep, so she grabbed Jasper's coat and walked to the sea. She nestled into the sand dunes and stared into the night sky.

The stillness was broken by the sound of a struggling outboard engine. Kate watched as a small boat rode the angry waves. Suddenly, it capsized. Men swam and waded to the beach. Their angry shouts soon turned into a fight.

She watched as the four men fell back into the sea. One grabbed the boat and tried to start the outboard motor; after several attempts, it spluttered into life. The men jumped back into the boat and disappeared into the darkness.

Kate waited for the blackness of night to turn into the greyness of dawn before she walked to the shoreline. Scattered along the beach were brick-like packages. She rummaged in Jasper's coat pocket, pulled out a penknife and pierced the plastic wrapping of each package. Caught between two rocks were two duffle bags and an attaché case. She picked them up and hid them in the dunes.

Chapter Fifty

The staff at River's End House had been silently waiting for Kate to return when Arthur, the chief constable, arrived with Jasper. Robert set a coffee in front of him.

"Will Kate be long?" Arthur asked, staring at Jasper, who was sitting on a stool drinking malt whisky. He was sweating as the events of the early hours played over in his mind.

Lord Blackthorn had arrived at his house in the early hours.

"Release Carmichael," Blackthorn had admonished as he pushed him from his front door.

Before he could answer, Blackthorn had stormed into the study and found the drinks cabinet. Arthur had been alarmed when he filled a whisky glass with malt.

"No one expected the Carringtons to interfere." He gulped the whisky. "After all these years. Never bothered with Isabel and left her to the mercy of Landon." Gulp. "I knew Kate was different." Lord Blackthorn refilled his glass.

"What are you on about?" Arthur had asked.

Lord Blackthorn turned to face him. "Kate's grandmother was Isabel Carrington before she married."

Arthur's mouth opened and closed. "The Carringtons? The reclusive Carringtons?"

"Yes, you bloody fool."

"Why didn't you say?"

"It was a secret."

"How do you know?"

"I'm… I'm a relation." Gulp.

"Blackthorn, just spit it out."

"Only by marriage. I've never met them. They're very private, particularly Phillip. Not many people know Phillip Carrington."

"I still don't understand."

"How do you think I managed to arrange for the Landon Trust Fund to be dissolved?"

"It was Kate's idea."

"Kate's a fucking Carrington."

"And they helped you out?"

"That's one way of putting it."

"Do Lords Ambrose and Devon know Kate's a Carrington?"

"Yes. Ambrose doesn't like losing, particularly to a woman, but he won't cross the Carringtons."

"But he could go after Jasper and indirectly get to Kate."

Arthur had sunk into the overstuffed couch while Lord Blackthorn refilled his glass.

"So, it's not about diamonds?" Arthur had asked.

"It's three birds with one stone: we blackmail Kate into giving us Jasper's diamonds; Ambrose gets revenge with Kate; and Carmichael gets put inside."

"I'm not getting involved with this jiggery-pokery. Carmichael stays put."

"You want payment in diamonds?"

"I'll deny that."

At that moment, Lord Blackthorn's phone had rung.

"All settled?" said a husky voice on the other end.

"No."

"Give me the phone," Arthur had said.

Lord Blackthorn handed it to him.

Arthur uttered, "Joanne. Pension. Family."

The phone went dead.

"What the fuck?"

"What did he say?"

"Joanne, pension and family," stuttered Arthur.

"Translated: your family will know about you visiting Joanne and you will lose your job and pension?" said Lord Blackthorn.

"I'll deny it. My wife will believe me," said Arthur.

"You're a fool, Arthur; they will have photographs," answered Lord Blackthorn.

Arthur looked across to Jasper. He was a mess: hair uncombed, dark rings below his eyes; his five o'clock shadow had become bristly, his white t-shirt was no longer white. They had locked him in their smallest cell, with dirty grey walls, a toilet in the corner and a three-foot-wide bed with a dirty blanket. Within a few hours, Jasper had become a shadow of his normal self. Arthur wondered how Kate would rescue him from the demons that were tormenting him.

The atmosphere suddenly lifted when Kate walked through the kitchen door.

Jasper twisted around to face her. Their eyes danced as she walked towards him. He wrapped his arms around her waist and rested his head on her stomach. Kate's fingers threaded through his uncombed hair.

Chapter Fifty-One

Jasper had relaxed as Kate stroked his hair and kissed his face, and when he had dropped off to sleep, she made her way to the kitchen.

Elsie's voice was low and harsh: "He treats her like shit."

Kate stopped just outside the open kitchen door.

"From what I've been told, he adores her," Ben said. "But this Carrington thing will put more strain on her. According to Wes Clayton, she'll need support."

"Well, she won't get it from him," said a bitter Elsie.

"Lord Carmichael has instructed us to let her sleep," said Robert.

"The selfish bastard probably fucked her until she couldn't walk."

Nearly right, thought Kate, *but this time Jasper's the one who's exhausted and sleeping.*

"Elsie, stop this," said Robert. "You know you won't leave."

"I only stay because of her. She treats me like I'm her friend, doesn't talk down to people."

"Should I put her cup out?" asked Ruby.

Kate hurriedly walked into the orangery and faced the new bifold doors.

"Lady Carmichael," Ben shouted so the others could hear him.

Robert rushed into the orangery. "Lady Carmichael, Lord Carmichael said you were to rest."

"Lord Carmichael is resting. I'm afraid his stay in jail has exhausted him. Ben, would you collect all my paintings and bring them into the living room. I'll go to the gallery tomorrow."

"Aye. But you do know it's Sunday?"

Kate smiled. "Yes, I know. Sunday is a good day for me to hang paintings in the gallery."

"Can I come? I'll be good!" shouted Little Jasper as he rushed to his gran, throwing his arms around her waist.

"Settled then," said Ben as he walked out of the orangery. "I'll do the hanging, and you do the thinking."

* * *

Little Jasper was skipping around the gallery. "Look, Gran, I'll be running soon."

Kate smiled. *He's getting more like Oliver every day*, she thought.

"Where do you want this one of Lord Carmichael?" said Ben, holding up a painting of Jasper.

"That's Grandpop!" exclaimed Little Jasper, staring at the painting.

"He was younger then," said Kate, thinking, *He loved me then*. "Your grandpop built this gallery for me."

"Wow! He must love you."

The glass doors to the gallery opened and in walked Von-Pitt, his sidekick, Margot, Lords Blackthorn, Ambrose and Devon and, standing at the back, Arthur.

Ben slowly propped the painting of Jasper against the wall, and Little Jasper stood at Kate's side.

"What do you want?" said a very miffed Kate.

Lord Blackthorn stepped towards her. "Jasper, Kate. Jasper."

"Jasper's at River's End, sleeping."

"A speedboat capsized in the bay."

Kate had completely forgotten about the money and diamonds. "Bay?"

"You know what I mean. The men returned safely, but the cargo ended up in the sea. Empty bags were washed up this morning."

"Let's see… it's Sunday morning, and Jasper was with me all night."

"For fuck's sake, Blackthorn, stop treading on eggshells." Von-Pitt's evil stare cut through Kate. "The boat was carrying drugs, bags of cash and a case of diamonds."

"We can't find them," added a distressed Lord Ambrose.

"Jasper was a mess when I left him with you, Kate. He couldn't have had anything to do with the capsized boat," said Arthur.

"If not Jasper, you, Miss Bloody Innocent, have got them," Von-Pitt began.

Ben stepped forward, blocking Von-Pitt's path to Kate.

"Phillip-fucking-Carrington won't save you. We know all about his visit."

"Arthur, before I involve my solicitors—"

"She means the Carringtons, Arthur," Von-Pitt interrupted.

"I don't need the Carringtons, Mr Von-Pitt. Security cameras will have all the evidence I need. Jasper had them installed."

"She's fucking lying."

* * *

When Kate, Ben and Little Jasper returned to River's End House, Jasper had gone. Kate wasn't surprised. Von-Pitt probably had phoned him, and he had gone looking for the cash and diamonds.

He won't find them though, she thought. *No one will.*

Chapter Fifty-Two

"Lady Carmichael," Robert said. "Chief Constable Arthur and Inspector Johnson to see you."

Kate looked up from her laptop. *What the fuck this time?*

"Arthur," Kate said as he entered the library. "Would you like a room? You almost live here."

Robert smirked and stood to one side to allow the chief constable to walk towards Kate's desk.

"Now, now, Kate, no need to be like that," Arthur said. "This is official business. I'm afraid I would like you to come to the station."

"You're arresting me?"

"You'll be helping us with our enquires."

Kate slowly saved her work and closed the laptop. She slid various papers into the middle drawer of her desk and put Phillip Carrington's phone number into her pocket. "Robert, make sure Little Jasper's picked up. I have no idea how long this will take."

* * *

Kate was sitting at the table of a police station interview room, staring at the mirror that filled one wall. The red light of a camera fitted on the far wall flickered on and off.

A young woman brought her a bottle of water. As she was leaving, Kate asked for her one telephone call.

Inspector Johnson appeared and held the door open. "This is unusual, for a call to be granted before the interview."

Kate stood and was directed to the public telephone.

Phillip Carrington's curt voice echoed in her ear. "Yes. I'm busy."

"I'm at the Wellsbury police station—" Before she could say another word, the call was abruptly ended. She stood for a moment, staring at the buzzing receiver.

Inspector Johnson escorted her back to the interview room, but before she could sit back onto the hard chair, Arthur flung the door open.

"My God, Kate," he said. "You're truly a Carrington."

"I, er, what do you mean?"

"My boss has had a call. Not from his immediate boss, but his boss's boss, the Home Secretary. You're to be released immediately. Basically, Kate, it's hands off Lady Carmichael. There's only one family with that kind of power and that's the Carringtons. I'm thinking you phoned Phillip Carrington, and he phoned his best mate, the Home Secretary."

An awkward silence drifted between them until Arthur said, "Where's Jasper?"

"I don't know; he had gone by the time I got to the house."

"His Range Rover is parked behind the Carmichael apartment block," said Arthur.

"You know more than me," said Kate.

"He looked as if he was struggling to control his Carmichael demons when he left here. But he used you to calm his demons and now he's left you. Carrington won't like this. Not one little bit," Arthur replied.

"Sir," said the young lady who had brought Kate a bottle of water. "Transport for Lady Carmichael has arrived."

"Must be Robert," said Kate, moving towards the door.

"Does he have a helicopter?"

* * *

Phillip Carrington, forever a gentleman, helped Kate into the helicopter and buckled her in. Kate was filled with nervous apprehension as this was her first time in a helicopter, so when his reassuring, soft touch sent a warm glow through her, she thought nothing of it.

They landed on a lawn not far from a beautiful Arts and Crafts house. Kate was mesmerised by its stone facade and slate roof. It was built on a slope and appeared to melt into its surroundings. There were two massive chimneys, and all the windows were set at different levels, adding to its charm.

"It's beautiful," she said.

"Glad you like it. Come." He grabbed her hand and walked down the gently sloping lawn to a cove and the gentle, lapping waves of the sea.

Kate was in awe.

"The family bought the house from the builder. He went bankrupt. It's been in the family since nineteen hundred." His grip on her hand tightened. "It's like this: the family has instructed me to sell it; I'm the only member that's captivated by its charm and I don't use it much. But the house deserves to be loved." He paused and glanced at their joined hands. "Does he make you happy? They say he is a skilful lover. I have the strangest desire to kiss you; it's this place, it casts a spell on me. Do you feel it?"

"I think we should go back to the house before we do something that we'll regret."

He continued as if she hadn't spoken. "I would like to get to know you. I'd read so much about you that I thought I knew the woman: Lady Carmichael. Now I've been in your company, I understand why men find you desirable. You're very attractive, intelligent, loving, caring, and you must be sexual otherwise Jasper wouldn't return for more. Is it true that you're the only woman he has shared a bed with?"

"Yes." Kate began to feel uncomfortable; she didn't like the direction this conversation was going.

"Incredible. I had the privilege of seeing you together. He didn't leave your side; you were his, and he made sure the whole room knew it. You outshone all the females in there, including my lover." Phillip's words tumbled from his mouth. "Alas, we are no longer together. She wanted more. She has turned down my monetary offer; I shall have to increase it. The family doesn't do scandal.

"You see, Kate, my wife and I live separate lives. I fucked her four times and produced four sons. I don't know my sons. They have been brought up the Carrington way, to be hard-nosed businessmen. My sons have never felt love like you freely give to Little Jasper."

Kate didn't look at Phillip; she tried to ignore him but that was difficult, as he still held her hand. He seemed confused as he started to talk about Jasper.

"They are after him. They will get him for his many crimes. There's not many left of the circle of men that have protected him since the massacre of those drug dealers. You were there, Kate; you know what he did. We have it on video. The only flicker of emotion was when he looked at you cradling your dead son.

"As we speak, he's developing an escape route. He'll want you with him, but you can't leave Little Jasper to people like me. When he's gone, leave that godforsaken house and go back to Isaacs House, where you belong."

"You people know nothing about our love."

"That's true, people like me know nothing about love. But these people you treat with contempt want revenge. They have lost track of him, for now. But he'll return to you."

Phillip could feel her anger. Her cheeks were slightly flushed, and the pink of her full lips was so inviting.

"When we know each other better," he continued, "I want you to tell me how Jasper makes you happy. I would like to make you happy.

"But I digress. This beach house is yours. The papers are in the system. You love the beach and you will fall in love with this house. It comes with a live-in housekeeper and handyman. Man and wife, Grace and Edward. They have been with me a very long time. They live at the back of the house, so you won't be disturbed. There's a garage where you will leave your car. There's a kitchen, so I hope you can cook. Grace will do whatever you ask, and Edward will sort out a painting studio.

"However, I don't want Carmichael to fuck you here. That pleasure will be ultimately mine."

"You're very confident."

"I get what I want, and I want you. But a lot must happen before I can have you." He brought her hand to his mouth. "One kiss, Lady Carmichael. Just one kiss."

Chapter Fifty-Three

River's End House was still. Little Jasper was asleep, and Kate had sent the staff to bed. At last, she was alone with her thoughts.

She shivered as she sat in front of the blazing fire; the house was cold, particularly the library. She poured herself a large brandy and pulled a blanket over her shoulders. The fire crackled and flames leapt up the chimney as thoughts of Phillip Carrington filled her mind.

He had cupped her cheeks and brought their lips together. His tongue teased her lips apart and entered her mouth. He sighed when their tongues met.

His hand had fondled her backside as his kiss deepened. His leg pressed into her legs, weakening her stance. She slowly fell onto the grass but, somehow, he was still kissing her.

Deftly, he'd opened her blouse and lifted her bra. She had tried to push him off as his hand gently massaged her breast and his tongue penetrated deep inside her mouth. She felt the button on her waistband open and his hand quickly move to her sex. He opened her folds and caressed her.

He skilfully inched her jeans down her legs while his lips and tongue massaged her mouth. He pushed her legs apart and his fingers explored deep inside her.

She had heard his zip. She tried to move, but his body had her firmly pinned to the ground.

"No." But her words had been meaningless to him.

He lifted her hips and gently entered her as his tongue circled her nipples.

His thrusts had become erratic as he filled her.

"I'm sorry," he'd said. "I didn't expect that to happen. No wonder Carmichael comes back for more. Come, we will shower."

"Shower?"

"You can't go home smelling of me, and I can't return to the office smelling of you."

He had gently washed every part of her and wrapped her in a white bath sheet.

"I want you, Kate, to be my lover. I want you to give yourself to me just like you did with Bruce."

He knows about me and Bruce, *she thought.* "That can't be. I'm married," she had said.

"You had Bruce."

"Jasper had left me. I needed…"

"You needed a man, as you do now. Jasper will be leaving you soon." Phillip had gently dried her body. "I want you on my arm when I attend these boring social functions. I want my hand on your back."

"Phillip, I'm older than you."

"What's age but a number?"

The logs on the library fire had long since died into glowing embers when she rested her head on the arm of the couch and fell asleep.

Chapter Fifty-Four

Kate sat at an outside table of her favourite café. She always maintained that she didn't favour one café over another, but this one was opposite her gallery.

"Lady Carmichael," said the waiter as he set a cup of tea and a pastry on the table.

Phillip Carrington was sitting in a window seat of the café, watching her. He noticed that she looked at the waiter and smiled.

Godfrey Clayton pulled up a chair.

"Not now, Godfrey," said Kate.

"You look tired."

Tired? she thought. *You don't know the half of it.*

"If you were working as hard as Kate, you'd be tired," said his brother Wes, who had joined them. "Kate, the work on the airfield has stopped. Is there a problem? Tiny is mad."

Kate took a bite out of the pastry.

Carrington moved outside.

She sighed. "Jasper left Tiny in charge of his bank account... Let's put it this way: the money wasn't going where it was supposed to. So, I put Jasper's bank accounts on hold."

"Jasper won't like that," said Godfrey.

"Jasper's not here," snapped Kate.

"I don't like it," said Wes. "Von-Pitt's on the warpath. His bank accounts have been raided. He blames you, Kate."

Kate finished her tea and pastry. "Von-Pitt blames me for everything."

"He's mad about Carrington getting you out of the police station."

"Wes, that's none of his business." Kate stood.

"Is that it?" said Wes.

"I've been here since seven, I reckon I deserve some me time. I'm going to the gallery."

"What about those three units?" asked Godfrey as she was walking away.

"Don't concern yourself, Godfrey. It's in hand."

* * *

Kate was standing staring at Jasper's portrait, when the gallery doors slowly opened. She guessed who it was; she smelt his aftershave.

"Phillip, why are you here?"

He locked the door. "I wanted to see you. Where's the office?"

"I don't have one."

He strolled around the gallery, looking at each painting. "You have a talent."

An awkward silence developed.

"We've lost him, Kate. Any suggestions?"

"No."

"I'm thinking that the pair of you had a special place where you could fuck all day and night."

"It was the beach house. I lived there, remember? And Jasper just turned up. No one knew and no one bothered us."

"These three units. I have a building company—"

"There's no need."

"You're a Carrington. We look after our own. You know, it doesn't matter if you don't tell me where your secret place is. We'll get him when he tries to get to you. Now, how do I get out of this place without being seen?"

Kate opened the rear gallery door.

* * *

The foyer clock struck two as Kate walked down the stairs. She was grabbed from behind and pinned to the wall. He lifted her negligee, and she wrapped her legs around the waist of the man she loved.

"I can't stay, I've got to deep disappear," Jasper said. "I don't know if I'll see you again."

Their mouths crashed together as he pushed inside her.

"Do what you have to do to survive," he said between kisses. "I tried to get to you when they put you in jail, but Carrington got there first."

Kiss.

"The chat is that he's in a spot of bother with his family. He's off his game."

Kiss.

"They blame his lover. He's under pressure to divorce and remarry."

Kiss.

"He'll want to fuck you. Carringtons look after their own."

Kiss.

"Don't trust Their Lordships or Von-Pitt. I will have my revenge, Kate. My way." He then wrapped her fingers around a linen bag. "Hide these well. I already miss you. If Carrington fucks you, imagine it's me."

She claimed his mouth.

"No divorce, Kate. Remember, I love you. That will never change."

They kissed as if it was for the last time.

* * *

Phillip Carrington's phone rang.

"This better be good."

"He's at River's End House."

"Get after him."

"He had a boat. We caught a glimpse of him disappearing up the river. I've got a team searching as we speak."

Phillip inwardly cursed. *He had to see her; he must love her.* "Did we capture any pictures?"

"I've sent them to you, but they're not very good. We opened the kitchen door. He must have heard us; he was leaving out the front."

Phillip downloaded the files. He cursed again; the images were poor, but he could make out that Carmichael had her up against a wall. He wondered how many times they had done that.

Next time it will be me fucking you up against a wall, he thought.

* * *

By the time Phillip Carrington's men had caught up with the empty boat, Jasper Carmichael had stolen a car that had been left by the roadside, and disappeared.

Chapter Fifty-Five

It didn't matter how many times Jasper left her, she always worried about him. Was he safe? Was he chasing diamonds? Was he fucking another woman? She knew that her strong feelings for him would be the end of her.

She was tired; sleep always evaded her when Jasper was away. She wandered into the dark foyer and turned towards the kitchen.

She had just put a teapot and china mug on a tray when the lights flickered and she fell onto the hard floor. The tea tray crashed beside her.

The noise woke Ben. He carefully walked down the stairs and eased the utility door open.

Three men were standing over Kate. A giant of a man was holding a knife.

Ben lifted a knife off the rack. He threw it at the giant, hitting him in the shoulder. The man stumbled, and his fellow intruders rushed to help him as Ben rushed to Kate.

"Call an ambulance!" Ben shouted. "She's unconscious."

* * *

Jasper Carmichael, who had been hiding in the bushes overlooking the old airfield, watched the blue lights speed around Wellsbury.

They must be going to River's End House, he thought.

He shouldn't have been anywhere near Wellsbury, but Tiny had arranged a meeting.

He reversed his stolen car out of the undergrowth and headed towards the crowd that had gathered outside the private hospital.

Walking amongst the crowd, he was unrecognisable, dressed in clothes he had swapped with a rough sleeper.

"What's going on?" he asked.

"Lady Carmichael's been attacked," said a woman.

"Broke into the house," said another.

He moved through the crowd, heading towards the hospital's rear entrance, but the police prevented him getting anywhere near the door. He slipped back into the crowd and waited for news.

He didn't have to wait long before Arthur appeared saying that Lady Carmichael was receiving treatment for a cut to her head from a fall.

"He's lying," said a man behind Jasper. "She disturbed burglars. One had a knife."

"Where's Carmichael?" asked another.

"Gone with his diamond friends."

The crowd was jeering, and Arthur was having a hard time being heard, but Jasper heard enough: Kate would stay in hospital overnight but was expected to be released in the morning.

Jasper returned to his stolen car and headed towards the disused Hill's Garage, which backed onto the airfield, for his meeting with Tiny.

When he got there, Tiny was sitting on a stool, and one of his men was trying to stop the bleeding from a wound to his shoulder. The offending knife lay on the floor by Tiny.

You bastards, thought Jasper. *You'll pay for attacking Kate.*

"You're late, Carmichael," snarled Tiny. "It's your lucky night." He pushed the man away and put his dirty paw on the bleeding wound. He had lost a lot of blood. "She would have been dead if she hadn't been carrying a fucking tray—she fell to the floor, and the fucking tray with her. But it's just a matter of time before Von-Pitt and his partners get her, along with you. He's paying big bucks for your head; I was going to be rich after tonight. Both Carmichaels dead." Tiny's head drooped onto his chest.

Jasper dived to the knife, picking it up and knocking the stool over. He threw it into the chest of the man that had been trying to stem the blood flow, then he jumped up to take the other man, but he had fled. Jasper dashed to the door just as the man was trying to start their car. He wrenched the car door open and dragged the man out. The Carmichael demons were in full flow as Jasper pressed his fingers into the man's neck and waited until he stopped breathing.

When Jasper returned, dragging the dead man, Tiny was struggling to stand. Jasper walked up to him, pushed him over with his foot and then stamped on his shoulder.

Tiny yelled in pain.

"That's for double-crossing me, you piece of shit. I trusted you. We'd been together so many years."

Tiny coughed as he looked into Jasper's evil eyes. "Von-Pitt pays more."

Jasper put more pressure on Tiny's shoulder, making him scream louder. Blood started to trickle from the corner of his mouth.

"I promised Kate that I was done with all this, but you crossed a red line when you went after her." He held his foot on Tiny's shoulder. "This is for putting her in hospital."

Tiny's screams echoed.

Jasper held his foot there until Tiny stopped screaming.

* * *

Arthur, Lord Blackthorn and Inspector Paul Johnson were standing by a burnt-out car. Three bodies had been taken for examination.

"The car was pushed from the woods above the airfield," said the inspector, pointing to the treeline. "The team back from the old garage said it looked as if it was being used. Tyre tracks from at least two cars, and blood on the concrete workshop floor."

Lord Blackthorn suspected Jasper was responsible; they had attacked Kate. "Does Kate still own the garage?" he asked, subdued.

"The owner of the garage is Lady Carmichael," answered Paul Johnson.

A uniformed officer was running towards them.

"What now?" mumbled Arthur.

"A man was seen in the doctors' changing room," the officer said while gasping for breath.

Jasper, thought Lord Blackthorn.

"Was a doctor's ID stolen?" asked Arthur.

The officer nodded. "A doctor's car was stolen, too."

"Different doctors?" said Lord Blackthorn.

"Yes. The car's been found at the railway station."

"How's Lady Carmichael?" asked Arthur.

"Waiting for the early morning scan results."

Arthur waited until the officer and the inspector had left before saying, "Don't know how he did it, but it's Carmichael. Left a car at the station to put us off his trail." He kicked the ground under his foot. "I told Von-Pitt to leave things alone, but he wouldn't listen. He's done everything to separate them." He paused. "Jasper proved to be the weak link; he couldn't resist Margot. But he turned when he discovered it was a trap. He'll go berserk now they've attacked Kate. There'll be no stopping him until he's had his revenge." He paused again. "Where's Von-Pitt? He should be here."

"He's got a bigger problem. His bank accounts are empty," answered Lord Blackthorn.

"What do you mean?"

"All his money's gone."

"Gone where?" said a nervous Arthur.

"Puff! Into thin air. He's desperately trying to raise money to pay certain people."

An awkward silence settled between the two men as their thoughts turned to their own bank accounts.

"The thing is," said Lord Blackthorn, "no one knows when it happened. It could have been months ago."

* * *

Jasper Carmichael entered the train station and retrieved a holdall from the left luggage. He then went into the toilets and changed his appearance again.

Chapter Fifty-Six

An elderly man dressed in joggers and a t-shirt was sitting on a bench outside the hospital, leaning on a walking stick. His left foot was heavily bandaged.

"Taxi, mate?" called a taxi driver.

The elderly man shook his head and waved a packet of cigarettes at the driver.

A Bentley piqued the elderly man's interest as it parked in Lord Carmichael's reserved parking bay. Phillip Carrington stepped from the Bentley and strode into the hospital as if he owned it. The elderly man stubbed his cigarette, hobbled to the car and stuck a tracking device in the left rear wheel arch. He then returned to the bench.

He didn't have to wait long before a porter came out and helped Kate into the Bentley. She looked ill; her green eyes were dull and set in a pale face.

What have they done to her? It took all his willpower not to run to his beloved.

For a second, their eyes met, and Kate half smiled. In that moment, Jasper changed his plans of disappearing.

A tearful Little Jasper ran across the car park to Kate and sat next to her in the car, nestling his head on her lap.

"Come on, lad," said Ben, taking hold of Little Jasper. "Gran needs to be safe. She's not safe here or home."

Phillip appeared with the doctor.

"Don't forget to forward all Lady Carmichael's notes."

The doctor gave him a paper bag. "Instructions are inside."

* * *

The evening sky was turning from grey to black as Jasper left his stolen car in a farm gateway not far from the Carrington beach house. He scrambled up the slope to look down on the house. Lights were on in the downstairs rooms; he guessed Kate was in one of them. Armed guards were patrolling the area, and Jasper considered that there would likely be more guards inside.

Phillip Carrington strode out of the house to the double garage. The doors opened, and seconds later, he left in the Bentley. Jasper watched him confidently speed down the lane.

It was midnight when he made his move. The first guard he neutralised was one that had lit a cigarette; the next was leaning against a garden wall reading his phone.

He tried a door; to his surprise, it was open. Jasper walked into a dark room. He stayed still for a moment to let his eyes adjust to the darkness.

He was in a small kitchen. It was so quiet that you could hear a pin drop.

Come on, Kate, send me a sign, he thought.

He quickly stepped into the shadows when a man and woman appeared.

"Is she asleep?" asked the man.

"I'll give her ten minutes to finish in the bathroom before giving her a sedative," replied the woman.

"Time for a cuppa then."

Jasper waited for them to disappear, then he left his hiding place and followed the sound of running water along a narrow hallway.

The bathroom door opened, and Kate walked into another room.

He stepped towards her, put his hand over her mouth and kissed her neck. She turned to face him and flung her arms around him.

"Not now, my love, we have to leave."

The moon poked its face out from behind a cloud as Jasper and Kate stood outside the kitchen door, listening to the crunching gravel. The crunching ended abruptly; Jasper's fist had met the guard's face.

Jasper grabbed Kate's hand, and they ran as fast as they could to where he had left the car.

* * *

Kate patiently waited while Jasper removed several car number plates; they were dumping the car at a used car sales garage and stealing a second-hand Range Rover.

"Tell me about Carrington," he said as they drove from the garage.

Kate hesitated. "Not much to tell."

Jasper turned his head; she was leaning against the passenger window looking straight ahead.

She doesn't look guilty, he thought, *but she did hesitate*. "Did he try it on?" he pressed.

Her lips were tightly closed.

"Kate?"

"We took a walk to look at the sea. He's obsessed with how you satisfy me. I said no and tried to push him off me, but he's a strong man."

The Range Rover skidded off the road and stopped at an all-night service station.

"He fucking raped you."

"I wouldn't say raped, I just… gave in. I thought getting it over with would be the best policy."

"You resisted, and he didn't stop."

Kate couldn't look at him. She could feel his anger. He thumped the steering wheel several times, then moved the car to the pumps and filled the tank.

As he walked to the kiosk to pay, he felt his temper rising and he struggled to control it. He was about to leave the country and disappear, but now he had Carrington to deal with. But he would have to be careful; Kate wouldn't approve—she might even leave him.

As they approached River's End House, he said, "Did he say why he took you to that beach house?"

"It's a gift. The family told him to sell it, and he wanted me to have it. It's very beautiful. The lawn runs down to the sea; the beach is nestled in a cove. It's idyllic."

"Let me get this straight, he's giving you that beach house?"

"Carringtons look after their own."

Jasper stopped the car in a lay-by. "You do know he's married, has a lover."

"He's trying to pay the lover off."

"He wants you."

"Maybe. He saw me being in hospital as an opportunity not to be missed."

"Kate, there's more… There's got to be more."

"I don't know. I'm not one of his socialites. In fact, I'm ordinary."

"Don't put yourself down."

"Jasper, can we go? I'm not feeling too good. I can't take much more: Von-Pitt sent Forrester to fuck me, but he failed; he then sent his thugs to kill me, and in the meantime, Carrington fucks me and then kidnaps me. Why is this happening?" Tears began to fall.

"Because you're heir to a very rich and powerful dynasty, and people want to control you. They want you dead."

As the Range Rover stopped at River's End House's kitchen door, Jasper said, "I feel there's something you're not telling me. What else did he do? Fuck you from behind. You hate that."

"Nothing. Except… we showered."

"He showered with you? Touched you all over? Saw you naked?"

"He said I couldn't go home smelling of him."

The car door flew open, and Jasper began to pace. He pulled at his hair and shouted. It had been many years since Kate had witnessed the Carmichael demons in full flow.

Inside the kitchen, the staff looked on. Ben tightly held Little Jasper who was struggling to go to his gran.

"Jasper." Kate gingerly stepped towards him. "It meant nothing to me."

He twisted round to face her. "Meant nothing? Not to you, but it's tearing me apart. I can understand why you gave in, but there was no need for you to shower with him. He saw your body, Kate, touched you."

"Tearing you apart? How do you think I feel when you fuck other women? The things you do to them. Do you think I'm immune to gossip? You tear me apart."

"They mean nothing, you know that. Do you fancy Carrington?"

"Suddenly, I've become easy game, and that's because you're making it clear that you don't want me."

"That's not true. I'm a jealous, selfish bastard, Kate, but I'm yours. You're the only woman that matters. I make love to you and only you."

"What's stopping you? It doesn't occur to you that I only want you? I have needs."

"I can't love you now."

"Well then, let's go inside before we say things we'll regret."

Chapter Fifty-Seven

Jasper didn't go inside with her; he wanted to be alone.

Little Jasper threw his arms around Kate's waist. "I thought you'd left me!" he sobbed.

She knelt so he could rest his head on her shoulder. "I'd never leave you," she said softly as she stroked his hair.

"Do you still love me?"

"I'll always love you; Carmichaels are my weakness."

His bloodshot eyes met hers and he tried to smile.

"Come, let's take you to bed."

* * *

The staff were still in the kitchen when Kate returned.

"I'm very tired," she said as she slumped onto a stool.

Ruby set her tea and a slice of toast in front of her.

"We've been talking," said Elsie, stepping forward. "It's like this, Lady Carmichael—"

"I'm becoming your driver and bodyguard." Ben interrupted.

"You're in danger, Lady Carmichael. We must do something," added Robert.

Kate finished her tea and toast. "I'm not going to argue. Ben, you can be my driver. The doors into the house will be always locked; it's not an open house, like some people seem to think. Use the intercom to vet any visitors."

"What about Lord Carmichael?"

"I wish I could answer that, Robert."

* * *

From inside the open garage doors at River's End House, Jasper Carmichael watched Little Jasper run and dive onto the back seat of the Evoque. Jasper smiled as Kate joined him in the car—she must have been telling him off, as she received the Carmichael smile. Ben was grinning as he started the engine.

They're happy, he thought.

Jasper made for the kitchen door and walked straight past Robert just as he was about to lock it. Without saying a word, Jasper went to the stairs.

Their bed looked very tempting. He hadn't slept; he had spent the night in the boathouse, thinking about Kate. He had left her many times to satisfy his diamond addiction. People have various addictions: smoking, gambling, drugs, alcohol—but his was diamonds, and her. He always returned to Kate. From the moment he first saw her, he'd been attracted to her like iron is to a magnet.

He stood for some time under the warm water of the shower. She was everywhere: the smell of her shower gel and shampoo lingered in the bathroom, the scent of her perfume drifted about the bedroom, and now, she dominated his thoughts.

His musing was abruptly ended by a booming voice. "Phillip Carrington to see Lady Carmichael."

Jasper threw on a pair of jeans and a white fitted t-shirt, and ran down the stairs as Robert was opening the door to the dining room.

"I'm not waiting in there," Phillip said.

"Why not, Phillip? Isn't it good enough for you?"

Phillip whipped around to face Jasper. "Carmichael," he snapped, his anger clearly showing. "The police will be interested to know that you're still here."

Jasper slowly walked towards him.

"I can't understand what Kate sees in you."

"You're jealous."

"Look at you. Jeans and one of those wretched t-shirts, bare feet."

"Kate likes me this way."

"What do you want to make you leave her for good? Diamonds? Cash? The family will have to agree, but I'm confident payment won't be a problem."

Phillip took a moment to take in the man Kate was in love with: his muscular chest, those piercing blue eyes, full head of salt-and-pepper hair. He thought of Kate's hand in that hair; he admired those full lips and imagined them kissing her body.

"Kate is very important to us Carringtons," he said in an unusual, dreamlike voice.

"Why has Kate suddenly become important? Your family ignored her for years. In the early days, when she was struggling to survive, you pompous lot—"

"We lost interest in her," Phillip said. "She has a habit of making the wrong choices, particularly with men." He stared deeply at Jasper, deciding if he should continue. "If you must know, it is your fellow criminal, Von-Pitt, that wants her dead. With her dead, you would fall apart, then he would step in and take your diamonds, and Wellsbury."

The two men stared at one another as if they were going to fight.

Phillip broke the stand-off. "Kate owns a lot of land. Is it true that she worked on peoples' accounts, saved their businesses, and they paid her in kind?"

"You can't understand that someone would help people for little or no return."

"That's not the Carrington way. But it's turned out to our advantage. Wellsbury is ripe for developing, and a Carrington owns the land. There's money to be made here."

Neither of the men knew Kate was standing by the kitchen door, listening.

"I'll ask again, what do you want to leave her?"

"What if I don't want to leave her?"

"Don't be ridiculous. You know as well as I do that Von-Pitt and Margot tempted you. How many times have you left her?"

"We have never divorced."

"But you will if the price is right?

Jasper glared at Phillip, but did not speak.

"Your silence tells me I'm right. She deserves everything we Carringtons can give her. She will have no worries, Little Jasper will go to boarding school, the shopping centre will have Carrington managers. She'll be free to deal in first-edition books, beach walk and paint as much as she likes."

"And she'll be in your bed."

"Yes." His voice rose. "Be on my arm at boring social occasions. It'll be my hand guiding her through the crowds."

"But will you have her love?"

Jasper heard something move and turned to face the kitchen door. His blue eyes met her watery green ones. She didn't smile but turned away from him and walked into the kitchen.

"She heard?" said Phillip.

"Yes."

Phillip ran his hand through his hair and stared at the empty kitchen doorway. Then he marched out of the front door to his waiting helicopter, without looking at Jasper.

"Lady Carmichael has left, sir," announced Robert.

Chapter Fifty-Eight

The Range Rover bounced along the track that led to Jasper's boatyard. He had lost count of how many boat builders had rented the yard and gone bankrupt, but the yard being empty had suited his purpose.

Tied to the jetty was his refurbished yacht. It was smaller than he would have liked but, as far as he was concerned, a smaller yacht was easier to hide in remote coastal inlets.

As he was securing the Range Rover in one of the workshops and collecting his belongings, he thought of Kate. He should be with her. The staff had been surprised when he left soon after Phillip. He had tried to convince them that she would be back. "She won't leave Little Jasper," he had told them.

Kate's emotional shield had been under attack since the storm destroyed her home. Von-Pitt was like a battering ram; he wouldn't leave her alone. Her resistance broke when Carrington raped her. Although she didn't think it was rape, it was in Jasper's eyes. Carrington wanted to control her, take all her land holdings in Wellsbury and make it a Carrington town; the Carrington family had become very rich by developing land.

And he, the bastard that he was, was leaving her.

* * *

Jasper dropped anchor as close to Kate's beach as he could. He carefully manoeuvred the dinghy past the rocky outcrop to the shore, then jogged to her favourite place, where they had loved one another.

Kate was sitting with her head resting on her knees. She looked up as Jasper was beaching the dinghy. He was an excellent sailor, talented diamond dealer and skilful lover, but he had the Carmichael demons.

"We have to talk," he said as he sat next to her. "I can't go with this hanging over us."

Silence.

"I let Carrington go on because I want to know what game he's playing."

"He wants to add Wellsbury to the Carrington portfolio. He also thinks that I know where your diamonds are." Her voice was soft and unusually flat, as if she didn't care.

"He wants you."

"As far as the Carringtons are concerned, I'm a loose end. They want me under the Carrington umbrella so they can control everything I do."

"When he's head of the Carrington family, he'll have his wife for formal occasions, a high-class mistress for when he's in London, and you."

"You're jealous."

"Of course, I'm fucking jealous! He'll be fucking my wife!"

"But it will mean nothing to me. Just like your many conquests mean nothing to you."

Jasper jumped up and started to pace. "My feelings mean nothing to you." His blue eyes were on fire and he ran his hand through his collar-length hair.

"Do my feelings mean nothing to you?"

Jasper stopped and stared at her. "I can't deal with you when you're like this." And began to jog back to his dinghy.

"Like what?" she called after him.

Suddenly, he stopped and ran back to her. He grabbed her arm and pulled her into him. Their mouths feverishly met; they were two people desperate for each other.

He gasped. "Does he kiss you like this?"

"I wouldn't know. He's never been given the chance," she said breathlessly.

Chapter Fifty-Nine

The Carringtons' London meeting house was hidden away in a secluded cul-de-sac. The family had invited Lords Blackthorn, Ambrose and Devon, Mr Von-Pitt and Margot to a meeting to discuss the properties owned by Lady Kate Carmichael.

Kate was proving to be more difficult than they had anticipated. Jasper rescuing her from the Carrington beach house had upset their plans; they had expected him to leave her and, consequently, without his support, Kate could have been easily persuaded to sell her properties.

The head of the family, who was referred to as "Auntie", sat silently watching the visitors, while trying to hide her immediate dislike for Von-Pitt, who was sitting opposite Phillip.

"Wellsbury would be under my control," Von-Pitt proclaimed in a loud voice, "if Phillip had increased the security around Kate."

Auntie coughed and moved in her chair, her dark eyes fixed on Von-Pitt. "Mr Von-Pitt." Her voice had lost its usual conciliatory edge.

Phillip Carrington's phone bleeped.

"Answer that," she angrily snapped, glaring at Phillip. "Put it on speaker."

"It might be best if I go outside."

"Phillip, don't defy me."

"Boss," said a gruff voice. *"They are at her beach, the one that the storm destroyed. We lost*

her in Wellsbury, but I had a tip off that Jasper has a yacht. I'm watching them. They must have had an argument; Jasper stormed off."

"That's all?" said Phillip.

Auntie turned her head towards Lord Blackthorn as he put his hands over his face. "Let him finish, will you."

"But he ran back to her and lifted her into a kiss. And what a kiss."

Auntie's eyes moved to the Von-Pitt party. Lord Blackthorn had lowered his head into his chest and Margot had gone bright red.

"She was wearing a big coat. Jasper lowered the coat onto the sand and her with it. Couldn't see much after that, but she's lying across him. He's pulled some of their clothes over her. What do you want me to do?"

Phillip looked at Auntie.

"Leave them alone," she barked.

Phillip ended the call and stood.

"Sit, Phillip. This changes everything. They are obviously still a couple. If we go for her, he will take his revenge—Carmichael style."

"Carmichael doesn't frighten me," said Von-Pitt.

"Well, he should," answered a distressed-looking Lord Blackthorn. "You paid Forrester to seduce her, and what happened to him?"

"He drowned."

"By the hand of Jasper Carmichael. He's a Carmichael, damn it; you harm Kate and the demons will surface. He will have his revenge his way." Auntie caught Lord Blackthorn's eye, but he was on a roll. "In his mind, Kate is his. She calms his demons. Take her away and all hell will be let loose."

"Jasper's mine," said Margot. "He made me feel like I was the only woman for him. She's old news."

"You mean he fucked you and left. Did he leave Kate? He could have just left her naked on the beach, but he didn't. You, and all the women like you, mean nothing to him."

"Now, now, Blackthorn, that's enough," said Auntie. "We will watch and wait, and if an opportunity arises, we will make a move into Wellsbury."

Von-Pitt stood. "That's it. I don't have the luxury of time."

"Mr Von-Pitt, you came begging for money to pay a debt and buy Kate Carmichael's shopping centre. We know all about your drug enterprise using Landon Hall and the shopping centre, but as Landon Hall is out of action and Kate still has control of the centre, I suggest that you sell Landon Hall to pay your debt. Phillip, make him an offer that he can't refuse."

"No. I won't sell to you. Landon Hall is mine."

"Mr Von-Pitt, you haven't registered the sale, and as such, Landon Hall is inherited by Lord Henry Landon's next of kin, and that is Lady Carmichael, also known as Kate."

Von-Pitt slumped back into his seat.

"I suggest you accept our offer with the utmost urgency before those bureaucrats realise that Lord Henry's estate has not been settled."

"What about diamonds?" said Lord Ambrose.

Auntie turned to him. "How can we discuss diamonds with Jasper Carmichael wandering about? Margot and Mr Von-Pitt have failed to control him, and we can't think about the diamond black market with Jasper free. I'll remind you all that Lord Jasper Carmichael is still the diamond king."

"We could hire a hitman," suggested Lord Ambrose.

"I have a horrible feeling that if we did that, we would see the other side of Lady Carmichael's nature. Revenge springs to mind."

* * *

It was approaching midnight when Kate returned to River's End House. Little Jasper raced out of the kitchen and flung his arms around her waist.

The staff stared at the woman who had her hand around Little Jasper's shoulder. Her eyes sparkled, her cheeks glowed, and she smiled. The cold dead eyes and worried expression had disappeared.

Chapter Sixty

Robert turned as the door opened and a bedraggled Lord Jasper Carmichael walked into the warm kitchen. Robert's eyes never left him as he eased himself onto a stool.

"Fetch Kate." Jasper's voice was low and tired.

By the time Kate appeared, the rest of the staff were in the kitchen and Jasper was sipping coffee and eating a bacon roll. He lifted his eyes to a sleepy Kate, still dressed in her silk nightdress and robe.

"Jasper, I thought you'd be long gone," she said as she sat opposite him.

"I, er, had some news."

Kate smiled at Ruby as she set a tea tray with toast on the work surface.

"I'll give you some background. The Carringtons have a house in London where they hold meetings. It's not easy to find, in a secluded cul-de-sac, surrounded by a high hedge, electric gate and armed guards."

"I've got the picture. Go on."

"My informant had suspicions that this house was owned by the Carringtons. They never make mistakes, but this time they did. A Rolls, driven by Von-Pitt with Margot in the front and Lords Blackthorn, Ambrose and Devon in the back, stopped at the gates. The guard took his time checking the paper Von-Pitt handed to him; my informant just had enough time to duck through the closing gate."

"Jasper, get on with it. What did he find out?"

"This is important, Kate. It involves you. I've been at his apartment all night. He managed to hear some of the meeting. The gist of it is that the Carringtons had a deal with Von-Pitt about Wellsbury. With me out the way, they anticipated that you would give in to Von-Pitt's takeover. Their plan was scuppered when I rescued you from the beach house and with our meeting on your beach."

"They were watching?"

"Auntie didn't like that we were together."

"Auntie?"

"The head of the Carrington clan. She wants to wait before they make a move on Wellsbury; Von-Pitt doesn't. For some reason, he doesn't believe I'm a dangerous man."

"There's more?" said Kate, pushing her tea tray for a refill.

Jasper pulled a plastic wallet from inside his shirt. "My friend has been researching Lord Henry and Lady Isabel for years. Your Landon connection ended with the disappearance of the American Landons, but Lady Isabel was a Carrington. She had a considerable fortune, but when she married Landon, her money and assets were frozen. When she died without any children, the Carrington estate claimed her fortune." He placed the wallet on the table and rested his hand on it. "This is a copy of the ownership record of the Carrington beach house. It belonged to her and now you." Jasper pushed the paper to her, his finger pointing to the names. "Only a Carrington can own it. Phillip Carrington would have to have provided proof of your birthright."

"That's a bit thin, Jasper."

"Kate, lift your head out of the sand. Somewhere, the Carringtons have proof that your grandmother was Lady Isabel."

Kate pushed her stool away and went to the window.

"Auntie's own words recommended that Von-Pitt register his purchase of Landon Hall, because if he didn't, it would go to you."

"Why don't they claim Landon Hall?"

"I'm betting that Lady Isabel owned it. A search would be made for her heir… Guess whose name would turn up."

Kate silently gazed out of the window.

"Why do you think Lady Isabel hugged you at that prize-giving?

Silence.

"Why do you think that the members of the Gentlemen's Club rejected Von-Pitt's offer of a slap-up dinner for information about you? You're Lady Isabel's granddaughter. It all fits."

"It's still circumstantial."

"Kate, I'll prove it to you. I'll put an offer in for Landon Hall."

"It still doesn't explain all the interest in Wellsbury."

"Von-Pitt wants it for his criminal activities; the Carringtons want to add it to their property portfolio. Think of a marina built where the old riverside café was. There's road access and river access. Big houses with moorings built all along the river's edge to the sea. Wellsbury would be put on the map, investments would flow into the town. The shopping centre would act as a hub: expensive designer shops, casinos, restaurants. Big money would follow." Jasper moved behind her. "Who's standing in the way of this? A Carrington. You're a silent partner in Hope's Farm, you're part owner of Carmichael Properties, you own the shopping centre, you own parcels of land all over the town."

"I haven't been approached about selling any land."

Jasper put his hands on her shoulders. "My love, they don't intend to buy the land. It will be a takeover. They will guarantee you a reclusive life of peace, beach walks, painting and books. They even will provide you with as much sex as you want. In return, you'll sign over all your assets."

"You've thought it all out."

"It wasn't difficult after talking to my informant and reading these documents. He's prepared to let you look at all his research."

"For money?"

"No. Just information for his book. He's changing the title to *The Lady That Owned the Carringtons*."

Chapter Sixty-One

Kate lay alone in bed, waiting for the hall clock to strike five. Jasper had had his way with her and left. Her hand gently touched her sore breasts. *My body will be delicate for days*, she thought. *I have no willpower when it comes to Jasper.*

The clock struck five, and she eased herself off the bed. Jasper filled her mind.

He had joined her in the shower, his large hands cupping her breasts while his soft lips caressed her neck.

"I love you so much it hurts. It's always been you. I'm sorry if I upset you."

His kisses meandered down her back, and her legs had buckled. His strong arm wrapped around her waist.

"The Carringtons are treacherous," he said. "They are going to use you. With their help, Von-Pitt will take what's yours, and then they'll get rid of him."

He turned her so her back was pinned against the tiles. "I love you, Kate. I need to feel your love." He'd lifted her legs around his waist.

She was putty in his hands, and he knew it. She wondered if she would ever say no to him.

* * *

The day had gone well until Kate returned home with Little Jasper. She had done the morning school run and spent the rest of the day in the office. She had asked Ruby to make her a packed lunch so she wouldn't have to go out into the shopping centre.

They were waiting for her: Phillip Carrington, Arthur, Lords Blackthorn, Ambrose and Devon, and Von-Pitt with Margot.

"I was not told you were at the office," said a miffed Phillip.

Kate slumped into the only unoccupied overstuffed chair in the living room. Robert appeared, set a small table next to her and placed her tea tray upon it. She lifted the warm liquid to her lips.

"What do you all want? I'm very tired."

"Jasper's given us the slip, Kate," said Arthur.

What's new? she thought.

"I have a consignment of diamonds," said Lord Blackthorn.

Robert reappeared. "Little Jasper's eating in the kitchen."

"I'll eat in the library," answered Kate, handing him her laptop bag.

"It's imperative that we know the whereabouts of Jasper," said Phillip.

Robert reappeared with a fresh teapot. "New potatoes or chips?"

Kate smiled. "New potatoes."

"No more interruptions!" snapped Phillip.

"I'll decide that," retorted Kate loud enough for Robert to hear. "I don't know where Jasper is and I have no knowledge about diamonds."

"But do you know if you're selling the old riverside café land?" asked Von-Pitt.

"Why would I sell? If anyone is going to develop along the river it will be me."

"I'll remind you, Lady Carmichael, that you know nothing about what's involved in such a large project," said a surprised Phillip.

"True. But Jasper does."

"You're lying!" Von-Pitt bellowed.

"Are you sure?"

"Jasper knows nothing about this," interjected Margot. "He would have told me."

"You think you know Jasper because he fucked you?"

"Kate, tell us where you think he's gone," said Arthur.

"He only tells me what I need to know, and I don't need to know what he's up to. I'm guessing that he's gone into chameleon mode."

"What the hell does that mean?" snapped Von-Pitt.

Arthur stood and made for the door. "Jasper can take on many disguises: tramp, rich exec, et cetera. He has safe houses, cars stashed. That's how he disappears. Only highly trained people can track him, and they come at a price." He walked out.

"We need Jasper's help, Kate," said Lord Devon, wiping a tear from his cheek.

Phillip Carrington opened the front door and turned. "Last chance, Kate. Where's Jasper?"

Kate stood and silently left to check on Little Jasper.

Phillip Carrington, the man that wanted her in his bed, pressed his phone to his ear. "Do it. Her and the lad."

Carrington business came before his sexual desires.

Chapter Sixty-Two

Fear gripped Kate as she raced into the kitchen. "Pack a bag of the things that are precious to you."

"Lady Carmichael?" said Robert.

"I have an awful feeling that we are all in imminent danger. Ben, do you still have that pickup? We'll need it."

She opened Jasper's diamond office, rushed to his wall safe and vault and emptied the contents into a canvas holdall. She rummaged through his desk, emptying everything into the bag. She placed the bag by the front door.

"Gran!" cried Little Jasper.

"Go and sit in the Evoque!" she shouted as she rushed into her library.

* * *

A speedboat beached onto the stony shoreline at River's End House. Six men dressed in black jumped out. Their leader instructed two men to the boathouse and one to stay at the boat. The other three jogged to the house.

* * *

Kate pulled her old computer from its hiding place at the back of the bookshelves. Robert joined her in the library just as she finished emptying her desk into another holdall.

"The Evoque?" he asked as he picked up her computer bag and the holdall.

Ben appeared. "Men are running in from the beach."

"Take the staff to Isaacs House," she ordered.

As Kate left the library, she heard the outside kitchen door shatter. She ran out of the front door and jumped into the Evoque.

"Gran, I'm scared!" cried Little Jasper.

Kate put her hand on his knee and floored the accelerator.

The leader of the group leapt out of the front door as Kate sped away from the house. He lifted his phone. "They've escaped. Staff and her."

"How the fuck did she know?" snapped an angry Phillip Carrington. *"Get over to Isaacs House."*

"They've taken all the transport."

When his men had finished searching the house, the leader emptied a can of petrol over the foyer floor and lit a match.

* * *

An extremely angry Phillip Carrington flew his helicopter over Isaacs House. Two vehicles were parked at the back.

"She's at Isaacs House," he said into his phone.

"What about Carmichael?" asked the leader of the hit team.

"Fuck Carmichael. She's the kingpin. She must die, along with the boy."

* * *

Kate was standing at the bifold doors of her Isaacs House studio, staring into the darkness.

Suddenly, the security lights came on. Three men were slowly walking towards the house. One stopped to answer his phone.

"Change of plan. The bitch can have a night's sleep."

Phillip Carrington had been overruled.

* * *

Jasper Carmichael was sitting outside a French quayside café, negotiating a diamond deal, when his phone pinged.

River's End House burned down. Kate's at Isaacs House.

Jasper stood, his eyes studying the man. The deal should have been finalised yesterday, but the man had been late. Jasper walked away.

"Trouble?" called the man, pulling his phone out of his jeans pocket.

Jasper stopped and hurried back to the table. In one swift move, the man's face met the tabletop and his phone was snatched out of his hand. Blood poured from the man's nose.

Jasper held his face to the table and whispered, "Tell them I'm coming for them."

Chapter Sixty-Three

Isaacs House hummed with activity. Little Jasper was following Elsie and Robert, who were trying to organise the house; Ruby was emptying the freezer.

The outside kitchen door opened, and in walked Arthur. His face was red and there were black rings beneath his eyes.

"I insisted that I come. I have always valued our friendship," he sternly said. "Jasper's up to his old tricks. Smashed a man's face into a table."

"Coffee?"

"You're not sweetening me up."

"I wouldn't dream of it. I'm making a fresh pot of tea."

"They want you at the station for a chat."

"Who are 'they'? Pick another venue."

Arthur started to pace as Kate set her tea upon the table. "I'm instructed to arrest you if you resist."

"Arrest me then."

"Think about it. If Jasper finds out, all hell will be let loose. I remember him rampaging when you had been roughed up. I think he's on his way here."

You could hear a pin drop.

"Kate, be reasonable. I don't want trouble."

"I'm not feeling reasonable. River's End House was torched. We escaped by the skin of our teeth, and you"—she hesitated—"and you want me to be reasonable?"

Kate's loud, angry voice echoed and her cold, green eyes pierced into Arthur. He stepped closer to the door; he had never seen her so angry.

"Everything was destroyed. We have no clothes, food. All my books and paintings."

"Just give them what they want, Kate, and everything will be fine."

A police officer pushed past. "Sir, you'd better come. A crowd has gathered outside."

"And so it begins, Kate. Jasper hasn't wasted any time."

"Jasper's not responsible for this, and neither am I. And you know it."

"They searched River's End House. There were no diamonds. They'll settle for diamonds."

"I don't give a fuck about them or diamonds."

"No one defies them."

"Well, it's time someone did."

"Kate, are you in there?" Godfrey Clayton called.

"Let him in and go to your masters," Kate said to Arthur as he left.

"Sorry about River's End House," said Godfrey, lifting bags onto the table. "The shopping centre traders have voted me spokesperson." He hesitated. "I know we have had our differences, but we're all sorry. A few of us got together." He pointed to the bags. "There's clothes, food, groceries to tide you over until you get organised." Godfrey fidgeted and his face reddened. "This isn't charity, Kate. You've always been there for us. Had our backs, so to speak. You've saved many small businesses, and we appreciate what you've done. This is our way of saying thank you."

"I don't know what to say, Godfrey."

"Just accept them."

Kate started to well up. She put her arms around him.

"Here, here," said an embarrassed Godfrey as Kate stepped away. "I don't want Jasper after me." He moved to the doorway. "I don't want you thinking I'm going soft. Normal service will be resumed when you return."

* * *

A small yacht sailed towards the boathouse at River's End House.

Jasper Carmichael had ignored the storm-force weather warning; he had fought the strong wind and waves all the way to the English coast.

He sailed past the charred remains of the boathouse and followed the river to a small, narrow inlet. The side of the yacht scraped the land until it stopped. Jasper jammed a metal stake into Hope's farmland and tied the yacht to it.

He took a moment to stare at what remained of River's End House. Through a pair of binoculars, he gazed at its blackened remains.

A small boy, running, caught his eye. It took him just a moment to find his love. His heart leapt. He would have recognised her anywhere: blue jeans, white blouse, hair flowing in the breeze. No woman stirred him like Kate.

The boy ran up to her and threw his arms around her waist. Her hands rested on his shoulders. A faint smile appeared on her face, but Jasper knew his beloved; she was putting on a brave face, but inside she was sad and hurting.

Someone will pay for this, he thought as he jogged away from the river.

* * *

Phillip Carrington strode into Auntie's study in the London house and slumped into one of the Chesterfield chairs. "There's been a whip round. Food and clothes."

"Can she recover from this?" Auntie asked.

"I'm not sure. Kate is resourceful. We didn't find her laptop."

"Diamonds?"

"Jasper's office was open, as was his safe, but no diamonds."

"So, she has them."

"We can't be sure."

"Stop thinking with your dick. She's the only person Carmichael trusts; she has his fucking diamonds."

"The team are preparing to break into Isaacs House tonight."

"She will have used every fucking hiding place."

"She'll tell us if we capture the boy."

"Where's Carmichael?"

"We think he's still in France."

"Think?" Auntie stood, her anger overflowing. "I don't fucking expect you to think, I expect you to know!"

"That storm broke records for this time of year. No one could have sailed through it."

"You do realise that Carmichael is an exceptional sailor, taught by an old-school captain? He relies on his instincts. Get a search team looking for his yacht."

"In France?"

"No, in bloody England! He knows we've attacked Kate. He'll move heaven and hell to be with her." Auntie returned to her chair, trying to calm herself. She looked at her heir apparent.

"This doesn't make any sense," he said.

"Neither does love make sense. I anticipate the unexpected; that is why I still run the Carrington business."

Chapter Sixty-Four

Jasper lay in the long grass that young farmer Hope had left to rewild.

Kate would approve, he thought as tiredness began to spread through his body.

He closed his eyes and Kate appeared. They were lying in the bath, her head on his chest and his hands cupping her breasts.

Sleep was hovering when voices stirred his senses. His eyes shot open. Jasper listened to a man talking into a phone.

"We're ready sir... Yes. I've got more men... Harry neglected the security."

Bloody Harry, thought Jasper. *How many times did I tell him to look after the security?*

"There's no sign of Carmichael, but I'll leave three men behind. Just in case... Entry from the back garden looks easy... I'm not underestimating her, sir."

* * *

Kate decided not to share her fear that there would be an attempted break-in with the staff.

She suspected that the fire at River's End House was an attempt to capture her, or possibly kill her. She suspected that the Carringtons were involved and that they would try again to get at her.

She figured that the security lights that surrounded Isaacs House would be the first target for the attackers, and then her studio's bifold doors. She needed an early warning of their presence.

She waited until the staff and Little Jasper were in bed before brushing her grandchildren's pile of seashells around the patio in front of her studio. They would break under heavy footsteps, alerting her to danger. After setting and double-checking the alarm system, she settled in the kitchen with a pot of tea and her old laptop, the one she'd used to hack into the NRJ bank accounts.

As she watched it go through its boot-up routine, a message appeared.

I didn't deserve your kindness.

For sticking by me through the most difficult time of my life.

This is better than the Carrington program.

It is safe and can't be traced.

Do your worst to these bastards.

Kate sat back and stared at the screen. There was only one person she could think of that could do this, and he had disappeared from her life years ago. Jasper had hired him, a genius with computers. She couldn't think of his name, but they called him "Whizz Kid".

Kate opened the program. She couldn't believe her eyes. Files on the Carringtons, Landons, Lord Blackthorn, Lord Ambrose, Lord Devon, Pieter Von-Pitt, Margot and Lord Jasper Carmichael.

Another message appeared.

I am surprised that you are part-owner of all Jasper's activities. He's a bastard, just like his ancestors. He doesn't deserve you.

Lord Blackthorn is a thief and should receive his comeuppance.

Lords Ambrose and Devon have embezzled money from the Gentlemen's Club for years. They intended to blackmail you into doing what they wanted. Screw them.

Von-Pitt and Margot are evil. Von-Pitt is the head of an organised crime cartel. He uses his high-class diamond and jewellery stores to launder money. He's developing a country-wide drugs network and, if the price is right, he'll traffic young girls. Margot leads an international diamond cartel and she wants Jasper's diamond network. They both are obsessed with power and money. They need to be got rid of.

There's nothing left of Lord Henry Landon's fortune; the Carringtons have seen to that. They have succumbed to alcohol, drugs, gambling and sex. Their direct bloodline is dwindling. The ruthless Phillip is the crowned heir apparent, but he's not a Carrington, only the stepson of one. Even Auntie's bloodline is questionable, but she's powerful inside and outside the family, and she wants Phillip to follow her. Study their family tree in the file.

They have known of your existence since you were born, but you weren't a threat until now. They want Wellsbury to become part of their massive property portfolio, but you own the land they want. Through their agent Von-Pitt, they have tried various ways to obtain the land—they have even tried to separate you and Jasper. Diamonds are a weakness of his, but you're his biggest weakness.

Lady Isabel, your grandmother, was a true-blooded Carrington, and you have her blood flowing through your veins. The Carrington empire is yours by right. With Little Jasper, you are the true Carrington bloodline. They will fight you, but you now have the wherewithal to beat them.

Keep this between us. DON'T DISCUSS THIS WITH JASPER.

I will watch your progress.

The sound of crushing seashells broke Kate's concentration. She leapt up and ran into her studio. She didn't wait to count how many men were slowly walking towards the bifold doors; she ran to the security control box and hit override. The backup system kicked in; all the security lights came on and the shrill of the alarm filled the night air.

She snatched her phone from her pocket and rang 999.

* * *

"This better be good," snapped Auntie.

"Kate called the police," answered a subdued Phillip.

"Arthur can handle that."

"She didn't involve him, she called 999."

"Bitch."

"We got Jasper. My men left him face down in a ditch. But when they went to collect him, he'd disappeared."

"Fuck. Clear this mess up and get onto Arthur."

* * *

Blood trickled down Jasper Carmichael's face as he staggered back to his yacht. The bullet had grazed his forehead.

He fired the engine and slowly reversed the yacht out of the narrow inlet.

His head began to throb as he navigated his way to his boatyard.

* * *

It was late afternoon when Auntie summoned her fellow conspirators to the Carringtons' London house.

She sat at the head of the table with a grim face. "The wolf in sheep's clothing is beginning to show her hand. Lady Kate Carmichael has outmanoeuvred us. I want the bitch to suffer. No one betters me."

Von-Pitt grinned.

"She will attack," Auntie continued. "You will have to check your bank accounts and your business dealings."

"What can she do? She's nothing without Jasper." Von-Pitt smirked.

"Fool. Her back is against the wall; she has nothing to lose. She will come out fighting. We have to assume that she has Jasper's diamonds and records of his network." Auntie looked at Margot. "She will go after you, Margot."

"My cartel is sound," said Margot.

"Nevertheless, be on your guard." Auntie diverted her gaze to Lords Ambrose and Devon. "What does she know about the Gentlemen's Club? Think back. If there's a crack in your organisation, she will find it. Lord Blackthorn, I suggest you stop what you're doing and disappear. You've been milking Jasper for years. She'll want revenge. And Von-Pitt, you have too many irons in the fire, so to speak. She'll be spoilt for choice as to where to hit you."

"You make her sound like a Mafia godfather," Von-Pitt said.

"Heed my advice, Von-Pitt. Innocent Lady Carmichael has a ruthless streak running through her veins."

* * *

Jasper awoke in the seat of his Range Rover, which he had left in the boatyard workshop. He staggered to the sink and ran cold water over his head.

He thought of Kate, but he had to be realistic; there was no way he could get to her. The Carringtons would have her surrounded.

He would have to lie low—after he'd checked the one place that she always returned to.

Chapter Sixty-Five

Jasper left his Range Rover in the bushes and trees behind Kate's wrecked beach house. He slid down the slope to the house and pulled the door open. He managed to find a dryish chair, and waited.

The sound of a diesel engine woke him. He gingerly peeped out of a broken window and smiled; it was his beloved.

The smile was wiped off his face when he saw that three of Carrington's men had followed her.

Three, he thought. *Phillip Carrington is superstitious, and odd numbers are bad luck.*

Number four appeared from behind Kate's Evoque and walked towards where her old beach house stood. The one that Bruce built for her.

* * *

"Lady Carmichael."

Kate's head whipped round to face a tall man with a beard and buzz-cut.

"You shouldn't be alone. Now, if you'll just come with us." His voice was polite but firm. "If you were hoping to meet Lord Carmichael, he's not here. We have been waiting for one of you to turn up. I can tell you that we wounded him. He was unconscious in a ditch, but he disappeared."

* * *

Jasper waited for number four to settle in before he slipped out of the beach house.

The man had lit a spliff and placed his phone and gun beside him. Catlike, Jasper approached him from behind. His large hands spanned the man's neck, and within seconds, number four lay next to the phone and gun, dead.

Jasper picked up the gun and checked it over before moving towards the three men that surrounded Kate. Without hesitation, he shot each man in the head.

Jasper's heart stuttered as he met Kate's innocent, water-filled eyes. She ran to him and flung her arms around his neck. Their lips hungrily met.

"I thought I would be safe," she said.

"The Carringtons and Von-Pitt won't stop until you're dead."

Kate stepped back and stared at his face. "You're hurt."

"Not so much that I can't protect you."

Kate slipped his coat off her shoulders and wrapped it around him.

He pulled her into him. "Kate, I didn't want our parting to be like this."

"What do you mean?"

"The Carringtons are too big and resourceful for me to take on, especially now they've joined forces with Von-Pitt. The smart thing for me to do is to lie low and fight them when they're not expecting it."

Kate's body tensed. "You're going with her." The words fell from her mouth. She swallowed hard. "You are going to form a diamond partnership."

"I feel nothing for Margot. Only you have my heart."

She pushed him away from her. Thoughts of the time, all those years ago, that he had left her for diamonds flooded her mind. But she'd had Bruce, Clare and Malcolm for support then. This time she was alone.

She began to walk back to the Evoque.

"Kate, say something. Even if it's only 'fuck you'."

Kate didn't look behind her. She carried on walking, her mind trying to recall how many times he had left her. But she'd had dear Harry.

Tears ran down Jasper Carmichael's face as he watched the love of his life disappear.

Chapter Sixty-Six

A space had been cleared on the bench in Kate's studio for her to work on. She was eating breakfast when Robert announced Arthur's arrival.

"This is getting tiresome, Arthur."

"Sorry to disturb you but I would like a quick chat. Just the two of us." Arthur couldn't take his eyes off the documents that surrounded her. *What is she doing?* he thought, as a printer churned out more pieces of paper. "I can see that you're busy."

She pushed her glasses into her hair and closed her laptop. "Why do you keep coming here? Have your masters sent you?"

"There's no need to be like that, we have been friends since you had the flower shop."

"You weren't chief constable then."

Arthur pulled up a stool and sat opposite Kate. His eyes moved over the documents.

Kate began to collect them into a pile.

"You'll be having visitors."

"Is that supposed to frighten me?"

Ben and Robert walked in carrying a table.

"Will this do?" asked Ben. "Found it in one of those outbuildings."

"Push the chaise lounge to the far end, the table can go there."

Elsie joined them, carrying a tea tray.

"Elsie, bring Arthur a coffee."

"How do you concentrate with all this going on?" asked Arthur.

"I've been working most of the night. This takes my mind off things."

"Carrington has four men missing. The last he heard, they were tracking you to your old beach house."

Elsie slammed a mug of coffee in front of Arthur.

"Von-Pitt reckons that Jasper killed them and you know where he is," he said.

"Here we go again. Four men missing so Jasper must have killed them. Where's the proof, Arthur?"

"My men have been over the beach and they didn't find anything."

"That's hardly surprising; the sea washes over the beach twice a day."

"Why do you go back there?"

"I like to be alone."

* * *

Arthur met Phillip Carrington and Von-Pitt at the car park of the derelict riverside café.

"Well?" snapped an impatient Phillip.

"She's using her old studio as an office. The worktable was covered in documents. She collected them so I couldn't read them. What I can say is that she's not mooning over Jasper."

"Margot said he's irritable, but that might be his head injury. He sleeps a lot," offered Von-Pitt.

"Or he's had a row with the bitch," said Auntie, who had joined them from the Bentley. "Where's Jasper now?"

"He's going to the Caymans with Margot," said Von-Pitt.

"To do what?"

"Empty a safe deposit box."

"How did Kate look?" asked Phillip.

"Tired and preoccupied," said Arthur.

Auntie walked to the water's edge. "So, this is worth millions," she said, staring at the river.

"She owns or part-owns all you can see. Turn around and she owns all you can see," said Phillip.

"And you say she's not a shrewd businesswoman."

"Kate is driven by emotion not business," said Phillip.

"How the fuck did she get all this then?"

Phillip took a step away from Auntie; he had no desire to be in the firing line of her temper.

"No one was interested in this place, and Kate didn't want it to go to a developer," said Arthur.

Auntie turned to face him. "What's your opinion of her as a businesswoman?"

"She saved the flower shop from bankruptcy and turned it into a profit-making concern. She held on to it as Carmichael Properties bought up all the shops around it."

"I would say that Lady Carmichael is a shrewd businesswoman," Auntie said. "She hung on to the flower shop until Carmichael had to pay top dollar. She's hanging on to this to reap the benefits of her investment."

"She hasn't the funds to develop it," said Phillip, following Auntie back to the car. "She would need a financial consortium to back her."

Auntie closed the rear door of the Bentley and wound the window down. "We have no idea how much she's worth, and we have no idea if she has Jasper's diamonds along with his records. All we know is that she hasn't moved any money from her Cayman Islands account, she's familiar with Jasper's business, she's his accountant and she rescued Harry's diamond jewellery business."

Auntie hit the shoulder of her driver. "My gut tells me that Lady Carmichael is an exceptional businesswoman. One we should be wary of."

The rear window closed.

Auntie stared at the back of her driver. Thoughts of Lady Carmichael swished about her brain. *A woman who' more than capable of taking over the Carrington business. A woman who's content with being the second in command. Kate may have been an innocent once, but she has developed into a ruthless businesswoman.*

Chapter Sixty-Seven

Jasper Carmichael was sitting enjoying the warm Cayman Islands sun and sipping an espresso while waiting for Margot. He was bored with Margot; her knowledge of the diamond trade was poor, and his dick wasn't interested. It had been her idea to come to the Cayman Islands so he could transfer money into her business.

His interest was piqued when the hotel concierge and a porter ran to the kerbside as a taxi arrived. He was more than a little interested to find out who commanded such attention. The concierge opened the rear door, and the porter lifted a large white messenger bag from the boot.

The lady was strikingly beautiful. Her white heels emphasised her legs to best effect; her silver, shoulder-length hair shone; her green eyes sparkled; a white V-neck dress fell over her curves. She smiled as she flicked her hair back.

Heads turned as she walked into the hotel.

Who can blame them? Jasper thought. *They are staring at an aristocratic beauty.* He shifted in his seat; his shorts became uncomfortable as he watched his wife walk into the hotel. *But why is she in the Cayman Islands?*

An out-of-breath Margot slipped into a seat beside him. "There's a big kerfuffle in the shops. A rich woman has just arrived. No one knows who she is." She gasped for breath and swung her designer bags onto the table. "Did you see her?"

Jasper glanced at Margot. Her hair was stiff, not like Kate's; she looked as if she had been poured into her dress, not like Kate; her feet were too big for her shoes, not like Kate's; she had so much make-up on her face that if she smiled it would crack. But above all, his erection had shrunk.

"I've got to phone Von-Pitt and tell him we have another prospective victim," she said as she rummaged in her bag. "Have you seen my phone?"

While Margot slept, Jasper had dropped it into the sea after transferring all her contacts onto his own phone.

"You know, you should see a doctor about your erectile dysfunction. I haven't had a good fuck for ages."

"My what?"

"I'm not like her, I need a good fuck."

"You uncouth bitch. You like to make people believe you're refined, but you're as common as muck."

"You should talk! The great lover Jasper Carmichael can't get it up."

An old Rolls Royce stopped outside the hotel and Kate got in. She had changed into a white shorts suit. The jacket was open, revealing a waistcoat open to her cleavage. The concierge handed her a white messenger bag.

"There she is!" exclaimed Margot as the Rolls pulled away. "Where the fuck is she going?"

To the bank, thought Jasper. *To protect her money and empty her security box.*

* * *

Kate didn't return to the hotel; the room, booked under an alias, was a ruse to throw off anybody who might be following her. From the bank, she went to the private airfield and the waiting jet. As she nestled into a seat, she reflected on what she had done.

The bank manager had been very obliging, but Kate put that down to the diamonds she had given him. From her messenger bag, she had withdrawn her laptop. The transfer of her money from one account to another went smoothly. The diamonds and cash from her security box were now in her messenger bag; they would be hidden, along with the remainder of Zak Cohen's cash and diamonds, and the diamonds Jasper had given her for safekeeping, in the secret compartment in Isaacs House's small library. The diamonds she had used to pay the pilot, cabin crew and customs man were from Jasper's diamond office.

Ben was waiting for her when the private jet landed. He didn't ask questions as they left for Isaacs House.

"Did you buy a Ford Focus?" she asked.

"Yep. Given it a service. Filled it with petrol. It's in the outbuilding."

* * *

Jasper and Margot were on the first available flight back to the UK. He hadn't told her that Kate had been in the Caymans. He suspected that Kate was going to take on the Carringtons, Von-Pitt and the Lords Blackthorn, Ambrose and Devon. He had to stop her because she wouldn't win. They would destroy her.

Chapter Sixty-Eight

While Jasper was on a plane, Kate was breaking into Margot's Wellsbury apartment. It was easy; she had the alarm code and safe combination from Whizz Kid's app. From the safe, she took diamonds, cash and a red notebook.

She stood by the open bedroom door, then hesitantly walked in. Deep down, she knew it was a mistake, but curiosity got the better of her. The room smelt of sex and Jasper's aftershave. Even without the lights, she could see that the room was in chaos—bed unmade and clothes strewn over the carpet. She opened a small wardrobe; his clothes were neatly arranged inside. Tears filled her eyes and her stomach nervously churned as she turned to face the bed. Her iPhone camera flashed.

By the time she reached the car, tears were dripping off her chin. Images of Jasper making love to Margot flashed through her mind. How many times had he whispered *"Only you, Kate. I love only you"*? And she had believed him.

She was still sobbing when she parked the Focus in the workshop.

Ben was standing in the shadows waiting for her. He watched as she leaned on the car, her body shaking as she cried. He wanted to comfort her, but she wouldn't want him to do that. The man she wanted preferred another woman.

If only I was lucky enough to have a woman like Kate love me, he thought.

* * *

"I'm ready!" shouted Little Jasper. "Are you coming?"

Kate was gazing out of the studio's doors. "I wouldn't miss it for the world."

He grinned and wrapped his arms about her waist. "Love you, Gran!" He ran into the kitchen.

Ben was waiting by the Evoque. "Thought I'd take some of the driving off you," he said as Little Jasper climbed onto the back seat. "Traffic is always heavy around the school."

All Kate could manage was a half-smile and a nod. She felt physically ill. Ben and the rest of the staff had noticed how tired she looked and that she wasn't eating again.

Kate walked with Little Jasper to the school gates, just as she had done with Harry and Oliver. But Little Jasper turned and waved, something her sons never had done.

"Office or home?" Ben asked as they joined the slow-moving traffic.

"Office. I should pick up the mail and have a word with Godfrey before he comes knocking on the door."

Ben turned towards the rear of the building.

"Go to the front. I want to be seen."

Kate punched the code into the control panel of the traffic bollards, and they lowered.

"I'll walk," she shouted to Ben.

Jasper was sitting in the bistro opposite Kate's office, sipping coffee. Margot was sleeping, but he didn't need sleep. He needed Kate.

"Kate," called Godfrey, "a word. What's happening with those three units? Work's stopped. Rumour has it that you have run out of funds."

Kate turned. "That's fake news. Work will resume shortly." She disappeared into the office and came out carrying a pile of mail.

Jasper had left the bistro by the time Kate returned to the car.

"Jasper was over the road," said Ben as Kate got in the passenger side.

"Were the rest of them with him?"

"No. He was alone."

When the Evoque pulled into Isaacs House, Jasper had his hands on the bars of the electric gate.

"I'll deal with this, Ben," said Kate.

Jasper turned to face the car as it stopped. His blue eyes were on fire and his cheeks were bright red. "He fucking won't let me in," he angrily said.

"I told him not to."

"What? I live here."

"No, you don't. You live with Margot."

Kate's calm voice irritated Jasper. "You're my wife."

"You can correct that any time you like."

Jasper took a step back and tried to calm himself. *She knows*, he thought.

"I can start proceedings, if you like. Of course, I'll name Margot. If you agree, we'll be free of each other in no time at all."

"I don't want a divorce."

"Think of that the next time you're fucking the living daylights out of her."

"Kate, this isn't you."

"Get used to it."

"I love you."

"Do you say that to her?" she snapped as she stormed through the gate. She didn't want him to see her tears.

Jasper was speechless. All he could do was stare at Kate's back. How did she know he had told Margot he loved her? Did she know it was only to get her trust and diamonds?

A taxi screeched to a halt and Margot ran out. "What did the bitch say? Has she agreed to a divorce?"

Jasper stared at the house he had bought for Kate to show his love. How happy she had been. They had loved, argued and had the most wonderful sex in that house. If only he could turn back the clock.

* * *

A church clock struck two as Lords Ambrose and Devon, Von-Pitt, Margot and Jasper gathered at the Carringtons' London house. Auntie and Phillip sat at the head of the table.

"Report, Ambrose?"

"Nothing."

"Von-Pitt?"

"Nothing."

"Margot?"

"I haven't checked. I've been busy."

"Busy fucking, no doubt," commented Von-Pitt.

"Jasper?" Auntie continued.

"If Kate has my diamonds, I've got to break in. And that's not going to be easy. By now, the security system will have been improved."

"You seem to be very confident in your wife's abilities," said Auntie.

"I know my wife. She's backed into a corner; she'll come out fighting. I was your only hope of controlling her. She's not interested in diamonds or being a Landon or Carrington. She wants to be left alone to live her life as she wants." Jasper stood and placed his hands on the table. "If you lot hadn't interfered, I would have had a lucrative diamond network, and you would have had Wellsbury."

Jasper kicked his chair out of his way and walked to the door. Margot jumped up and followed him.

The journey back to Wellsbury was a silent one. Margot had never seen Jasper like this; he frightened her.

Jasper opened the apartment door, and Margot raced to her safe.

"They're gone! My red book is gone!"

Jasper put his hand into the safe, searching for the diamonds. "Fuck."

* * *

While Jasper and Margot were pondering the loss of Margot's diamonds, Kate was following the instructions from Whizz Kid's app. She wasn't surprised to find that Lords Ambrose and Devon had substantial funds in their personal bank accounts while the Gentlemen's Club was in the red. She had just finished transferring funds from their accounts into the club account when she received another message from Whizz Kid.

This was recorded earlier from their meeting.

We mustn't judge yet, but don't trust Jasper. He could be on your side—after all, he is in love with you—or he could be a double agent. But, knowing Jasper, he's on Jasper's side.

If it's not too much for you to cope with, I'd like to buy you dinner when this is all over.

Suddenly, she heard Jasper's voice.

"I know my wife. She's backed into a corner; she'll come out fighting. I was your only hope of

controlling her. She's not interested in diamonds or being a Landon or Carrington. She wants to be left alone to live her life as she wants."

She heard the sound of a chair moving.

"If you lot hadn't interfered, I would have had a lucrative diamond network, and you would have had Wellsbury."

Kate welled up.

Chapter Sixty-Nine

The Gentlemen's Club accountant was dreading the morning AGM meeting. How could he explain to the members that the club was on the verge of bankruptcy? He opened the bank account to check his figures before printing off his report. He stopped and stared. The balance, instead of being in debit, was in credit. His eyes scanned the columns of figures, looking for a mistake, when he spotted there had been two large deposits.

He called the bank to make sure they hadn't been a mistake. Miraculously, the club had become solvent.

He didn't concern himself with where the money had come from; he pressed "print", and the pages of the revised annual report filled the out tray.

* * *

Phillip Carrington was leaving the Carringtons' London house when his phone rang.

"Yes, what is it?" he snapped.

Margot was crying. *"The diamonds are gone, with my red book."*

Phillip hit the brakes and reversed to the front door. "Are you sure?"

"Of course I'm bloody sure. Jasper's gone berserk."

Phillip ran through the house to Auntie's office. As he got to the door, his phone rang again. It was Lord Ambrose.

"Our personal accounts have been emptied, and the club is solvent."

Phillip ended the call and marched into Auntie's office. Auntie stared at the distressed Phillip as she stood from her desk.

"Margot's diamonds are gone, and Lords Ambrose and Devon have apparently just saved the Gentlemen's Club from bankruptcy."

"Fuck. Fuck!" she shouted as her arm cleared the desk of papers. She slumped back into her leather desk chair. "So, Miss Innocent is attacking, just like Jasper predicted."

Phillip had never seen Auntie like this. He began to pick up the papers that were scattered over the floor. His eyes quickly scanned them; they all had the heading "Final Demand" in red. One in particular caught his eye:

Demand for mortgage repayment from a South American solicitor.

"You remortgaged Carrington Towers?"

"I had no choice."

"Who is Anton Perez?"

"You don't want to know."

"Is there anything left?"

"Isabel's trust fund for her son, now her granddaughter. Isabel was always difficult. Her fund can only go to her blood. I can't touch it."

"Who knows about Isabel's trust fund?"

"No one except me and our solicitors, Sinclair's law firm."

"Is there anyway Kate could find out about it?"

She hesitated. "No, all copies of Isabel's papers have been destroyed…"

"I sense a 'but'."

"Isabel's private papers were missing from Landon Hall."

"Shit. So there could be a copy hanging around."

"Look, all that's immaterial if I can't get a loan."

"The house of cards is falling down, Auntie."

"We have never been this close to losing everything."

"Why bother with the Wellsbury project?"

"Perception. If we start on a long-term project, investors will assume that we are solvent, and the rumours will be forgotten."

"But they know we are involved with scum like Von-Pitt?"

"That is not public knowledge. The idea was to use his money, with Margot's and Jasper's diamonds, to get us out of this cesspit."

Phillip sat in one of the Chesterfield chairs. "But we don't have diamonds, and I have a feeling Von-Pitt doesn't have money. We are well and truly fucked."

* * *

Jasper Carmichael had spent the night in a stolen Ford Focus parked in the street that led to Little Jasper's school.

The Evoque went past him; Kate was driving.

Where's Ben? he thought.

She stopped in the drop-off lay-by and followed Little Jasper to the school.

Jasper's eyes never left her as she returned to the car and filtered into the line of school traffic.

He became impatient as he crawled in the traffic towards Wellsbury. He could just see the Evoque stopped at the junction, but he couldn't tell whether she turned right or left.

By the time he got to the junction, there was no sign of the Evoque. He thumped the steering wheel and cursed.

* * *

The Evoque had left Wellsbury and travelled to the country offices of Sinclair Law.

Kate stopped at the high, steel gates. A camera was focused on her.

A voice came from a security box. "Name?"

"Lady Carmichael."

The gates opened, and she followed the "Visitors" signs.

Two men watched her park and lean on the driver's door to change her shoes, then walk to the front door, carrying her black messenger bag.

"So, that's Lady Carmichael," said the younger of the two.

"No, my boy, that's the living image of Isabel Carrington, aka Lady Landon. Today, we will have to tread carefully. There are murmurings that she's at war with the Carringtons over some land she owns—it's all a bit hush-hush due to the Carringtons' financial problems. Of course, Lady C is the true heir to the Carrington and Landon estates; none of the pretenders have a legal claim like Lady C.

"The stakes are high, and the trick is to be on the winning side. We have to decide that today. I have it on good authority that Lady C has no knowledge of her trust fund and that all copies of Lady Isabel's will, except the one in our safe, have been destroyed. But her granddaughter is a very determined lady with a hidden ruthlessness. At the end of the day, we will be working for one of two Carringtons—if not both."

* * *

Three hours later, Kate was sitting outside a pub drinking a pint of shandy. She needed time to reflect on the meeting with the two Sinclairs.

She opened her laptop and began to type.

There were two Sinclairs in the meeting, both called Peregrine. The younger insisted that I called him Perry.

The elder Peregrine turned the conversation to Lady Isabel. "Back in the day," he recalled, "when I was a mere boy, I fancied Isabel. A beauty and a Carrington; they didn't come much better. But an American swept her off her feet."

When I produced documents copied from the ones I took from Isabel's bedroom proving I am the heir to the Landon estate, he declared that there was "No need for those, we all know who you are. That is, the members of the Gentlemen's Club."

Perry, the younger Sinclair, continually tried to turn the conversation to Landon Hall. He left the meeting a couple of times, leaving Peregrine to reminisce about "the good old days".

Peregrine told me there was a group of them at university that shared the same women, competed in the same sports and exams. Apparently, over the years it hasn't changed much; they still share women, but compete in the world of law. Perry is the result of such a liaison. His mother was Peregrine's lover for years. She brought him to the house one day and said, "Peregrine, meet Peregrine."

Perry phoned the Landons' solicitors and confirmed that Landon Hall is still for sale as no money has changed hands. I instructed him to make a claim that I'm the rightful owner of the Landon estate, including the hall.

I can't decide if it was a good idea to hire Sinclair Law. Peregrine is a wry old fox; it's difficult to pin him down. Perry is his apprentice. A big plus is that they seem very discreet, and they operate from a country mansion, not a big city office, where I could be seen.

They were reluctant to discuss money.

Kate closed her laptop, finished her shandy and drove back to Wellsbury.

Chapter Seventy

The night was cool and still when Kate parked the Evoque at her old thinking spot, the confluence of the rivers Wells and Bury. Her thinking bench was in ruins, but there was still a grassy path that led to the old river café.

She was very troubled. She longed for the sea, but the river would have to do. Her pace was slow and her thoughts were heavy—until she heard voices carried on the wind.

She stopped and waited until she heard them again.

"Landon Hall is her birthright." Kate recognised Jasper's voice. "I couldn't give a flying fuck that Von-Pitt's drug business is finished."

The moon popped out from behind a cloud, and Kate moved into the bushes to get closer to the voices.

Jasper and Phillip Carrington were having a heated conversation.

"Von-Pitt is a vital part in our development of this site," said Phillip.

"What the hell do you mean by that? You can't trust him. You must be desperate."

Jasper stepped away from Phillip. "I know you need money, and he needed the drug business to pay off his creditors." He paused. "And to join the Carrington family's latest project." Jasper ran his hand through his hair. "Let me try and put in all the pieces of this puzzle: Von-Pitt's been selling diamonds, paintings, anything to repay his creditors; Kate foiled his drugs business in the shopping centre and at Landon Hall; he has been unsuccessful in getting her to sell; he came to you for a loan and told you about his plans for Wellsbury, which you saw as the answer to your cash flow problems."

"You couldn't be more wrong, Carmichael."

Jasper ran his hand around his chin. "You needed diamonds, so you sent Margot to persuade me to trade mine. You were going to use the Gentlemen's Club as a fence, but that's when you found out it was nearly bankrupt. Every way you turned, Kate was involved. She saved the shopping centre from Von-Pitt; she wouldn't save the Landon Trust Fund; she wouldn't sell her properties; she wouldn't accept that her grandparents were Lord and Lady Landon. You've even tried to kill her twice. But you killed her son, Harry. She'll never forgive you." Jasper twirled and clapped his hands. "Kate is the blood heir to the Landon and Carrington estates! What are you hiding, Carrington?"

"You don't know what you're talking about, Carmichael. There are many heirs to the estate."

"It all fits. The Carringtons are behind this massive, duplicitous con. You owe money big time, probably got a loan to fill the hole. Why else would you involve Von-Pitt, Their Lordships, Margot and me? Von-Pitt approached you for a loan for his Wellsbury project, but instead of lending him money, you want his! What a shock you must have had when you realised he had none, that he *owed* money."

"You're making this up. You have no proof."

"It's always been smoke and mirrors with you Carringtons; you hide behind a veil of secrecy.

Is there anything left of the Landon-Carrington legacy?"

"All that we can touch, we have."

"That means there's some part of the legacy you can't touch... probably a trust fund that only Carrington blood can touch. Kate."

* * *

Kate stumbled. Her hand reach for a tree, but her legs buckled and she slumped to the ground. She fought to breathe as a waterfall of tears covered her mouth.

She didn't hear their cars leave; all she could think of was her beloved son, killed at the hands of the people that now wanted her dead. Harry was sacrificed for her.

The drive back to Isaacs House was a blur. She saw the staff staring, and heard Little Jasper crying, "Gran!"

She didn't stop. She couldn't speak. She was consumed by thoughts of revenge for Harry.

She went to her en suite bathroom and sat under a shower of warm water. Scratches from the undergrowth covered her face and body, and her hair was tangled with twigs.

She wrapped herself in a large towel, and slept.

* * *

It was midday when she left the bedroom. Little Jasper was waiting. He ran to her and wrapped his arms around her waist.

"Come," she said to the staff. "I have something to tell you all."

They all sat in the overstuffed chairs in the living room.

"I, er, I'm going to ask for your loyalty and support. It may require you to lie for me. I know it's a lot to ask. If you feel that you can't do it, there will be no hard feelings on my part."

"Can you tell us more?" asked Robert.

"I have been subjected to emotional pressure from various people for far too long and it's got to change. It appears that Wellsbury has become the jewel in the crown for some people, and when Jasper left, I was expected to just give in. However, I own the most sought-after jewels and I'm not going to sell them."

"We all know the pressure you've been under," said Robert. "If it wasn't for you, we would have all been burnt to death. You can rely on our support."

Kate sighed. "I'm going to lock myself in my studio. I have something I must do that requires concentration. If there are visitors or enquiries, say I'm not well, that I've caught a stomach bug or something. Little Jasper can stay away from school."

"How long to you anticipate being in the studio?" asked Robert.

"No more than a week. I would appreciate food and tea," she said with a smile. Then the smile faded. "I'm relying on you to keep this secret."

Chapter Seventy-One

One by one, they all took their seats at the grand oak table at Carrington Towers, the home and headquarters of the Carrington family. A tired looking Auntie sat at the head; Phillip, her heir apparent, sat next to her; Their Lordships, Blackthorn, Ambrose and Devon, sat along one side of the table; and Von-Pitt, Margot and Arthur sat the other side.

A heavy silence filled the room as they waited for Auntie to speak.

"It's fair to say that Lady Carmichael, Kate, is responsible for your financial problems. None of you listened to me. Margot has lost her diamonds, Von-Pitt's lost Landon Hall and his drug operation, Lords Ambrose and Devon have lost their fortunes to the Gentlemen's Club. Lord Blackthorn and Arthur have been busy trying to hide theirs. We are expecting her to attack the Carrington banking assets as well, but for the moment she has left us alone.

"It's come to our attention that she visited the Cayman Islands. She closed one bank account and opened another. Her Swiss bank account remains but is not being used. We are trying to find all her accounts, but that will take time. Time we don't have."

"Where is she getting all the information from?" asked a subdued Von-Pitt.

"We don't know," said Phillip. "It could be internet searches."

"She has made a mistake by contacting the trustees of the Landon estate," said Auntie. "It's public knowledge now that she is the grandchild of Lord and Lady Landon. She has become fair game for the media."

"Where's Carmichael?" asked Von-Pitt.

"Gone," said Margot.

"If you have any money in the NRJ bank, move it," said Auntie.

"Too late," said Lord Blackthorn, looking at his phone. "NRJ has just announced that their system has had a serious cyberattack. Too early to say how many accounts have been hacked."

"I assume that we all have lost money," Auntie said.

* * *

On the off-chance, Kate had checked the NRJ accounts of her adversaries: Von-Pitt, Margot, Lord Blackthorn and the Carringtons. The bank gave high interest rates but poor security.

Will they never learn? she thought as she emptied their accounts.

* * *

Jasper sat on Carmichael Castle's quadbike with his binoculars trained on the construction company tearing down Von-Pitt's drug workshops.

He had fled to his ancestral home after he left Phillip Carrington. He had taken on the disguise of the groundsman.

* * *

Kate worked into the small hours, studying Whizz Kid's file on the Carringtons. She didn't want to mess around hitting their peripheral assets; she wanted to go for the jugular, and that was proving to be difficult. The Carringtons had woven a complicated web of false companies with fictitious assets that led to a shell company.

In frustration, she typed her name into the search engine.

Lady Carmichael, née Reynolds, Kate – birthplace: Wellsbury – married Lord Jasper Carmichael – two sons, both deceased.

Mother: Laura Spencer, deceased – Grandfather: Meredith Spencer, lawyer, deceased – Father: Henry Landon Jr., deceased – Grandfather: Lord Henry Landon, diamond dealer, deceased – Grandmother: Lady Isabel Landon, née Carrington, heir to the Carrington fortune, deceased.

Kate was sure that she had seen a copy of Lady Isabel's will in the papers from Landon Hall. At the bottom of the box file that contained the papers was a sealed envelope.

Last Will and Testament of Lady Isabel Landon, née Carrington.

Peregrine, Sinclair Law.

Kate's hands shook as she read. Bank accounts, jewellery, diamonds, sapphires, shares in companies, a book collection—all bequeathed to Kate Reynolds, granddaughter.

There were strict, sealed instructions about a trust fund. Lady Isabel had been a rich woman.

There was also a handwritten note.

My dearest Kate,

My heart is bursting with love for you. My greatest wish was to walk with you, share a meal, go shopping. But alas, that was never to be.

My son, Henry, is your father, and Laura Spencer is your mother. You are their love child.

Forgive me for letting Lord Henry talk me into letting Reynolds look after you. If you had been a boy, I'm sure life would have been very different.

I've tried many times to see you and been thwarted. I'm old now, and the fight has gone out of me since my beloved Henry left me. It won't be long before I join him. But I have managed one last trip to Landon Hall.

If you're reading this, you have found the secret compartment in my desk. Press hard on the back and you'll find my most precious jewellery and the most valuable of Henry's diamonds. They are yours, along with the trust fund I have set up.

My dying wish is that you honour your Carrington bloodline. Many years ago, the first Carrington decreed that the Towers was only to be owned by Carrington blood. I forfeited that right when I married Henry, but if the bloodline is followed, you are the rightful owner of Carrington Towers.

With all my heart, I hope you are loved like Henry loved me.

All my love, your grandmother, Isabel.

Kate leaned back in her chair and cried.

Chapter Seventy-Two

Robert gently moved Kate's shoulder. "Lady Carmichael," he said.

Kate's head was lying across her laptop. She opened one eye.

"It may be a good idea to rest in bed."

Robert's words floated over her head.

"You've hardly slept and eaten. We are worried about you."

Kate slowly lifted her head. She had a thumping headache and her watery eyes were stinging. "What time is it?"

"Eight."

"I'll have breakfast after I've showered." She tried to stand but lost her balance.

Robert gripped her arm. "You can't go on like this. You must rest."

"I've got to finish it, Robert. Open the bifold doors. I'll have breakfast outside."

* * *

Jasper Carmichael drove the quadbike to Landon Hall.

"What's going on here, mate?" he said to one of the workmen.

"Waiting for the new owner. She's supposed to come yesterday."

Jasper nodded. "What's happening over there?"

"Flattening all those workshops. Wicked shame, but she wants them destroyed."

A white van stopped in front of the hall.

"About bloody time," said the workman, marching over to it.

Wes Clayton and his team of six men jumped out of the van. The Clayton pickup pulled in behind them.

"Come on," said the workman to the men as he headed to the hall.

The Clayton team followed, carrying boxes.

Jasper started the quadbike; he'd seen enough. Kate was moving the Landon books.

Wes turned as Jasper drove away. "Who's that?" he asked the workman.

"A nobody, poking his fucking nose."

"Where's he from?"

"Carmichael's Castle. General dogsbody."

* * *

Kate, fortified by fresh air, tea and a bacon and egg breakfast, left the paperwork for a drive to Landon Hall.

* * *

Jasper's gut told him Wes Clayton had recognised him. He parked the quadbike in the workshop and checked how many cars were parked outside the apartment building.

The first empty apartment he broke into only had a small amount of cash, but in the second and third there was jewellery as well.

He quickly showered, cleaned his room and wiped the quadbike clean. His gardening clothes and towels he burnt on the smouldering bonfire.

He took his wedding ring off and placed it in a used jiffy bag with a short note.

Look after it for me.

The wolves are circling. They want revenge for my past deeds.

I love only you, Kate, and that's never going to change. I would ask you to wait for me but I'm going to be away a long time. I'll be as jealous as hell of the man you share a bed with.

All my love.

Jasper handed the jiffy bag to the clerk at the sub-post office. "First class," he said. He pushed a ten-pound note through the opening in the glass screen.

Jasper's eyes never left the jiffy bag as the clerk dropped it into the letter sack.

As he walked back to the car, a white Evoque flashed by him. He would know his beloved anywhere, and she was driving unusually fast. He wished he could follow, but the wolves were snapping at his heels.

Two hours later, Jasper parked the Range Rover in the yacht owner's car park of the marina he'd once owned. He scanned the moored yachts until he found one that would suit his needs.

With confident strides, he walked to the yacht and dropped his bag on the bridge. He fired the engine and slowly moved out of the marina.

* * *

While Jasper had been escaping England, Kate had been emptying the secret compartment in Lady Isabel's desk. She didn't have time to study the jewellery or the diamonds, she had to get back to Isaacs House and hide them.

Three hours later, Kate was back in her studio, studying the published accounts of the Carrington Company. She couldn't see anything wrong with them until she read "Anton Perez Holdings". It was the name "Anton" that shot shivers down her spine as memories emerged. She knew "Anton" as a South American businessman that dealt in diamonds, property, drugs and money laundering. Jasper had had dealings with him.

An internet search for "Anton Perez Holdings" was very brief: a South American property company. She couldn't find any photographs of Anton Perez, but she had a gut feeling he would resemble Jasper's Anton.

She closed her laptop, her mind mulling over what the Carringtons had to do with Anton.

Chapter Seventy-Three

"The chief constable is at the front door. He says he must speak to you," said Robert. "And this came for you."

Kate stared at the jiffy bag. Jasper's handwriting. "Put Arthur in the living room and offer him coffee."

Kate opened the bag and out dropped Jasper's wedding ring and the note. She welled up.

An image of him filled her mind. He was walking out of the sea; she was painting in a flimsy dress. She couldn't take her eyes off him—the broad, muscular, tanned chest with beads of seawater dripping from him. His blue eyes shone with desire and his face was alight with the irresistible Carmichael smile. He slowly took the brush from her hand as he kissed her. Her dress floated onto the sand and he lowered her onto a large towel.

She walked into the living room still thinking of Jasper, but it wasn't him she was looking at but Chief Constable Arthur.

Arthur placed his coffee on the table and stood. "Kate, I'm here as a friend. If you have any idea where Jasper is, tell me, for his own good."

Kate sat opposite Arthur and poured herself a tea. "Arthur, I have no idea. Jasper just left."

"He always contacts you."

She had no intention of mentioning Jasper's note. *I love only you, Kate.*

"Phillip Carrington and Von-Pitt have joined forces to hunt him down. They intend for him to pay for his crimes."

The wolves are circling, Kate. They want revenge for my past deeds.

"Lord Blackthorn is singing like a canary," Arthur continued. "They have men everywhere. Jasper was seen at Carmichael Castle, posing as a handyman; he was seen at Landon Hall; he stole jewellery from several apartments. His Range Rover has been found at the marina and a yacht is missing."

"I don't understand why there's a manhunt."

"They claim he's fiddled them out of diamonds, but that doesn't make sense. Why would he then steal from the apartment owners?"

"Where does Lord Blackthorn fit into this?"

"He's maintaining that Jasper stole diamonds from him and his clients."

You'll regret this, Blackthorn, Kate thought. "This is news to me."

"If he's got a yacht, where would he be going?"

The Greek cottage flashed into her mind. She was lying naked across his chest, his fingers caressing her back. "My guess is Europe, but the yacht may be a ploy to fool you all."

"So, do you think he could still be here?"

"Arthur, he could be anywhere. Jasper is a master at deception."

I would ask you to wait for me but I'm going to be away a long time.

* * *

Phillip Carrington, Von-Pitt and Lord Blackthorn were waiting for Arthur.

"Well?" snapped Von-Pitt.

"She knows nothing. I told her more. Jasper just left."

"Did she ask about me?" said Lord Blackthorn.

"No," Arthur lied.

"What is she working on?" Phillip Carrington's voice had an edge to it.

"Didn't see. Robert showed me into the living room."

"Diamonds? Did she mention diamonds?" asked an anxious Von-Pitt.

"Kate doesn't do diamonds."

* * *

Before Arthur had reached Wellsbury, Kate had reviewed Lord Blackthorn's, Phillip Carrington's and Von-Pitt's NRJ accounts. All three had safety deposit boxes at the Wellsbury branch. Lord Blackthorn, number ten; Von-Pitt, number three; Carrington, number eleven; Jasper Carmichael, number one.

Jasper had given her two keys to his safety deposit box. *"This is for my box, and this is the bank's key. NRJ breaks all the rules; there are two keys. The bank has a master key for all the boxes, while all the customers' keys are the same."*

She changed into her more formal "Lady Carmichael clothes" and drove to the Wellsbury branch of the NRJ bank. She parked the Evoque in the visitor's car park and confidently walked into the building.

Her grey skirt was above the knee, showing off her legs, and her white blouse was open to her cleavage. A Mr Smith hurried to greet her, his hungry eyes travelling up and down her body. His sweaty hand clasped hers as he craned his neck to look down her cleavage. She began to feel sick.

On the way to the safety deposit boxes, Mr Smith explained their security setup. He pressed a switch, and the steel doors to safety deposit box area opened.

Kate noticed that above the door switch was another switch labelled "Camera". *Sloppy and careless*, she thought.

As he gave opening the door his complete attention, Kate switched the cameras off.

They turned the keys to Jasper's box at the same time. Kate made a display of turning the key just enough for her blouse to open and show the top of her white lace bra. Beads of sweat formed on Mr Smith's forehead.

"Excuse me, Lady Carmichael," he said, adjusting his trousers and leaving the room.

Kate slipped off her heels and opened all four boxes. She brought her briefcase over and emptied their contents into it.

She was just closing Jasper's box when Mr Smith returned. She ran her hands down her skirt and smiled at Mr Smith as she slipped her shoes back on.

Smith was beside himself as she stood close beside him as he locked the steel doors. Discreetly, she switched the cameras back on.

"Tea, Lady Carmichael? Or probably something stronger?"

Kate was about to politely decline when the receptionist joined them.

"Head office on the phone, Mr Smith."

"Rain check, Mr Smith?" said Kate.

A disappointed Mr Smith nodded.

He gazed out of his office window at Kate putting her briefcase on the back seat of her car, changing her shoes and stepping into the driver's seat. Her skirt moved up to her thighs when she stretched to close the door.

"Smith, are you bloody listening?" bellowed a stern voice down the phone.

"Yes. Yes, sir."

"Till tomorrow, then."

Chapter Seventy-Four

Lord Blackthorn's safety deposit box had contained a black velvet wallet with a diamond-studded necklace inside, six bags of diamonds and a black notebook; Von-Pitt's box had diamonds, cash and a notebook; Carrington's box was full of used fifty-pound notes and a black notebook. Kate hid the cash and diamonds in the small library at Isaacs House.

The notebooks she moved into her studio, to read. She was looking for one named "Anton Perez". She got lucky with Carrington's book. The Carringtons had borrowed five million pounds off Perez; the collateral was Carrington Towers.

A slip of paper fell from the notebook.

JC finished valuing the diamonds. Over five mill.

Her heart raced with nervous energy and her hand shook as she opened Lord Blackthorn's notebook. It consisted of columns of dates, diamond IDs and valuations by "JC".

Jasper was valuing diamonds for Carrington to pay Anton Perez.

* * *

"Are you sure that's Lady Carmichael's car?" asked Anton Perez, staring at Kate's Evoque parked in front of the shopping centre office.

"I'm positive. That's what she drove to my office," answered Peregrine Sinclair as he guided Anton to the hotel's restaurant for lunch.

Von-Pitt stood and waved to them. He had arrived early to reserve a table.

The wine waiter appeared and dropped the wine list onto the table before rushing to the restaurant door.

"What the—?" exclaimed Peregrine as he turned to see Kate talking to the concierge.

"That is her," said Anton in disbelief as the three men watched Kate being directed to Jasper's reserved table. "Blue jeans, white fitted blouse, boots and a waistcoat."

"Forget her clothes," said Peregrine. "Von-Pitt, who is that at her table?"

A tall man with a full head of dark hair and rimless spectacles that hid the colour of his eyes. A radiant smile was kissing Kate's cheek.

The wine waiter poured red wine into their glasses and ignored Peregrine's table. Peregrine and Von-Pitt's displeasure increased as they watched Kate and her mystery guest talk and smile at each other.

"She is very attractive when she smiles," commented Anton.

* * *

"I've been trying to contact you all day," Von-Pitt snapped.

"I had urgent meetings," answered Phillip Carrington. He wasn't going to let on that he had been negotiating with their creditors.

"The bitch had lunch with a mystery man."

"Carmichael?"

"I don't think so."

Phillip's patience was non-existent. "Was it Carmichael?"

"He was tall, dark hair. Couldn't see his eyes, he wore glasses, but they never left her."

Phillip poured himself a large malt and slumped into his favourite leather chair. He put his phone on speaker. "Where's the search team?"

"Looking along the coast of France."

"How about the team here?"

"France."

"No one's watching her?" Phillip shouted.

* * *

The Evoque bounced along the lane to her beach house. Kate switched off the engine and lights.

She was pulled from the driver's seat and pinned against the side of the car.

"I want my Kate," he said as their lips crashed together. "I don't want Lady Carmichael." His fingers nimbly flicked a button of her blouse open. "I don't want Lady Landon." Another button opened as his lips caressed her neck. "I don't want Lady Carrington."

He whisked her into his arms and carried her to the beach.

"My Kate," he murmured as her clothes fell onto a blanket.

They lay naked on the blanket, his fingers brushing her hairline.

"My innocent Kate is changing."

"I've had a good teacher."

His lips kissed her eyes and cheeks before claiming her mouth. "This may be our last time, my love."

"Then love me, Jasper, as if it were the first time."

An invisible spark passed between them as their bodies touched. She rolled on top of him, kissing his chest. He rolled on top of her and sucked her nipples in turn.

She sighed. Her hands threaded through his hair as she wrapped her legs around him.

His lips slowly moved to her mouth. "Kate," he whispered as their tongues danced.

"Don't make me wait," she murmured.

She sighed as he inched inside her. Her hands were on his buttocks, coaxing him in.

His mouth covered hers as he slowly moved.

"Cum for me Kate. I need to feel your love." His thrusts became harder and deeper.

Her hands gripped his shoulders when the orgasmic wave moved through her. His movements quickened when she cried his name and fell into the abyss.

"Kate, my love." His words were soft and full of love. He wrapped her in his arms and waited while her heart slowed.

* * *

Dawn was breaking as they strolled, arms wrapped around each other, back to the Evoque.

"I've brought you something," she gulped, fighting back the tears. She knew this was goodbye and it was highly likely she would never see him again. She clicked open the attaché case. "There's your diamonds from River's End House; Lord Blackthorn and Margot were only too willing to help you out. I've divided the cash."

He pulled her into him and kissed her hair. "You're going after them?"

"I've got to stop them. I'm at my wit's end." She paused. "I can't keep denying who my father was.

Only the Carrington bloodline owns Carrington Towers."

"And that's you?"

"Yes."

"I've got to hide. The word's out. Phillip Carrington is willing to pay big money for me. He'll come after you. Divorce may be the price we pay for my freedom."

"Do you know Anton Perez?"

"No, but he sounds dangerous. Keep away from him."

"He owns the Carringtons."

"That must be where Phillip's getting his money from." His index finger stroked her forehead. "Kate, I sense you're in danger. And I can't help."

"Kiss me. It's going to have to last a long time."

Chapter Seventy-Five

The front doorbell at Isaacs House rang.

"Robert?" called Kate.

"A Mr Anton Perez to see you."

Kate hesitated; she hadn't been expecting him to call. "Show him into the living room."

When Kate joined him, Anton was staring at her paintings that were hanging on the living room walls. "I spent some time viewing your paintings in your small gallery," he said. "You have an alluring talent that captured my imagination." He turned to face her. "You are an unusual woman, if I might say so." He walked slowly to a seat and picked up his espresso, which Robert had placed on a small side table.

Kate sat opposite him.

"You are probably wondering why I'm here. I like to do business with the person who has the power to negotiate." He paused and ran his fingers along the side of his espresso glass. "The Carringtons have duped the true Carrington bloodline out of their birthright. You are that bloodline."

"What do you want?"

"I want you to buy the Carringtons' loan. Of course, there will be interest, but I want diamonds. Before you tell me you don't have diamonds, your husband does."

"How much?"

"Straight to the point. I like that. You disappeared yesterday, snuck out when you were sure you were not being watched. You went to meet him. You and Carmichael have an overpowering sexual attraction. You refer to it as love; I don't believe in love, but sex is another matter."

Kate's gut somersaulted. Her senses were on high alert. Was he guessing that she had seen Jasper or had he had her followed?

She had no intention of playing his games. She stood and went into her old office that was now being used as a storage room. She opened the wall safe and removed the diamonds.

Memories of Harry flashed through her mind as she opened the diamond box. There were two envelopes inside, one labelled "Fake" and the other with no label. She opened the fake envelope and removed a smaller white envelope from within it.

Returning to Anton, Kate slipped a white cotton glove on her hand. His eyes glowed as she slowly slipped the diamonds into her palm. She inwardly smiled; Anton had shown her his weakness.

"May I?"

Kate closed her fist.

He laughed. "Jasper's diamonds?"

"No. Mine."

"You are full of surprises, Lady Carmichael. Do you have a solicitor?"

"I will have."

"Not Mr Sinclair, I hope."

"Mr Sinclair has divided loyalties."

Anton smiled, reached inside his jacket and dropped a long brown envelope onto the table. "You have shown your hand, Lady Carmichael. I hope you won't regret it. In the envelope are copies of the documents proving I'm not lying. Will Jasper be involved?"

"I doubt it."

"Shame; I would love to meet him."

Robert and Ben joined Kate to watch Anton's car disappear.

"Can we increase security?" she asked.

"There's one or two things we can do," replied Ben.

"Do it."

Chapter Seventy-Six

Anton Perez gazed up at the Sinclair Law mansion. His meeting with Kate hadn't gone exactly to plan, but he was satisfied he had the upper hand.

The front doors of the mansion opened, and Perry Sinclair stepped out. "Mr Perez. Perry Sinclair. This way."

Anton followed him to a large office with a large fireplace, large desk, large free-standing safe and a large man, Peregrine Sinclair. Anton hated everything that Peregrine had achieved; he used the Sinclairs only because of their reputation of being the best where client confidentiality was concerned. He had experienced it first-hand when he was approached about the loan on Carrington Towers. Anton had been only too willing to help, providing he was given the Deeds to the Towers.

Anton sat opposite Peregrine with a contemptuous air he knew would irritate him. He had refused the offer of refreshment; he wasn't there to socialise.

"I want to view Landon Hall," he said. "I want to make an offer." Anton considered Landon Hall to be an ideal place for his UK business.

"It's not for sale," Peregrine warily said.

"She will sell. Everyone has a price."

"Is there something else?" asked Peregrine.

"She wants Carrington Towers and is willing to pay in diamonds."

"Are you sure? Jasper has left the country."

"She has diamonds; I've seen them. Prepare the necessary paperwork."

"Do you have a price in mind?"

"Twenty million."

Peregrine's mouth opened then closed.

"Don't look surprised; she will get some back from the sale of Landon Hall."

"That's a lot of diamonds."

"That is the idea. I've already put the word out so Jasper will know she is in trouble."

"We suspect Jasper is in Greece."

"I disagree. He's somewhere in the UK. They have already met; Lady Carmichael has that well-fucked look, and Carmichael is the only man who can give her that. They will meet again to satisfy their sexual needs, and I will be waiting." Anton's voice suddenly developed an angry tone. "I have a bone to pick with Jasper Carmichael."

* * *

Lord Jasper Carmichael strolled into the Gentlemen's Club as if he owned it. He said to the elderly doorman, "Tell Lord Ambrose I'm here to see him."

Minutes later, he sat opposite Lords Ambrose and Devon in Ambrose's private office.

"This better be good, Carmichael; there's money on your head," snapped Lord Ambrose.

Jasper emptied a bag of diamonds onto Lord Ambrose's desk. "I need you to fence these."

Lord Devon stretched across the desk and examined the diamonds with his eyeglass. "They're genuine," he said.

"I know about the rough deal you've had. This is between us, not the club." Jasper pushed a slip of paper across the desk. "The bank account number to pay the five mill into; phone number, just in case there's a problem. Don't try to double-cross me; I'll come after you and your precious club."

"Does Kate know you're here?" snapped Lord Ambrose.

"This has nothing to do with Kate."

Lord Devon leaned across the table, his chin hovering above the surface. "Do you know Anton Perez?"

Jasper shook his head. "Should I?"

Lord Devon's index finger circled the diamonds. "He owns Carrington Towers. Has the Deeds. She's willing to pay in diamonds."

Jasper began to feel uncomfortable.

"Peregrine Sinclair is representing him," Devon continued. "But Anton is becoming impatient. He wants Landon Hall for his business. Kate has workmen in there now; Lord Henry Landon's library is empty. Our source tells us she's been in the study and Lady Isabel's bedroom. Both rooms were locked."

Lord Ambrose pushed a photo towards Jasper. "Anton Perez."

Jasper's heart raced. *Anton? Anton's dead*, he thought, staring at the photograph. *Is Perez a grandson, grandnephew, a bastard son?* It didn't matter; Jasper knew what had to be done.

He rested a finger on the photo. "He has the Deed, you say? Surely Peregrine has them?"

"No. It never leaves Perez. He has them in his inside pocket along with other documents."

"I don't understand. How do you know this?"

"Change that five into a four."

Jasper did as requested.

"The club members had a party to celebrate that we avoided bankruptcy. In their drunken stupor, they recalled that Peregrine saved the Carringtons from bankruptcy by arranging a loan with Perez. The loan is due, and Perez is not going to extend it."

Their Lordships watched Jasper leave the office. As the door closed, they looked at each other and grinned.

Lord Ambrose lifted a bottle of Glenmorangie from his bottom desk drawer. "Let the fireworks begin!" He laughed as he poured two generous portions of malt.

Chapter Seventy-Seven

Kate was standing outside the bifold doors, gazing at the bushes at the bottom of the garden. Memories of Harry and Oliver filled her mind. She thought she could see Clare, Malcolm and Jasper looking at her. Jasper was walking towards her, smiling—a smile that said one thing: make-up sex. Isaacs House was full of memories. Some of them were sad, but most were happy. A rogue tear trickled down her cheek. She was beginning to doubt that she could live there amongst the memories.

There was the shuffling of feet and a soft cough. "I'm sorry to disturb you, but Landon Hall is on the phone."

A tearful Kate took the phone from Robert.

"Yes," she said.

"Police are here. Anton Perez was found dead in the foyer."

A wave of nervous energy passed through her. "I'm on my way."

* * *

Kate pulled the Evoque onto the grass verge outside Landon Hall. There were police cars and vans everywhere, along with police and forensic technicians wearing their standard white coveralls. To her surprise, Arthur was marching towards her.

"He's done it this time," snapped Arthur. "They've sent the top team from Scotland Yard."

"Who are 'they'?"

"People well above my pay grade that make these decisions."

"Why are you here?"

"Top brass called me in; I know you and Jasper."

"Lady Carmichael, I'm Detective Chief Inspector Smith. You own Landon Hall?"

"Yes."

"Do you know Anton Perez?"

"I wouldn't say *know*."

"He came to see you at Isaacs House."

"That was business."

"Did he make you an offer for Landon Hall?"

"No."

"What was that business? I'll remind you that this is a murder investigation."

"He offered me Carrington Towers."

The chief inspector looked surprised; the Carringtons had signed the investigation authorisation form.

"To save you a lot of digging," Kate said, "Mr Perez loaned the Carringtons money, providing he had the Deeds to Carrington Towers."

"Are you sure?"

"I've copies of documents proving the truth."

"Did he mention Landon Hall?"

"I've already told you, no."

"You haven't asked where he was found."

"You haven't given me the chance."

"Rooms were locked."

"I locked them."

"Why?"

"I didn't want workmen poking around."

"Where's your husband?"

"Ask the chief constable."

The chief inspector hesitated and stared at Kate.

Arthur stepped forward. "We believe he's somewhere in Europe. We've tried all his old diamond haunts. There's an Interpol warrant out—"

"I have a right to know what happened," interjected Kate.

"It appears that Mr Perez was trying to kick Lady Isabel's bedroom door open. We have his bootprint on the door. One scenario is that he leaned on the banister to give him leverage, lost his balance and toppled over onto the foyer floor. But we will know more after the post-mortem. If your husband contacts you, you must tell us."

"Do you know that the hall was damaged by a fire?"

"Yes. But we believe that the previous fire had nothing to do with his death."

"How do you know it's Mr Perez?" Kate asked as the body was being removed from the house and slid into a white van.

"Mr Perez was under surveillance."

* * *

Kate began to walk to the hall as the chief inspector sped away. She stopped at the door, where a man gave her shoe covers and gloves.

The forensic team was still working as she stepped inside the foyer. There was an outline of the body drawn on the floor. A police officer suddenly appeared at her elbow as she walked up the stairs to Lady Isabel's room.

The desk drawers had been opened. However, she noticed that the secret compartment hadn't. In the middle of the room were clear plastic bags of papers, clothes and jewellery.

Kate walked out to the landing and momentarily watched the forensic technicians going over the banister with a fine-tooth comb. The study was receiving the same scrutiny as Lady Isabel's bedroom.

Once outside, the foreman appeared. "I've sent the men home. The police wanted their names and addresses." He went to walk away but then turned to face Kate. "The police suspect Lord Carmichael murdered him."

Kate's phone rang.

It was Robert. *"The police are here with a warrant."*

She ran back to the Evoque and floored the accelerator.

Chapter Seventy-Eight

Kate skidded to halt across the gates to Isaacs House and cut the engine, blocking the police cars in. The front door was wide open and men were carrying boxes into a van. The jingling ignition keys caught her attention. Without a second thought, she lifted them out of the ignition.

She pushed past the men to find Arthur ordering police officers about.

"Warrant," she angrily demanded.

Arthur reluctantly pulled the warrant out of the inside pocket of his jacket.

"You bastard!" she yelled.

"It wasn't my idea, Kate. I just follow orders."

"Stop. Stop!" she shouted.

"She's blocked us in," called an officer.

"Key's missing," said another.

"Ben, Robert, make sure these officers bring the boxes back inside," Kate said. "Elsie, Ruby, stop making drinks and clean the kitchen."

"Kate, can we talk about this?" asked Arthur.

"No, we can't."

"Hand them Jasper and all this will stop."

"I'll send you a bill for the damage you've caused."

"He's no good, Kate. He deserves his comeuppance."

* * *

Kate wandered around Isaacs House, looking at the chaos the police had left. Papers were strewn around her studio and her laptop was open; she wondered if they had copied any of her files.

Ruby was in tears; the kitchen cupboards and freezer had been emptied. Elsie was on the verge of tears looking at the clean bed linen and towels that were scattered on the floor. Robert and Ben were putting the books from Landon Hall back into boxes and then into the outbuilding.

The doorbell rang, and Kate ran to open it.

"Lady Carmichael?" said a young courier holding a A3-size box.

"Yes," she snapped.

He handed her the box. "Delivery."

Kate stared at the handwriting on the address label. Jasper's.

"Sign here."

Kate cleared a space on her studio's workbench and gingerly opened the box. She opened one of the two large envelopes that were inside. It looked old and worn; the document inside was also old and was titled "Carrington Towers".

Kate carefully read the loan agreement for five million pounds between Margaret Carrington and Anton Perez. Her legs began to wobble as she dragged a stool to the bench. The Carringtons didn't own their ancestral home; Perez did.

There was another official document listing the past owners of the Towers. Her name, Lady Kate Carrington, was below Lady Isabel Landon's name. The stamp of Sinclair Law was below the signatures of Margaret Carrington and Anton Perez.

Kate assumed that the remainder of the documents detailing the history of Carrington Towers would be in Sinclair's safe.

She found a bottle of brandy and poured herself one. Nursing the glass, she walked through the open bifold doors. Her anger was still simmering at the wrongful police search of Isaacs House, and Perez breaking into Landon Hall.

Someone will pay for all that I've been through, she thought, taking a big swig of brandy.

She had to calm herself and think, but act she must. The old Kate would have dismissed the fact that she was the legal owner of Carrington Towers; the old Kate wouldn't want to own such a building. But she was Lady Isabel's bloodline that had been cheated out of her birthright. She must do something.

Her thoughts were interrupted by Robert. "May we have a moment of your time?"

The staff and Little Jasper were sitting around the kitchen table when Kate joined them. Robert had placed the bottle of brandy on the table. The only sound was Ruby blowing her nose between sobs.

"I can only apologise for what happened today," Kate said. "The police were in the wrong, and I intend to make a complaint."

Robert coughed. "If you don't mind me saying so, you have been acting very strangely."

"If any of you, or all of you, want to leave, I understand. Everything is coming to a head. There are a number of people that want me out of the way." Kate walked to the kitchen window. "When Harry was killed, I felt I had lost everything… except, he lives on in his son. I can't desert them.

"And, er…" She hesitated. "I have discovered that I've been cheated out of my birthright. I know none of this is your problem, but the stakes are high, along with the risk. If I'm successful in regaining my birthright, you all will be working in a very grand house."

"I don't speak for the everyone, but I've nowhere else to go, and you're the best boss I've ever had. I'm with you, Lady C," said Ben.

"Can you be more specific about this grand house?" asked Robert.

"Carrington Towers. I'm not sure if I told you, but I'm the true bloodline of the Carrington family. Lady Isabel Landon was my grandmother."

Loud intakes of breath filled the kitchen.

"I'll be busy then," commented Ben.

"What about me?" asked Little Jasper.

Kate walked over to him and kissed his hair. "You're with me."

"Lady Carmichael, you can count on us all," said Robert.

"You should all be aware that I shall be acting out of character again."

Kate spent the rest of the day with Little Jasper. They didn't do much talking but a lot of cuddling.

When he was fast asleep, she returned to her studio and opened the second envelope that was in the box Jasper had sent. The Deeds to the Carrington beach house, which Phillip Carrington had signed over to her, fell onto the workbench, along with a note with the address of the Carringtons' London house.

An outline of a plan began to take shape.

Chapter Seventy-Nine

Kate relied on the satnav to guide her to the Carringtons' secluded London house. She had a lot on her mind after the phone calls to the trustees of the Landon estate, the ombudsman for the conduct of lawyers and the Home Secretary's office. She was amazed at the cooperation she had from the various offices when she introduced herself as Lady Kate Carrington, née Carmichael.

"You have reached your destination," said the satnav.

The Evoque coasted to a stop behind some trees. Cars filled the Carrington driveway, and the gates were open.

A meeting, Kate thought.

She walked to the back of the house; the door was wide open and loud voices echoed towards her. She eased open the door to the room where the voices were coming from. Sitting around a table were Von-Pitt, Margot and Lords Blackthorn, Ambrose and Devon. Auntie was at the head with Phillip to her right and Peregrine Sinclair on her left.

Auntie froze when she saw Kate. Then all eyes turned to her.

"Come in, my dear," said a grinning Lord Devon.

"I would ask what you're doing here, but my gut tells me you've come to claim your birthright," snapped Auntie.

"Now, let's not jump to conclusions," said Lord Devon. "I'm sure Lady Carmichael has come to have a conversation about Carrington Towers."

Kate's eyes blurred as she looked at the conniving, greedy bastards that had caused her so much pain, had killed Harry and taken Jasper away from her.

"The old man you're staring at is your great-grandfather. Good-looking man, don't you agree?" said Auntie.

Kate ignored her and addressed the group. "Auntie Carrington," she began. "She that must be obeyed. Head of the Carrington clan. However, she shouldn't be in that position for she is not a true Carrington."

Auntie went as white as a sheet.

"I'm not sure how she came to be head of the clan, but I am sure that she's desperate for diamonds to pay off a debt.

"Phillip Carrington," she continued. "Heir apparent; also not a true Carrington. Does as he is told, ruthless in business, feared by many. But he has a weakness: women.

"Lord Blackthorn, also a member of the clan. Made a deal with Jasper to keep the authorities off his back, providing Jasper sourced and valued diamonds for him. I imagine he has a nest egg from cheating clients, and Jasper.

"Lord Ambrose and Lord Devon. The dynamic duo, using the Gentlemen's Club as a front, have fenced diamonds for many years. They took umbrage when I wouldn't support the Landon Trust Fund—a fund that was built on diamonds—but Lord Blackthorn came to their rescue with the help of his Carrington relatives.

"Margot, diamond queen that wanted Jasper's network—"

"Your husband fucked me more than once," Margot snapped.

"Jasper has fucked many women, but he has only shared a bed with me. Get over it.

"Mr Von-Pitt," Kate continued to a speechless room. "A rich gangster whose fortune has dwindled away. I wouldn't have given you a second glance if you hadn't interfered with the shopping centre. You wanted everything Carmichael: Jasper's diamonds and my properties.

"And Peregrine Sinclair, the best for last. You've done your last dirty deal. You represent the Carringtons and yet willingly accepted my job. Though, it wasn't much of a job; you probably had all the information you needed in your safe. When Anton Perez became your client, you couldn't lose."

"Anton was your client?" exclaimed Auntie. "You bastard!"

Kate would not be diverted from her task. She continued as if Auntie hadn't spoken. "All I wanted was to be left alone, but you all kept battering me, and everything changed when you killed Harry. You will all feel the wrath of Lady Kate Carrington; I shall take my birthright and all that it involves."

Auntie stood and pointed her finger at Kate. "Anton's dead, and with him goes our debt."

"I think his lawyers may have something to say about that. I have certain documents that will interest them."

"There were no documents on him."

"The police didn't know where to look. I believe the signatories on the Deeds to Carrington Towers are Lady Isabel Landon and Lady Kate Carrington. Interesting… Lady Isabel gave up her birthright when she married James Landon, and I have never signed such a document. On paper, ownership of the Towers is the Carrington bloodline, but in reality, we all know that's not true."

Lord Devon jumped up in his seat, clapping.

"Sit down, you old fool," barked Lord Ambrose.

"I will take you to court," said Auntie.

"Do that and you will lose. I have many documents proving who I am and DNA samples from Lady Isabel."

"Impossible."

"Why do you think I locked her bedroom door at Landon Hall?"

Auntie turned to Phillip. "Say something."

"Nothing to say," Phillip said. "It's obvious that Kate has built her case. She was careful not to use her Lady Carrington title until now. I'm thinking Lady Carrington has a lot of sway in high places. I think the prudent thing to do is just leave." He paused. "I would have been a better lover than Jasper, Kate, but I guess we can't turn back the clock and enjoy the beach house."

"Where is Jasper, Kate?" asked Lord Blackthorn.

"I'm sure the people around this table know more than me."

Chapter Eighty

Three months later
Jasper

Jasper had known that his beloved wouldn't live in the grand Carrington Towers, or Isaacs House – that was too full of memories she would prefer to forget. The beach house would be her home, next to the sea she loved.

He hadn't had much time to fix his cameras in the newly renovated Arts and Crafts house. Someone had hired an experienced team to catch him. He guessed Lord Blackthorn had joined forces with some of his criminal associates.

From his yacht, Jasper had watched the workmen gutting the inside and extending the house. The new side extension blended perfectly with the 1930s house and was Kate's private space. Her studio had bifold doors that led to the long lawn and the sea.

He had touched her new easel and sat on her new chaise lounge. She had a small desk away from the bifold doors and empty shelves for her books, but painting was the main purpose of the room. He had walked up the spiral staircase and into her bedroom. He had been tempted to lie on the bed, but it would have been torture thinking of making love to her. The en suite bathroom was fitted with a bath and a large shower. Memories of their love-making under cascading water flashed through his mind. He had moved to the state-of-the-art, open-plan kitchen with accompanying seating area, designed for the staff. The living room had a cosy feeling, with its large fireplace. The staff all had their own spaces, with en suite facilities. There was only one upstairs bedroom in the original house, and that was Little Jasper's.

When Jasper was satisfied that his internal cameras wouldn't be detected by the beach house's new security system, he had moved to the outside, fitting cameras around the house and garage.

Darkness was falling as he hurried back to his yacht. He lifted the anchor, preparing for the tide to take him out to sea, when he caught sight of headlights on the private lane to the beach house. The wind carried the sound of the diesel engine.

I know that sound, he thought.

He trained his high-powered binoculars onto the vehicle and followed it to the garages.

The security lights came on as Kate jumped out of the old Evoque. She was talking into her phone. One of his outside cameras picked up her end of the conversation.

"Robert, I just want some alone time. So, make sure you're delayed tomorrow... The sea will heal me... Lie... I'll deal with the PA. I want a new crest, that's it. She'll have to put up with it. I've got to go."

The call ended, and Jasper checked that he had tracked Kate's new phone number. He'd guessed that she had more than two phones; the one she had just been using was her personal one.

Minutes later, he watched his wife kick off her shoes, roll her trousers up and step into the sea. She removed the tie that was holding hair back and shook her head. The breeze caught her hair as it fell to her shoulders. She removed her blouse and unclipped her bra, freeing her full breasts.

I like this Kate.

Kate pushed the bra into her trouser pocket and draped the blouse over her shoulders.

You need me, Kate, and I need you. I've got to find a way for us to meet and make love.

Three months later
Kate

Kate was walking down the grassy bank to the beach from her new beach house. Little Jasper was running ahead, laughing and shouting with his new, energetic, Labrador rescue puppy, Blackie. He had persuaded her to let him have a dog, saying that he deserved it after all he had been through, and she hadn't the heart to argue. After all, he was right.

She hadn't completely settled in the beach house with her staff and Little Jasper; a home takes time to build. However, she needed alone time to adjust to her new life as Lady Carrington without Jasper. Her feet had barely touched the ground since being declared Lady Isabel's granddaughter and heir to what was left of her estate.

There had been meeting after meeting with various lords who were either lawyers, chairmen of banks or police commissioners. The outcome, although there were still some loose ends to tie up, was that she was the legal heir to Lady Isabel Landon's estate. Auntie and Phillip Carrington had tried to contest Kate's claim, but it was thrown out.

It had upset her that so many lords, dukes and judges had all known about her birthright; these people had ignored her when she'd needed help. Lady Isabel had wanted to bring her up as a Carrington, in a life of privilege, but they had allowed her to be brought up by that evil bastard Reynolds.

Her official home-cum-business centre was Carrington Towers with its army of staff and cold rooms, but her real home was the beach house.

She hadn't realised that her life had to be signed off by her PA, who had tried to prevent her altering the beach house and moving in with her personal staff and Little Jasper, but that was when she discovered that, by being rich and knowing the right people, she could do what she wanted. In record time, the local authority signed off the plans for the beach house to be extended and remodelled.

She didn't regret moving from Wellsbury; that part of her life was over. Isaacs House would only be used when she had business in Wellsbury. Godfrey Clayton had agreed to run the day-to-day affairs of the shopping centre, as she had more than enough to do sorting the Carrington business.

The smell of freshly cut grass drifted into her senses, breaking into her thoughts.

She kicked off her trainers to feel the sand between her toes. After a short walk, she stood with the gentle waves lapping over her feet. The sounds and smells of the sea had started to make inroads into the stress that had accumulated over the past months.

However, there were still some private loose ends that she had to deal with—the computer genius, for one, without whom she would never have had the confidence to tackle the likes of Von-Pitt. There had been a message left on her laptop.

Till we meet again. You owe me dinner, and I may need a friend in a high place.

She wondered what he meant by that, but she would cross that bridge later.

Von-Pitt had disappeared and so had Lord Blackthorn, but she was sure that they would resurface. Lords Devon and Ambrose had offered to assist her in any way they could. She wasn't sure what that meant, but she had a sneaky feeling it might have something to do with diamonds. She still had Jasper's diamonds hidden away with the remains of Zak Cohen's cash.

Kate's fingers moved to her Carmichael wedding ring; her heart ached for Jasper. Godfrey had told her that he was living with Margot. She was dreading the day that her solicitor contacted her with divorce papers.

Every bone in her body told her that he had been at Landon Hall when Anton Perez died, but there was no evidence of foul play. The verdict of the inquest was accidental death. But how had he got the Deeds to Carrington Towers and the beach house?

Little Jasper was running towards her with Blackie, who was carrying a branch bigger than himself. She wished that he wouldn't run so much; it was putting too much strain on the leg that had been broken.

"Did you see that yacht?" he said. "It was pretty close!" He play-fought with Blackie for ownership of the branch.

Kate turned and scanned the sea, and butterflies filled her stomach.

Jasper.

Six months later

Summer was coming to a close as Kate was putting the finishing touches to a painting. She was at the far end of the cove, away from everyone. This was her private time, no watch, no phone or interruptions.

A small sailing yacht caught her eye as it beached. Her heart trembled as a tall figure walked towards her. Her mind raced. He would be the only person with the nerve to blatantly approach her.

He stopped in front of the easel and removed his sunglasses. Two piercing blue eyes stared deeply into her green eyes. He slowly removed the brush from her hand. Her mouth opened, and Jasper Carmichael was not one to miss an opportunity.

Author Profile

As I approach my twilight years, my industrial and academic life is a fading memory. Time is precious, so now I indulge myself in the world of fiction, and when the dreaded writer's block appears, I escape to the tranquillity of my garden. The fragrance and colourful blooms of my roses always inspire me. The sowing of seeds and nurturing of the plants to bear fruit is also a source of delight.

Jasper's Wife is the fourth book in the Jasper Carmichael Series.

I have tried to put Jasper and Kate to bed, but these old friends soon take over any new stories. I am writing book five; I wonder if this will be the last of Jasper and Kate.

* * *

What Did You Think of *Jasper's Diamond?*

A big thank you for purchasing this book. It means a lot that you chose this book specifically from such a wide range on offer. I do hope you enjoyed it.

Book reviews are incredibly important for an author. All feedback helps them improve their writing for future projects and for developing this edition. If you are able to spare a few minutes to post a review on Amazon, that would be much appreciated.